THE PRINCE OF CARENTAN

FG and DC Laval

THE PRINCE OF CARENTAN

DOUBLE DRAGON

Dedication

In memory of
Martin Alexander Laval

With thanks to
Barbara Robertson for reading, editing, cupcakes
and coffee. Thanks to Litopia Writer's Colony for
their insightful critiques in the Houses.

Billy, William and Damien for their love, support
and encouragement.

A massive debt of thanks to Charlotte Laval for her
continued support in reading, editing and suggesting
changes and just being there in more ways than
anyone can imagine.

Thank you to all our family and friends for their
continued enthusiasm and interest and last, but by
no means least, the authors would like to thank You,
the reader, for coming along with us on this journey.

Chapter One

The blood pounded in Gereinte's ears. He sprinted away from the Tower, then chanced a glance over his shoulder. The older boy was gaining on him fast. Sweat beaded his skin. His hands tingled in the cold, damp air. Surely the castle guards would have seen him from their vantage point? He took a deep breath, put his head down and pelted for the forest. It would be too humiliating to be caught out in the open, in front of the men he would one day command.

His foot caught a tree root and he fell, protecting his face with his hands. His whole body stung, with the pain of the fall and the bitterness of knowing what would come next. The boy descended upon him and kicked him hard.

Crunch.

The blow to his side was excruciating.

Something cracked, a rib? The air was sucked from his lungs. He gasped. Each short, shallow breath punctuated the pain. He tried to roll onto his side, but a coarse leather boot pressed on his shoulder like a dead weight.

"Not so tough without Warmaster Alaric looking over your shoulder, eh?" the boy said.

He looked up the stocking covered leg; it was Drayton, squire to the knight, Fulk. Gereinte coughed, winced and a spear-like pain lanced through the side of his body.

He gauged Drayton's size. If he were to get out of this in one piece, he would have to be quick. Quick witted and as quick on his feet as his small, wiry frame allowed.

"Let me up and we'll do this man to man." Gereinte's voice sounded distant, as though it belonged to another person, someone strong and confident, not weakened by pain and humiliation. Drayton grinned. The weight lifted and Gereinte stole a short, pain-wracked breath. He rolled nimbly onto his side drawing his knees into his chest before thrusting out his feet as hard as possible into Drayton's chest. It was worth it to see the shock on Drayton's face; his eyes nearly popped out of their sockets and his mouth worked like a fish, fighting to catch his breath.

Gereinte knew he had only a split second to make his escape. He sprang to his feet, ignoring the burning sensation in his side, launched into a sprint and slammed straight into the body of another person.

First, he was relieved as he slumped to the ground; someone from the castle guard had been sent to find out what was going on. Then, crushing defeat as he realised he had run headlong into Drayton's training partner, Squire Charrock. Charrock loomed above him with a mean grin. Charrock and Drayton were given a wide berth by most squires or pageboys who had even the slightest instinct of self-preservation. It was well known that the duo preyed on the small and weak for sport, but they were subtle enough to get away with it. To top it, they were good, loyal squires and tipped for joining the Queen's Guard once they were knighted.

Gereinte backed away on his hands and feet. Drayton appeared at his shoulder and hissed like a snake. Gereinte looked up into unforgiving eyes, trying to imagine this pair of jesters in the Queen's

8

colours.

"Purple wouldn't suit you anyway," he said to himself.

"What did he say?" Drayton said, still labouring for breath.

"Dunno," Charrock said, grinning. "Something about purple... how hard did you hit him?"

"Not hard enough," Drayton said, rising above his victim. Drayton's next blow caught him across the face, snapping his head back with the force. The salty, metallic taste of blood filled his mouth. Instinctively, his hands flew to his face. He had a gash on his upper lip and was sure to have visible bruising. This time, he had them. They couldn't get away with it, too much evidence. Charrock knew it too.

"What the darkness do you think you are doing? No marks, remember?" He stepped over Gereinte and pushed Drayton away. "Now what are you going to do about it? This was you, not me. Remember that when you are summoned before the Queen Regent," Charrock said.

"Whatever happened to 'we'll stick together, no matter what'? Got cold feet have you? Some friend you are," Drayton said. But Charrock continued to jab him in the shoulder to emphasise his point.

"If I get chucked out, my father will disown me."

"This is different." There was a look of delight on Drayton's face and Gereinte decided it was time to start inching away. He managed to roll onto all fours while the squires continued to argue and push each other. If he moved slowly enough, the noise of his escape might be muffled by the brawl going on.

Inch by inch, he sneaked away.

9

At two, three yards, he dared to look over his shoulder and saw the argument had descended into violence. Slowly, he stood up. Drayton aimed a punch at Charrock, who dodged it and slammed an uppercut into Drayton's chest, just at the spot he had been kicked. Drayton's face flushed red with rage and pain. Gereinte crept away. Light burst out of the clearing ahead. If he could just make it that far, someone would surely see him from the castle walls. Just a few more… wretched… steps.

His foot was wrenched forcibly from behind him and suddenly, he was being dragged backwards through the woods. Bits of stone, twigs and tree roots battered his hands and face, cutting little nicks in his skin. It was like he was lying still and the ground was being pulled from under him. He closed his eyes as dirt and debris filled his eyes, nose and mouth. The earthy scent of decay was overwhelming. Then, a sudden crack to the side of his head and the world started spinning. Nausea rose from the pit of his stomach. He opened an eye. A large oak tree blocked the path.

"Idiot. That could have killed him." Drayton's voice.

"I thought that was the idea," Charrock said.

"Not before I've had my fun." They laughed.

"This'll do," Charrock said. "I hope you brought some rope."

Rope? Gereinte panicked. He tried to get up, but his legs buckled.

"No you don't. You're not going anywhere," Drayton said, striking Gereinte's face again. An explosion of stars danced before his eyes. Drayton pushed Gereinte flat to the ground and held him there, while Charrock fumbled around by his feet. The rope was pulled so tight, his feet went numb. They yanked him up while the rope was tied around the tree. Then forced his arms behind him around the tree trunk, each wrist bound so tight, he could no longer feel his fingers. The boys took their time to forage around for the biggest sticks and branches they could find.

Gereinte let his head loll to his chest. What would his father have thought? He tried wriggling his hands and feet, but he couldn't feel them. Not much hope there. *Never give up hope.* His father's words drifted into his thoughts. Deep breath. Don't show them how much it hurts. Don't give them the satisfaction.

Gereinte Andolin, Prince Royal and heir to Carentan raised his head and levelled his eyes with his persecutors. Drayton's piggy black eyes stared back at him and for a moment, Gereinte indulged himself with imagining a large snout to replace that button nose. Yes, much better. He smiled. Drayton flinched, eyes widened with surprise. Gereinte had won on a different level, a level that these two were unlikely ever to understand. Drayton swung his stick with all his might and Gereinte was ready for it. The blows pelted him over and over. Drayton and Charrock swapped and changed; head, body, legs. All the time, he kept his gaze fixed ahead until eventually, he let his eyelids slide shut. His chin dropped softly to his chest and he slipped thankfully into unconsciousness.

***

Gereinte was aware of pain. Had he been sleeping? He wanted so much to sleep, but this gut-wrenching agony kept bringing him back from the edge of darkness. He slipped away again. Blissful peace. He yearned for the quiet that sleep would bring, but something kept dragging him back, making him feel the pain again. Gods, why can't they leave him in peace?

The rhythm of his heart was erratic and slow, but there was another beat - strong and determined, it craved his indulgence and was not going to give up. His heart picked up the beat and ran with it, coaxing the breath from his lungs. He could not resist. It was playing the tune of his life, daring him to get up and move on.

A sharp intake of breath, then his eyes flew open. He was on his back, a canopy of trees overhead. He squeezed his eyes shut again, blinded by the light. Gasping for breath, he dug his fingernails into the dirt in which he lay, slowly opening one eye to try and get a grip on his whereabouts. Every breath he took was speared with pain.

There was a giant who towered above him, huge paw-like hands cupped above his chest. It must have been the panic on his face, because the giant backed away and held his hands aloft in a gesture of peace. His huge, muscular body was dressed in the green and browns of a forest ranger. Then Gereinte remembered; the boys, the tree, the sticks.

What was a ranger doing in the castle grounds? His face was oddly familiar, but there was something missing, as though it didn't match the place or the occasion. The rope binding on Gereinte's feet and hands had been cut, he was lying flat on his back and there was a dull ache in his chest.

12

The giant disappeared and was replaced by officious looking royal advisers and castle guards. They swelled around him, fussing and cursing and shouting at one another. All he wanted to do was to shout and holler, but his voice had deserted him.

He was carried on a make-shift litter by several men, who were still cursing each other even as they reached the castle, where the royal medic awaited. He was safe at last, to sleep.

Chapter Two

Seneschal, Nils Martan, hurried towards the Western staircase which led up to the Great Hall, where the Queen Regent, Caitlin Andolin, was holding court.

"Seneschal, please," a small voice said.

He whipped around, startled by the sheer panic in the voice. Nils's crimson robes swished to a halt, echoing the movement of his tall, thin frame. He looked at the pageboy who stood wringing his hat with his hands and shifting his weight from one foot to the other. Nils lifted an eyebrow.

"It… it's the Prince," the boy said. "I saw him go and two squires went after him. I know I shouldn't say… but they hurt other boys, smaller boys. I just thought… I tried to tell a castle guard and he just told me that I didn't see anything. So… I didn't see anything, but they went into the woods on the west side of the Tower and they didn't come out."

Nils knelt down and prised the felt hat out of the boy's hands, straightened it out and placed it back on top of his head.

"You did the right thing," he said. "You know you can tell me anything and I will make sure you are safe. Now, go back to your duties and I will see to the Prince."

The boy smiled with relief and he headed back the way he had come. Nils doubled back towards the Western wall sighing. Not again. How did the Prince keep getting caught up in these games?

The guards on the Western wall were chattering and exchanging playful banter when Nils appeared. They stood to attention and tried to look busy, scanning the horizon and looking out across the farmlands that surrounded the castle and beyond. He ignored the momentary lapse of concentration; he would deal with that later. For now, his priority was the Prince. He knew which guards he could trust and those that could be bribed by outsiders looking for a spy inside the castle grounds. The likelihood that some of these men were being paid not only by the Queen Regent, but by other noble houses was a certainty he had to live with. Since the death of the King, every eye in the nation was on the throne of Carentan. It was a fine line between protecting the Prince until he came of age and allowing him the freedom to fight his own battles.

The transformation of the castle guards was instantaneous as the Seneschal swept along the Western wall. He stopped beside a guard who appeared alert; gaze focused on the woodland inside the grounds.

"How long?" Nils kept his voice low, but didn't try to hide his urgency.

The guard's focus did not waver for an instant.

"An hour, maybe more, Seneschal, Sir."

Grief. Where in this gods forsaken castle was the Prince's personal guard? Nils sprinted back down the staircase towards the garrison, barking orders to servants and rounding up a team of guards who followed in his wake. Servants were fleeing and shouts for the royal medic and the Prince's personal guard echoed around the corridors. The Seneschal had a reputation for being all-seeing and all-powerful. Well, he was kicking himself now. Something had gone wrong and the Queen would hang him from the nearest balustrade if anything

15

had happened to the Prince. The search party swept out of the Western gate and marched towards the woodland; there was no hiding this little excursion and Nils hoped that the only mistake he had to face today was his overreaction to the Prince's latest escapade.

***

Nils stood, head bowed. Caitlin Andolin, Queen Regent of Carentan paced up and down her palace living quarters. The view from the window looked out over the castle gardens and beyond, to the woodland that encircled the inner and outer walls. As she paced, her fur trimmed magenta robes cut a swathe in her wake. She stopped every so often, as though pausing for thought, before resuming her rhythmic pattern. This always made Nils feel uncomfortable. It either meant she was about to come up with some impossible idea or that it meant trouble for whoever was in the room. Some of the barons likened her to a caged tigress. The tigress epitomised her fiery spirit and the cage was the kingdom she was bound to rule.

Prince Gereinte. Nils bowed his head lower, studying the red and beige woven mats beneath his feet. The shame of it. He should have been aware of the Prince's movements at all times. The boy's face had been barely recognisable when they found him. And his body... the royal medic predicted weeks before he would fully recover, if indeed he'd be able to walk at all. It was his fault; Nils had appointed the Prince's personal guard and it was his responsibility. He wrung his hands together over and over and tried not to be intimidated by the Queen's continual pacing. But she was absorbed in her own thoughts. They had been over and over the scene. Nils had told her everything he knew, but she was still not satisfied. She stopped and turned to face Nils, her emerald eyes glared out from beneath the jewelled head dress.

"Ah ha."

There was finality to her tone, which he knew meant that whatever came next would be yet another episode in the royal game plan. It was like being in the backdrop of a large tapestry, unable to see the whole picture.

"You said that there was binding around his feet and hands. That it had been cut by the time you got there?" she said.

"Yes, yes, Your Highness. He had been bound before…" the words stuck in Nils's throat.

"I spoke to the Medic, who said that there was a circular bruising to his upper chest, not in keeping with the deep welts created by whatever had been used to beat him." The Queen fixed her gaze upon Nils and he shrank away from her intensity.

"Which would indicate," she said, "that someone got there before you?" That possibility had not crossed Nil's mind, but on reflection, it seemed obvious. "Someone saved his life and I need to find out who."

"But, Your Highness. How do you…?"

"Well, if this person wanted him dead, he would be dead. It is not as if he was going anywhere," she said.

"No, quite."

"And until Gereinte regains consciousness, this person is a crucial witness. Find him, Nils. Use all of your networks. Bring Gereinte's saviour to me.

17

That is all."

Dismissed, Nils retreated. The sooner he talked to his people, the sooner he would come up with a result for the Queen. Anything less than success would be inconceivable.

***

The chamber door closed behind the Seneschal. Caitlin sighed and let her shoulders droop.

She wanted to scream and shout the walls down, but knew that the servants would come running at the noise. Instead, she screwed up her face and let the tears stream down. To have almost lost her son so soon after her husband… it was almost too much.

A platter of cold meats, cheese and a jug of wine lay untouched on the table. Caitlin's hands trembled as she poured a cup of wine and forced herself to drink. She couldn't yet face the rest. The wine began to warm her insides and she started to pull herself together. She could not afford to indulge her maternal instinct for too long; there was so much to do. This was not the first attempt on Gereinte's life, if indeed an assassination attempt it was, and it certainly would not be the last. It was, however, the most violent, which is what disturbed Caitlin the most.

Gereinte's personal guard would have to be replaced; preferably with someone a little less gullible. The boy was becoming quite a strategist; it was just a shame he didn't yet have the physical strength to back it up. But that would come. That was all part of the plan. Caitlin nearly choked on the wine. Dear gods… the plan. That had very nearly gone out of the window, had it not been for one man's intervention in the woods that afternoon.

Caitlin needed to know who it was. Never before had it been so crucial to know your allies as well as your enemies. There was no mistaking the curious mark on Gereinte's chest. She had once watched Reiner bring back the life of a small boy he had found, nearly mauled to death by a wild animal in the forest. They never spoke of what he had done for fear that folk would accuse them of being cursed by witchcraft.

The two squires who had perpetrated the attack had been rounded up and brought before their Queen. It made her sick to her pit to see them stand there with barefaced denial of ever having been near the woods that afternoon. Several witnesses including a pageboy and a castle guard had confirmed their identity despite having to cajole this information from them with promises of royal protection. What worried Caitlin more was who had put the squires up to this attack. It was easy enough to banish them from the kingdom, but Carentan's real enemies were still close at hand. Despite Nil's best efforts to cleanse the palace of spies, it was still not safe to assume that all the castle staff were loyal to her interests. Caitlin sat and picked at the food. She was going to need her strength in the hours and days ahead.

The door to her chambers opened and Caitlin scrambled to her feet, quickly straightening herself out and adopting an air of aloof authority. Audan Borsa, Caitlin's mother glided into the room, closely followed by Ladys Autin, the Queen's Chief Lady in Waiting and two servants. Caitlin embraced her mother, while Ladys instructed the servants to replace the dishes with fresh ones and refill the jug.

"Ladys, don't fuss so," Caitlin said. Ladys tutted under her breath and continued fussing. She had a gentle demeanour, which matched her rounded face and creamy complexion. Ladys always had a smile and a cheery word, for which Caitlin was especially grateful at a time like this. Despite the Queen's constant chiding, Ladys refused to do anything less than a superb job of looking after Caitlin.

Audan Borsa looked like an older, slightly plumper version of Caitlin. Her dress was conservative, due to the amount of time she spent in Royal children's living quarters and her hair was white. Lines of worry were etched into Audan's expression.

"How is he?" Caitlin said.

"He has regained consciousness. I thought you would want to know," Audan said. Caitlin released a long sigh.

"Thanks the gods," she said. "I must see him."

"Of course. But first, you must eat." Audan took Caitlin by the elbow and guided her towards the seating area where a trestle had been set up with fresh food and drink. "Then Ladys will return to help you freshen up before you visit Gereinte."

"Sit with me," Caitlin said, lowering herself onto a bench. "Tell me how the children are." Audan smiled warmly and sat down while Ladys shooed the servants away.

Chapter Three

Alliane sat on a window seat in the royal children's quarters and looked out across the castle gardens towards the woods. She hugged her knees into her chest and thought about her elder brother, Gereinte. She didn't like this. She didn't like it one little bit. Ger was lying in his room looking like a rotten squashed tomato and everybody was bumbling about as normal, like nothing ever happened. She sniffed loudly and fiddled with the jewelled headgear that kept her long dark hair in place.

Celie, the nursemaid, tutted from across the other side of the room. She was standing behind her twin sister, Nerys, piling up her hair beneath a similar garment. The dressing mirror split the room into two separate areas; one for sitting and one for dressing, so Celie couldn't see the face that Alliane pulled. Alliane was tired of being told how unladylike it was to sniff in the company of others. It just made her want to do it all the more, just to annoy everyone. Of course, Nerys would never do anything like that, she was far too dignified. Pish, posh. Nerys, just hid it well. Nerys was the prettier of the twins; a classic Carentan Princess, father would often say. Her hair was dark brown, nearly black and ran down her back like a long glistening river. She had a petite face with a delicate nose and all the squires crooned over her from a distance. Nerys's greatest ambition in life was to marry a prince from another realm, thus cementing a crucial political alliance and then having lots of baby Neryses. Euek... how could two girls so similar be so different? In contrast, Alliane's hair was dull and lifeless and her face full and round which betrayed her sweet tooth. Alliane would much rather be tramping around the woods building fires with the rangers, than wearing stupid headdresses and smiling coyly at visiting dignitaries.

Besides all of that, there was Ger. Somebody needed to look out for him. Alliane knew that as soon as he had recovered, he would be allowed to go off again, creating his own brand of mayhem with no one there to pick up the pieces when it all went wrong. It wasn't that he went looking for trouble, just that trouble seemed to find him wherever he went. She hoped that this time, their mother would take the matter more seriously. She had already taken the first step by dismissing the personal guard. In case the Queen was not prepared to take drastic action, Alliane was.

She turned away from the window when the chamber doors opened. Roda, their elder sister, swept into the room, carrying baby Josselin. At ten months, he was the youngest of the Andolin children. Josselin had been a big surprise to all of them, after their mother had years of difficulties conceiving followed by several stillbirths. Roda was closely followed by Josselin's nursemaid and one of the guards, who kept a vigil outside the door. The personal guards did not enter the Princess's living quarters, but were always there whenever they left. Frankly, it got on Alliane's nerves being watched all the time and she was not at all surprised that Ger had been driven to devise some ingenious strategies to escape their presence. Apart from Josselin, Gereinte was the only boy. He had his own living quarters adjacent to those of the Princess's. Josselin's high-pitched squeal cut through Alliane's thoughts.

He was squirming in Roda's arms and the nurse maid was hovering nearby, arms at the ready, to alleviate Roda of her burden.

"Oh shush, you little rascal." Roda wouldn't take any nonsense from anyone, least of all her baby brother. She was tall for her sixteen years and bore an uncanny resemblance to their mother. She wore the same aloof expression that mother often used.

Roda lowered Josselin to the floor and before the nurse maid was able to scoop him out of harm's way, he had shuffled on all fours, over to where Alliane sat and started to pull insistently at her robes, trying to stand up. Alliane sighed and lifted him to her knee.

"He doesn't understand any of it," Roda said, "but he likes listening to Nana telling the Pygmies Tale." It was a favourite story of the Andolin children; they all knew it by heart, but no one told it quite like Nana. "We met Nana and mother when we were visiting Ger and Nana promised."

"How is Ger?" Alliane said. Roda looked irritated by the interruption but smoothed away her frown and replaced her mask of indifference.

"Remarkably well, under the circumstances," she said. Roda was a peacekeeper and Alliane knew that sometimes she rubbed Roda up the wrong way but she couldn't help being impulsive.

"Is Nana still there?" She stood up and lifted Josselin into the waiting arms of his nursemaid. Josselin squealed his displeasure. "Yes, yes, little one. I'm going to get Nana." Alliane had found a great excuse to re-visit her brother, if only for a few moments.

"Where are you going, Ally?" Nerys always knew when Alliane was up to something and it irritated her to no end. She couldn't do anything without her twin sister being suspicious and Nerys knew that once Alliane got something into her head, there was no stopping her. Nils told her that she was so like her mother in that respect. Why couldn't she have inherited something useful, like good looks or the art of persuasion?

"Going to see Ger," she said in passing as she slid out of the door. She could hear Nerys's muffled protests behind the closing door.

"But Nana said…" Yes, yes. Nana said they should not bother Ger. But it was Nana who was needed and she didn't have time to explain this to Nerys.

One of the guards outside the door shifted his weight in anticipation of moving off after her, but as soon as he realised Alliane was entering the Prince's chambers across the corridor, he settled back. Alliane glared at him over her shoulder. She knew it wasn't his fault, he was only doing his job, but it still irritated her and unlike Roda and mother, she wasn't able to bottle up her feelings.

She opened the door to Ger's chamber softly and stood by the entrance. Nana, seated at the foot of his bed, glanced up briefly. Her eyes sparkled and she put a finger to her lips. Her mother sat beside Gereinte, softly stroking his hair and crooning like she had never seen her do before. It was a surreal vision. The light streamed in through the window, just enough to illuminate Gereinte and mother.

24

Words flowed continuously from her lips in a soft whisper, but Alliane could not hear what she was saying. It was like a soothing mantra, spoken over and over. The mask had lifted from her mother's face and for the first time Alliane could remember, she saw raw emotion in her expression. Alliane stood transfixed by this vision. It seemed so right. She fidgeted, as though her presence was intruding on a very personal moment and as she turned to leave, her mother looked up and caught her eye. For one brief moment, Alliane saw the woman behind the mask and felt the awful burden she carried. All the loneliness and the unshed tears. Like a rabbit startled by the hunter, Alliane could not draw her eyes away from her mother.

"Ma..." It came out like a strangled cry. A lump sprang to her throat. Her mother beckoned to her and Alliane ran to her side. She folded Alliane into her arms and together they looked down on Gereinte who slept. She didn't even hear Nana leave the room.

Chapter Four

A great while ago, when the world was full of wonders, there lived an earth-born giant, named Antaeus, and a million or more of curious little earth-born people, who were called pygmies. Nana's melodious voice filled the room. By the time Alliane had returned, the Pygmies Tale had begun. Roda and Nerys were ensconced in the window seat with Josselin in between them and lots of cushions to add to their comfort. Josselin lay on Roda's lap, his thumb stuck in his mouth. His expression was one of attentive bliss. Nana sat on a seat in front of the children, her hands in her lap and her smile warm and inviting. Alliane grabbed a cushion and joined her siblings, though somehow the whole situation seemed unreal without Gereinte.

This giant and these pygmies being children of the same mother (that is to say, our good old Grandmother Earth), were all brethren, and dwelt together in a very friendly and affectionate manner, far, far off, in the middle of hot Africa. Nana often told them stories about far off lands. Alliane found it hard to comprehend that there were other places further than the Western Isles. She had heard Warmaster Alaric instruct Gereinte in the strategic possibility of people coming from another land to conquer Carentan and the Western Isles. That was how father had died. Protecting them from invaders in the South. She shivered despite the warmth of the cushions and the proximity of her siblings. It was unsettling to think of... she focused in again on the story.

One day, the mighty Antaeus was lolling at full

length among his little friends. A pygmy chanced to climb upon his shoulder and he beheld something, a long way off. As it came nearer and nearer, what should it turn out to be but a human shape, not so big as Antaeus, it is true, although a very enormous figure in comparison with pygmies. The pygmy scampered to the giant's ear and shouted lustily into it. "Halloo, brother Antaeus! Get up this minute and take your pine-tree walking stick in your hand. Here comes another giant to have a tussle with you."

"Who are you?" Thundered the giant. "And what do you want in my dominions?" There was one strange thing about Antaeus. Whenever this redoubtable giant touched the ground, either with hand or foot, or any other part of his body, he grew stronger than ever he had before. The stranger did not seem at all disturbed. He carelessly lifted his club and balanced it in his hand, measuring Antaeus with his eye, from head to foot.

Alliane thought about their own giant, the knight Fulk, who towered above all other men in the castle. She had never spoken to him, in awe of his strength and he always fell silent in her company. She thought perhaps she made him feel uncomfortable, being the only female to take any interest in the forest rangers. Or perhaps it was the fact that she always had a guard and umpteen other officials trailing along behind her horse. Perhaps that was it. Mother always said it wasn't really appropriate for her to go out with the rangers. She started to fidget now, anxious that she makes it to the rangers' afternoon ride-by. All she needed was to capture the interest of their giant, just once. Once, she hoped would be enough, in order to enlist his help. Just like Antaeus helped the Pygmies.

"Who are you, I say?" Roared Antaeus.

"You are a very discourteous giant." Answered the stranger quietly. "And I shall probably have to teach you a little civility, before we part. As for my name, it is Hercules. I have come hither because this is my most convenient road to the garden of the Hesperides."

"Caitiff, you shall go no further!" Bellowed Antaeus. The giant strode tower-like towards the stranger (ten times strengthened at every step), and fetched a monstrous blow at him with his pine tree, which Hercules caught upon his club; and being more skillful than Antaeus, paid him back such a rap upon the sconce, that down tumbled the great lumbering man-mountain, flat upon the ground.

But no sooner was the giant down, than up he bounced again, with tenfold might. Hercules let drive again, and gave him another knock-down blow, which sent him heels over head, but served only to increase his already enormous strength. Now, Hercules began to be sensible that he should never win the victory if he kept knocking down Antaeus. So, throwing down his club, the hero stood ready to receive his antagonist with naked arms. As the mad giant made a rush at him, Hercules caught him round the middle with both hands, lifted him high into the air, and held him aloft overhead. Hercules gave his huge body a toss, and flung it about a mile off, where it fell heavily, and lay with no more motion than a sand hill.

Alliane's mind wandered to her current dilemma. How to get Fulk to keep a protective eye on

Gereinte. People thought him a little slow, but Alliane had seen him fight. He had passion in his heart, just like the little pygmies. She had to somehow get him away from everyone, as you never knew whose spies were lurking around. That was something she had learnt from Nils. He had his bank of spies who mostly worked in favour of House Andolin, but sometimes against. Nils was at pains to point out to the Andolin children, which ones could be trusted and which ones could be bribed.

So... where were they? Oh yes, weary after his exertions, Hercules had fallen asleep and the pygmies were so angry thinking that their friend and protector, Antaeus had been killed, that they attacked him with their little weapons while he slept. Nana's voice smoothed her back into the story.

Waking up, surprised at the shrill piping of so many little voices, Hercules espied the innumerable assemblage of pygmies at his feet. He stooped down, and taking up the nearest one between his thumb and finger, set him on the palm of his left hand.

"What in the world, my little fellow," ejaculated Hercules. "May you be?"

"I am your enemy," answered the valiant pygmy in his mightiest squeak. "You have slain Antaeus, our brother. We are determined to put you to death; and for my part, I challenge you to an instant battle, on equal ground." Hercules burst into a great explosion of laughter. "Upon my word," cried he. "I thought I had seen wonders before today – hydras with nine heads, stags with golden horns,

six-legged men, three-headed dogs, giants with furnaces in their stomachs. But here on the palm of my hand stands a wonder that outdoes them all! Your body, my little friend, is about the size of an ordinary man's finger. Pray, how big may your soul be?"

"As big as your own!" said the pygmy.

Hercules was touched by the little man's dauntless courage. "My good little people," said he. "Not for all the world would I do an intentional injury to such brave fellows as you! Your hearts seem to me so exceedingly great, that, upon my honour, I marvel how your small bodies can contain them. I sue for peace, and, as a condition of it, will take five strides and be out of your kingdom at the sixth."

For once, Hercules acknowledged himself vanquished. The Pygmies Tale was handed down over the centuries to future generations of pygmies, telling tale of the day that the valiant pygmies avenged the death of the giant Antaeus by scaring away the mighty Hercules.

But finally, I must tell you that Antaeus was not really slain, but somewhat dazed, and after a while, picked himself up and wandered away to find himself a home with better luck and as far away from Hercules as possible.

Josselin wriggled down and shuffled away, this time behind a chair. Alliane sighed and stretched her legs.

"Good grief," she said.

"Don't worry about us," Nerys said, arching an eyebrow. "We'll deal with Joss – you go and play at being a ranger."

"It's more interesting than primping about the palace pretending to be a lady." Alliane sneered at her twin.

"For goodness sake, Alliane, just go if you're going." Roda whipped up the squealing Josselin into her arms and started to rock him back and forth.

"Enough, now." Everyone was quiet when Nana spoke. "We don't need this, with the way your brother is feeling at the moment." Alliane skulked towards the door, knowing that Nana was right, but unable to stay. Somewhere between Hercules falling asleep and the Pygmies attacking him, she had had an idea. Whether or not it would work, remained to be seen.

***

Nils Martan sped down the corridor towards the royal children's' quarters where he hoped to find the Queen. His news could not wait. The identity of the Prince's saviour would throw into question his safety and future as heir to Carentan. A thousand possibilities swarmed around in Nils's mind and despite the chill of the castle corridors, he was starting to feel hot beneath his robes. He was pleased to note that the guards were keeping a vigil outside the doors and nodded to them as he hurried into the Prince's quarters. The receiving room was empty, except for a few guest chairs and two servants standing either side of the door to the Prince's chamber. The Queen emerged from her son's sleeping quarters just as Nils's entrance was announced by the servants. She closed the door to his chamber and gestured Nils to enter the living quarters on the opposite side of the entrance. It was a large, bright room that overlooked the castle

31

gardens. Most of the Prince's formal education took place in that room and the large oak table was precariously piled with books and scrolls on a variety of subjects from strategic defence and weaponry to the history of the Western Isles. Caitlin turned her full attention to Nils, who began to sweat profusely under the heat of her gaze. The expectation in her expression was uncompromising.

"Your Highness." Nils glanced nervously at the servants standing to attention. The Queen nodded to the two young men who left the room. When Nils was sure they were alone, he said, "Fulk Borsa is your man."

A flicker of surprise escaped Caitlin's measured gaze. Then she nodded, a smile tugging at the corners of her mouth. Nils could visualise the thoughts and possibilities running amok inside her head.

"You are sure?" She said.

"Absolutely. I have it on good authority that-" The Queen raised a hand.

"I don't need to know how, just that it is so." Nils nodded, pleased that the Queen trusted his word without explanation. "Does anyone else know or suspect?"

"No, your Highness."

"Good. Let it stay that way. I want you to invite Fulk Borsa to the Great Hall later today, use whatever excuse you can think of, just get him here. We have hearings to carry out, but I will see him afterwards. Inform Chancellor Lorquin that his presence will be required." Nils nodded and bowed as the Queen turned away, silently dismissing him. He backed out into the corridor, closing the doors on his exit.

Great gods, she worked fast. He could see from her expression, that she had already formed a plan, while he was still reeling with the possibilities. He nodded again at the servants and guards. Normally he would find time for a few friendly words of motivation, but there were duties that could not be delayed.

33

Chapter Five

"Bitch!" Reynald, Lord of Borsa, slammed his fist down on the oak table making the cups and plates jump to the tune of his anger. Fulk stood in the background, impassive and mighty in his silence, observing the reaction from his cousin to the news that Reynald's sister, the Queen Regent, had banished two Borsa squires from the realm of Carentan.

The messenger shifted nervously from one foot to the other.

"Dismissed," Reynald said. The messenger dropped his scroll lightly on the table and scurried out. Reynald strode around the table and swiped at the scroll, sending it and several cups flying across the room. This was exactly the kind of behaviour Fulk had grown to expect from this man.

Reynald had taken him into his employ at a young age, much to the pride and honour of Fulk's family. Fulk was really only the son of a distant cousin, but Reynald had been looking for an heir after the Borsa line had died out. Joffrey, Reynald's younger brother had disappeared some years ago in unusual circumstances. A few years later, Reynald's two young sons and their mother had been taken by the fever. His current wife, Lady Amelia, had just produced her second daughter.

Fulk shuddered when he thought of the recent bruising around Amelia's arms and on her face. Her pale and delicate features carried the burden not only of recent childbirth, but also of a disappointed spouse. Fulk longed to take her away, somewhere safe. This was not a house for children. His initiation into House Borsa was proof enough of that. He vowed not to let another young person suffer at the hands of Reynald. He would find a way somehow, to get Amelia and her children away from there, before it was too late. Fulk narrowed his eyes as he watched Reynald storm about the room.

Though older, Reynald was fit and strong for his age. He bore the heavy shouldered, thickset countenance of his northern ancestry, but had the fiery temper often attributed to lowlanders. The native people of Carentan were genial and slow to wrath, but when unfairly treated were capable of incandescent temper – Fulk had seen this trait before in the Queen. She was exceedingly tolerant of the provincial barons, but when one of them stepped out of line, her power to command was legendary.

"Well? Have you nothing to say?" Reynald turned to glare at Fulk who returned the look with an impassive, levelled gaze. Fulk shrugged, knowing that this simple gesture would add fuel to the fire. Reynald hated the fact that Fulk was uncommunicative and he hated that he could not be drawn into an argument. He often dismissed Fulk as a simple-minded fighting man, incapable of articulate speech and unable to grasp the political nuances at play in the Western Isles. But Fulk had developed his own measure of protection. He was a fighting man, a powerful warrior, undefeated in combat and no one could touch him physically. Reynald's only hold over him was with words as he tried, unsuccessfully, to shape Fulk into the political schemer that he himself had become. Unlike his sister, Reynald was unable to control his temper and was eaten up by a bitter jealously that burned inside him.

"What is the point of having you spend your days serving Queen and country if I don't get some benefit from it?" Reynald said.

"Benefit?" Fulk frowned.

"Good gods, man, do you not see what is happening right under your nose? She is playing us all for fools. Rumours abound from the kingdoms to the south and west of Carentan. They are waiting in the wings for civil war before marching in to claim Carentan as their own. And all the time, she is buttering up the barons with her lies, stalling for time until that snivelling little brat grows up to take his father's shoes." Reynald threw up his hands in despair then stalked over to the door where the servants waited for his call. "Clear this mess up," he said, then turned to face Fulk, who recoiled a little in the full glare of his attention. "We await the company of an esteemed visitor. It might surprise you to learn that Baron Issoire is open to negotiations. I need not remind you that we should pick our allies carefully now that the future of Carentan lies in the balance. Whatever the outcome of this meeting, I want you to be mindful of who it is you really work for."

***

Baron Chanac Issoire arrived at House Borsa behind a tight screen of his elite knights. Fulk watched from behind the many officials and staff lined up to greet him. Reynald's eyes narrowed at the sight of the man and his entourage, as though he didn't trust him. With his massive master knight-at-arms at his right side, Issoire was introduced to the

36

assembled company by Reynald, who displayed a touch more enthusiasm than was customary. Issoire's wealth and holdings made him a potentially strong ally in Reynald's battle against House Andolin.

Issoire was a slender man of medium height. His sharp features and fathomless black eyes revealed nothing of the real man. He did not smile as he shook hands with each official in turn. He only hesitated when he was presented with the Lady of the House, Amelia. Fulk was surprised at Reynald; he usually liked to roll out Amelia at times like this as she had such delicate and pretty features and a winning smile. However, in her current state, Fulk doubted she would be winning any hearts that day. Perhaps it was a calculated risk. Issoire took Amelia's hand and his eyes rested on her face for a brief second longer than any of the others. Fulk noticed a fleeting look cross behind his eyes; was it empathy? Horror?

Before Fulk could ponder further, Issoire had moved on. Despite his slight frame he had a firm handshake, which served to re-enforce his reputation of a skilful and accomplished swordsman. Fulk was under no illusions about the man's personal power. He wondered if Reynald had considered this when he decided to engage in dealings with a man like Issoire. The entourage quickly passed and Reynald glared over his shoulder at Fulk. Had he been staring too long at their guest? He never could understand what it was that Reynald wanted of him.

Issoire was directed towards the meeting room, which had been cleared and replenished with refreshments. Fulk held back for a moment, reticent of getting involved in the kind of politics Reynald indulged in. Reynald caught his eye and with a frustrated nod of his head indicated that he should sit. Issoire glanced at the exchange between them, revealing nothing in his expression, but Fulk was certain that Issoire was a man who never missed the slightest social nuance.

"I trust your journey was comfortable," Reynald said as the servants busied around pouring goblets of wine and serving cheese. Issoire nodded politely, taking a seat. His personal guards stood by the door and Reynald seemed uncomfortable with their presence. Issoire waved a hand towards his men.

"Please, don't be offended. I take them everywhere, just a precaution, you understand," he said.

"Yes, quite," Reynald said. "So, to business." The door swung open and a wary face peered through the gap. Fulk recoiled inwardly as Sir Denzl Charrock stepped into the room. It was all he could do to remain seated and not run him though with a broadsword in recompense for what his son had done. It was better than the weasel deserved. But Fulk remained seated and impassive.

"Ah, my good man. Baron Issoire, may I introduce Sir Denzl Charrock?" Issoire rose slowly from his seat, his eyes fixed on Charrock's face, his expression unreadable. He took Charrock's proffered hand, then sat back.

"Terrible business at Helmstedt, I understand. Shocking." Issoire's voice had a soft velvet undertone, which belied the obvious threat beneath his words. "I believe the Prince will make a full

38

recovery, though."

Charrock looked like a deer, frozen in the path of the hunter. His eyes, normally narrow and piggy looking, were wide and searching, unsure what to make of Issoire's words. He hesitated, then took a seat.

Reynald lead the ensuing discussion, which turned into something of a monologue. What were Issoire's ambitions for himself and Carentan? How good was his relationship with the Andolins? Did he think Carentan had a stable future? Statements, questions and innuendos on these and allied topics flowed from Reynald's lips. To all this Issoire was largely silent and answered briefly, if at all, in terms both vague and ambiguous.

Finally Issoire smiled and for the first time since his arrival the atmosphere seemed to relax a little. Fulk was convinced that there was no depth behind that smile; it was a political smile. He got the impression that Issoire was a man who spoke convincingly, but said nothing. Even his silences revealed little of substance. He was a master of equivocation and deception. Fulk wondered whether Reynald truly appreciated the danger of getting involved with a man like Issoire. What seemed so obvious to Fulk, who was continually scolded for being socially inept, seemed to have been overlooked by Reynald, blinded as he was by his own self-importance. Issoire was certainly a dangerous man, but dangerous to whom?

Chapter Six

Three weeks after the Pygmies Tale, Alliane returned to Castle Helmsted after riding out with the forest rangers.

"What in the world happened to you?" Nerys flew to the doors of the chamber to help her sister, who was caked in mud and had a large bruise on the side of her face.

"It's nothing really, don't fuss so, Nerys. I just fell off my pony, while out with the rangers." Well actually it was a carefully orchestrated bolt and tumble that she had been practising in order snare the attention of a certain giant named Fulk Borsa, but there was no need to divulge that bit of information to her nosy twin. Nerys frowned at Alliane as though she found it all rather hard to swallow.

"But you are the most accomplished rider of us all – you never fall."

"Yes, well you know what they say," Alliane said, "first time for everything. Now, help me get out of these muddy clothes." Nerys stared at her, rooted to the spot. "What?" Alliane said. Nerys raised an eyebrow. "Why can I do nothing without you suspecting that I am up to something?"

"Because usually you are." Nerys put her hands on her hips. "Come on, tell. Else, I'll go to Roda and you'll wish you'd shared it with me then," Nerys said.

"Oh, you are so annoying. Help me get cleaned up and I'll tell you then," Alliane said.

Nerys bustled Alliane towards the bathing area, an annexe to their sleeping chamber, and popped her head around the door to that lead to the living area.

"Celie, can you get some hot water and towels?" Nerys said.

"Is Princess Alliane all right?" Celie said.

"Yes, she'll be fine. I'll look after her, just get some water and towels, please," Nerys said.

"Only, there is a knight waiting outside the door to the quarters and he won't go away until he has news of the Princess. He is most insistent," Celie said. Nerys frowned and glanced back at Alliane who would not have been able to hide her blush were it not for the mud smeared across her face.

"A knight? Heavens. Let me sort out Alliane and then we'll see to the knight. Thank you, Celie." Nerys shut the door gently behind her and turned to face Alliane, who had begun to disrobe. Alliane turned to see her sister with that disapproving frown on her face and her hand on her hips again. Gods, she hated it when Nerys made everything her business. "Apparently there is knight waiting outside the door who will not leave until he has news of you. Know anything about that?" Nerys said. Alliane fought back a coy smile, as she recalled the concerned look Fulk had given her, as he had deposited her at the chamber door. He had carried her all the way from the forest where her pony had tossed her, nearly knocking herself unconscious in the process. Perhaps it had worked a little too well. She had dug her heel in a bit too forcefully and the little pony, Erith, had dutifully bolted and chucked her further than she had at first calculated. Of course, the other thing she had not expected was the large stone embedded in the earth where she landed. In fact, she had been so dazed that she had forgotten why she was doing it in the first place. And then, as predicted, Fulk was at her side. He seldom said anything and many of the girls in the castle joked about him being a simpleton, but Alliane wasn't bothered about that. It was his good nature and brawn that she was counting on.

There was rap on the door and Celie entered carrying a jug of hot water and clean towels. After several trips to and fro with jugs of steaming water, the maid stood in the doorway waiting for further instructions.

"Thank you Celie," Nerys said. The maid curtsied and left the room. Alliane sat in the tin bath and let her sister pour water over her face, hair and back. She ached all over and the water felt good. Yes, perhaps her plan had worked too well. She hadn't even had the chance to talk to Fulk about Gereinte.

"Ally, you worry me sometimes. What were you playing at?"

"Nerys," Alliane lowered her voice to almost a whisper. "You know the knight Fulk? I am trying to get him to help us, to help Gereinte. But if I tell, then everyone will know and Gereinte will not like it. You know how he hates it when people follow him about. But Fulk is perfect, he will just be there, in the background if anything goes wrong again." Alliane was so excited and animated, she forgot her fatigue and began washing herself vigorously.

Nerys sighed. "Ally, you can't manipulate people like that. Have you asked this of the knight yet?"

"Well, not exactly… first I want to get him on my side," Alliane looked sheepish.

"So you figure that playing the dumb princess who can't control her pony and then knocks herself senseless is going to win his favour? Which school of courting did you go to? No don't tell me, you've been taking lessons from baby Josselin."

Alliane was hurt by her sister's mockery and sucked in her lower lip, sitting still in the tub. "Oh don't sulk like that. If you want to know how to attract someone's attention, you should have come to me. I could have half the squires in the palace eating out of my hand," Nerys said.

"That's easy when you look like you. Look at me. Dumpy, plain and boring. Who would take a second look at me?" A lump rose in Alliane's throat. She felt battered and bruised and for what reason? Maybe she should just go out and tell Fulk what a fraud she was and how she only did it for her brother and she was really using him. She had thought she was so clever and as usual, Nerys brought her back down to the ground with a thump.

"Ally, don't cry," Nerys pulled her soapy sister into her arms and hugged her. "Gereinte will be okay. Nana says he will be up and about soon and the best we can do for him is to let him be. He needs to grow and find his own way without interference from busy body sisters. He is going to be king one day."

"You are right," Alliane said. "Why are you always so flaming right? It makes me sick." Nerys giggled and playfully splashed her sister. Then Alliane dumped a handful of water on top of Nerys who then threw the remainder of the jug into Alliane's face. The twins descended into a squealing water fight, much to the angst of those standing behind closed doors.

***

The nursemaid, Celie, popped her head out from behind the chamber door.

"The Princess Alliane is fine. Thank you," she said. The knight Fulk heard the girls' squealing from inside the chamber. The nursemaid shut the door and the knight slipped quietly away, deep in thought.

Chapter Seven

It was several weeks following Alliane's accident that Gereinte finally emerged from his chambers and ventured outdoors. There was a faint sense of freedom, despite the retinue of guards and servants following in his wake. He sat on the bench at the far end of the training ground, watching the knights go through training drills with their squires. Heaving a long sigh, he moved one bench closer to the action. Without even glancing behind, he knew that his personal guard will have mimicked his movement and further closed the gap between them. Not even up for one day and already he was starting to feel the constraints of being Prince Royal, pressing down on him.

His whole body ached with pain and his ribs were tight with the bandage that squeezed his middle. However often he played the scene over and over in his mind, he always ended up at the same place; being slammed in the chest by a huge bear-like creature clad in green. He winced and shifted his weight, trying to alleviate the stabbing pain in his chest. He supposed that a few broken ribs were a small price to pay for his life. It was a miracle. A strange and unholy thing that he could speak to no one about, lest he be accused of at best, insanity and at worst witchcraft. His father once told him a secret about the forest rangers. That they had the power to bring someone back from the dead. Is that what had happened? A forest ranger had found him and brought him back?

In the distance, beyond the walls of the training ground, he saw a group of riders approaching the castle grounds. Probably his sisters returning from their ride; he hoped they wouldn't start fussing at him being outdoors. It really was getting ridiculous. He couldn't move his big toe without someone popping up to tell him where to go and what to do. He glanced over his shoulder at the burly chap that Nils had recently recruited to stand guard over him. He looked primed and ready to leap over the benches and pin Gereinte to the floor if he moved again. Great. How in the world was he going to get out of this one?

Gereinte turned his attention back to the squires, who had now paired up with their knights for sparring practice. There was one knight, a huge thickset man, who didn't have a squire. The knight was going from pair to pair, shouting encouragement and correcting the young squires in their posture and technique. Gereinte stood up and inched further forward to get a better look at the knight. The hairs on the back of his neck prickled. It was Fulk Borsa; no need to question why he had no squire. Gereinte leaned forward, holding onto the wooden railing which surrounded the training ring and squinted to get a better look at him. He had the right build. And Fulk was a forest ranger, which would explain the green attire. But, why? To be nearly killed by one Borsa, only to be saved by another? It didn't make any sense to him. The knight looked up from his tutoring and stared right back at him. He held Gereinte's gaze for a moment before returning to his tutoring.

Over the other side of the training ground, Gereinte saw Alliane and Nerys trotting towards the stables on their ponies accompanied by a guard. He looked around again at his own personal guard who was accompanied by two servants, three knights of the Queen's Guard, one Royal Adviser and bunch of people from who knew where. Good grief. He really was going to have to do something about this.

Alliane spotted him. He watched her dismount, hand her pony's reigns to Nerys and come running around to his side of the training ground.

***

Fulk held the young Prince's gaze for as long as he dared before looking away. He put his hands on the squire who was sparring ineffectually with his knight. The knight was batting the squire about with the wooden practice sword like a cat that had just caught a mouse and this was not really helping the boy improve.

"Turn your body this way," Fulk said. He positioned the young squire so that his body was side on. "That way you become less of a target." The squire nearly toppled sideways, just regaining his balance in time to fend off another barrage of attacks from his training partner.

Fulk watched impassively. His mind was distracted by the complexities of the political landscape. As Reynald was trying to manipulate the most influential barons to back him in opposition to House Andolin, it appeared that the other local barons were busy manipulating each other. Everyone tried to remain impartial, waiting to see who would come out on top. Who didn't want to be on the winning side? And then Fulk appeared to be stuck in the middle, purporting to be a knight of the realm, yet invited to witness at first hand Reynald's treasonous plotting. And yet, nothing was ever said

47

out loud, everything was implied. That was what he found so frustrating; why couldn't these people just come out and say what they wanted to say? Fulk knew full well that that the Queen's little 'informal chat' with him was a plea for help to protect the Prince, so why could she not just come out and say it? And why did she have to have that lap dog, Chancellor Lorquin, standing by scrutinising Fulk's every gesture, every breath. And how was he supposed to act on such an implicit request? From the Queen's perspective, it would be foolish indeed to entrust the care of the Prince Royal to the person closest to her most active enemy.

Confused and torn, Fulk continued his rounds of the sparring squires, stopping every now and then to impart some words of wisdom or correct a failure in technique. Another young squire stepped into the advancing thrust of a seasoned knight and Fulk winced inwardly as he watched the boy crumple in pain around the wooden sword. He would be bruised for sure, but would be less likely to make the same mistake twice. Next time he might find himself impaled on the end of a broadsword.

Fulk glanced over again at the activity on the spectator benches. The Princess Alliane joined her brother. A Carentan Princess; prized for their beauty, charm and intelligence. Reynald never tired of telling the story of how stealing Carentan girls was a time-honoured sport among the young men of the bordering tribes of Salat and Tordre. Fulk bristled with anger at the thought, but Reynald seemed to find it amusing in a perverse kind of way. And he always managed to gloss over the end of the story; how King Reiner established the ranger

48

border patrols. To Fulk, that was the interesting bit. There was swift and brutal retribution visited on any village found to be harbouring anyone engaged in the activity of kidnapping girls. Fulk's pride as a ranger would never allow kidnapping on his watch. Reynald had balked at Fulk's request to train with the forest rangers as well as a knight, eventually giving in when Fulk managed to persuade him that it would bring him ever closer to his enemy and give them even more insight into the internal network of Castle Helmstedt.

Alliane glanced over at him, and then looked away. She was alluring in a way that was different from the classic Carentan girl. She looked more like the northern girls. Every time Fulk looked at her, he felt a pang in his heart for home. He knew he had done the right thing, as he was now able to send money and food back home to keep the family comfortable, but he missed his freedom, he missed his homeland. Somehow, being with Princess Alliane felt like going home. He frowned; the previous day's accident bothered him. Alliane was an accomplished rider, there was something not quite right about it. And when he had carried her in a daze back to the castle, she had said some disturbing things.

"Sir Fulk Borsa," the knight said. His squire had taken a blow to the ribs had been left without a partner. "May I indulge your expertise in a round?" The knight bowed low and Fulk retrieved a discarded sword, saluted his opponent before taking up a stance.

***

Alliane averted her gaze. He had seen her

49

looking. He must think her such a fool, falling off her pony like that. Her cheeks reddened, despite the distance between them.

"Ally... look." Gereinte shook her and pointed back towards Fulk, who had begun to circle another knight with his sword held ready. "Watch, if you want to see how it is really done."

"Really?" Alliane folded her arms across her chest and feigned a look of boredom, though she could not take her eyes off the action. The entire field had downed arms and backed to the edges of the arena forming a circle of spectators. The knights circled one another, each waiting for the first attack. Fulk's opponent feinted with a left thrust, then drove his sword forward; Fulk batted the sword away as though it were an annoying fly.

"Did you see that? He parried the thrust before his opponent began the feint... amazing speed for such a big man." Gereinte watched in awe.

"It's not speed, he's just good at reading body language," Alliane said. She was rewarded with a glare from her brother and decided it was probably better to keep quiet. After all, what did she know about fighting? She was 'just a girl'.

The knight attacked again in a whirlwind of strikes and thrusts, each blocked at every point by Fulk's sword, as he side-stepped and circled allowing his opponent the space to make his attacks.

"He's playing with him," Gereinte said, staring into the arena. "At any point, he could step in and finish it, but he's just letting the knight attack."

"If you ask me," Alliane said.

"Which I didn't," Gereinte said. She glared at her brother.

50

"If you ask me, that knight will be flat on his back before Sir Fulk even breaks a sweat."

Gereinte glanced at Alliane and frowned at her before looking back towards the action. What was it? Did she give something away in her tone; the way she talked about him? She never could keep a secret from Ger.

She was right, though. Fulk had barely broken a sweat and the other knight was visibly racked for breath, flailing ineffectively at his opponent. Fulk had obviously decided that enough was enough. He stepped on the inside of a weak thrust, parried and drove forward, knocking his opponent off his feet. The sword was like an extension of his arm, but he controlled it with perfect precision. The knight had landed on his back knocking the wind from his lungs as Fulk finished up with one foot on the knight's chest and the point of his sword just touching his throat.

"Ally," Gereinte said. "I've just had a fantastic idea." Alliane turned to look at her brother and shook her head. Please, she thought, for all that is good in this world, protect us from another one of Ger's crazy ideas.

Chapter Eight

"No, absolutely not. I forbid it." His mother's eyes challenged Gereinte, and he squirmed under her scrutiny. Fine. He would take it, like the man he longed to be, but he would not let her see the defeat in his own eyes as he held her gaze, steady and sure.

At first she had seemed angry, which is what he expected; when the Queen was really angry, she smacked you with her eyes. Then, there, her words were firm and there was no denying their meaning, but there was a softness around her eyes; a faint crinkling in the corners. It confused Gereinte, but also intrigued him. There were many layers to his mother that he could not begin to fathom. "The Prince Royal does not act as Squire. Not under any circumstances. It has never happened in the past and is not about to change." His mother's eyes flashed dangerously for a moment before she gathered her robes and strode towards the rectangular window at the far end of the Great Hall. Her skirts swished a royal magenta in her wake.

Chancellor Lorquin cast an anxious look at Gereinte before scurrying after his Queen. The Queen's hearings had just finished for the day. Gereinte had been waiting for the last of the commoners to leave, so he could talk to her. He had only this single-minded notion of gaining some experience and at the same time some independence from this prison-like existence. He couldn't shout 'boo' without some royal adviser popping up to advise on his use of language.

The Chancellor and the Queen conversed in hushed tones, a view of Carentan stretched out before them. From where he stood, Gereinte could just about make out the winding route of the River Caren, carrying its cargo loads in and out of the realm. He visualised himself on a boat, travelling the length of the rich lands of the Western Isles; Malvas to the North; Vermondie to the South.

What was the problem anyway? Gereinte paced up and down; a habit he had acquired from his father. It helped him to alleviate nervous tension, while at the same time adding to the air of authority he was trying to cultivate. There had to be some give and take. He desperately needed to cut his teeth at ground level and this was the ideal opportunity. Fulk was without a squire due to recent events, so it made sense for him to step into that role and take his training like a real warrior, not like the pampered little prince everyone was trying so desperately to protect. How would he ever learn to take care of the country when he couldn't even take care of himself? Gereinte stopped pacing and stared above the heads of the Queen and Chancellor. He shuddered, visualising his ascension to power only to be cut down in the flesh by the first challenger to his throne.

Rupert Lorquin, the Chancellor, cast an apologetic look at Gereinte as his mother continued to rant in whispers at a distance. Gereinte smiled at the Chancellor, who appeared to be the only person in the room who was flustered by the whole scenario. He wondered what was going through the man's head, as mother and son played a game of royal chess. Lorquin had no doubt spent the afternoon in the company of the Queen, presiding over the common disputes brought before the

Crown by the people of Carentan. His expertise was traditionally in areas of finance, but Lorquin acted in his capacity as adviser on many fronts. Gereinte also noticed the little tell-tale signs displayed by Rupert Lorquin when in his mother's company; the way he leaned in closer to her as she talked – perhaps a little closer than would normally be acceptable for the Queen's adviser. The way he would catch her gaze and hold it for a second longer than most men would dare. Neither did it escape Gereinte's notice that his mother appeared to encourage this attentive behaviour from her Chancellor.

The Queen came back to face Gereinte, as cool as a winter's day. The Chancellor hovered nervously by her side.

"Tell me, my son," her eyes glittered with mischief, "what do your lessons in the history of Carentan tell you about the duties of a Prince Royal?" Gereinte squared up to his mother, fully prepared for a battle of wits, when a curious idea struck him. He opened his mouth to respond, then snapped it shut with a hollow 'clop' sound. The Queen smiled, her expression dared him to find a counter to her argument, but instead Gereinte chose to remain silent. "Nothing to say?" his mother said sweetly. "How refreshing." Gereinte flashed an angry look at his mother before turning on his heel and striding away. Beneath the mask of discontent, he smiled to himself. He paused by the door without turning as he heard his mother 'tut' to herself and mutter "So like his father." Gereinte left without a backward glance.

***

The sun had begun to drop, giving a timeless feel to the evening still of the Great Hall. Caitlin turned towards her Chancellor and smiled. Rupert Lorquin basked in the glow of her gaze.

"Do you think it will work, your Highness?" He said.

"Oh yes, my dear Chancellor. If I know my son, it will work," she said staring at the empty door.

***

"This is never going to work." Alliane stood with her arms folded and frowned at him. He looked down at his clothes, which matched that of a squire in training and grinned at his sister. It was all he could do not to start hopping from one foot to the other with glee. It was perfect. And even if it didn't work, it would be such fun to see everyone running around in confusion for a while. His strength had returned in the few weeks after he had failed to persuade his mother to let him train as a squire. Enough time also to come up with a plan.

"You're mad. I think you must have landed on your head a few times during your beating." Alliane had no shame in speaking the truth.

"Will you stop doing the sister thing. You're not even older than me. I'm the one who should be looking out for you." Frustration was beginning to wear him down. If she could only see how important this was to him.

"A lot of use you'll be twitching on the end of a broadsword," Alliane said.

"How can I ever be a king if I don't know how to fight? Warmaster Alaric tries, but no one will come near me since the incident for fear of being banished if they touch me. I can't do anything, learn anything. This is the best way." Gereinte smoothed back his dark hair and fixed a golden wig upon his head. Alliane burst out laughing and this time Gereinte stood with his arms folded across his chest. There was a light knock on the door and both brother and sister turned expectantly as a young lad, about the same height and build as Gereinte entered the prince's chambers. "Ah. This is Devlin. Devlin, this is my sister, Alliane," Gereinte said. The boy bowed his head towards Alliane. "Give us five minutes and you won't be able to tell the difference."

Gereinte and Devlin disappeared into his sleeping chambers, while Alliane remained outside. He could hear her pacing up and down, as they swapped clothes. He glanced out the window. Beyond the Inner Ward and on the other side of its moat, lay the training ground and the armsmen's quarters. He could just about make out someone in the garden, picking herbs – one of the nursemaids, perhaps. Beyond that, it was impossible to see what the knights and their squires were up to.

Was this as ridiculous as Alliane insisted? Would he get away with passing himself off as a squire without anyone recognising him? And if the Queen found out what they were up to, he would never be allowed out of the castle again. And now, Alliane was an accessory to this deceit. When they were done, he opened up the door to the outer chamber and the two boys walked out side by side. Alliane looked from one to the other and smiled. She nodded her approval.

"Now that's not bad. Say something," she said.

Gereinte glanced sideways at Devlin who drew a

sword, went down on one knee and laid the sword on the floor in front of them. Then he spoke, in rather faltering Etanese.

"Prince Gereinte, at your service."

Alliane looked from Devlin to Gereinte, and then back to Devlin, who grinned and shrugged his shoulders.

"Okay, so maybe you need to keep your mouths shut," Alliane said.

57

Chapter Nine

Sunlight cast a yellow hue across the floor of the Great Hall, where Caitlin presided over a dispute between a local freeholder and his Lord. The argument, as was so often the case, was over unpaid taxes. The local man was clearly impoverished by a bad season's crop and was offering his services in the Lord's household as recompense. Unfortunately, the Lord was having none of it. Caitlin sighed. This Lord was a pompous idiot with an over-inflated ego and this wasn't the first time he had washed his dirty laundry in public. She cast a disparaging glance in the direction of Chancellor Lorquin who spread his hands as if to say 'your call, Highness'. Why was it always she who had to settle this kind of nonsense? She wished now that she had paid more attention to how Reiner had handled such petty arguments. Right now, her head was too full of bigger things. But perhaps she could turn such a tedious duty to her advantage.

"Your Highness," began the idiot in the yellow tunic and thigh length boots.

"As you know, I have considerable experience of dealing with such disputes on my own estate and would not want to waste-"

"Thank you." Caitlin held her hand out to stop him mid sentence. "I have made my decision. I shall buy your services, Messer," she said, turning to address the freeholder. "Which will earn you enough to pay off the debt to your Lord." She turned back and waved her hand dismissively. "Now go," she said to the Lord, whose face fell as he realised he had been robbed of the chance to earn some interest on the debt. "Messer, stay, and I will tell you what I need," she said to the freeholder who managed to look both dumbfounded and apprehensive. As the Lord retired from the Great Hall, Caitlin turned to look at Lorquin who looked as equally dumbfounded as the freeholder.

"Your Highness," the Chancellor lowered his voice. "Be wary of starting a precedent."

"Oh nonsense, Chancellor. These are petty Lords who know their place. The barons are quick to remind them of that. And we all know who pulls their strings," Caitlin said with a sly smile.

Chancellor Lorquin shook his head in disbelief. "Perhaps you might let me hold court on your behalf occasionally, Your Highness? These small-time issues are clearly beginning to bore you." His smile was ironic and Caitlin, who took it in the vein it was intended, returned a barely stifled yawn. She raised an eyebrow.

"Oh really, Chancellor, I haven't had so much fun in weeks." She returned her attention to the freeholder, who now looked utterly bewildered.

"Right," she said. "What can you do for me, I wonder? Come closer, Messer, and tell me what is going on in the territories outside Castle Helmstedt. My eyes and ears tell me there is much civil unrest. Is this true?"

"Y... your Highness." The freeholder took a few steps forward, then went down on one knee. "Had I been able to settle this in the local court, I would not have dared bring such a petty matter before your Highness."

"Yes, yes, we've done with all that, I've settled the debt and in return all I ask of you is

59

information," Caitlin said. The man flinched at the sharpness of her tone, then continued.

"Your Highness, that is what I am trying to say. The reason I came here today is because the barons are controlling everything through the local courts and yes, there is much civil unrest. The landowners are being squeezed by certain Lords who have sworn fealty to certain barons."

"Certain this, certain that... you can name names here, Messer. I may hazard a guess that Baron Borsa might have something to do with this?" The man flinched again at the mention of Borsa. She sighed. Up to his old tricks, no doubt.

"Issoire-"

"What?" Caitlin sat upright.

"Has been seen in the Eastern Territories, visiting House Borsa."

Issoire. Now why would Chanac Issoire be negotiating with her rat of a brother? That seemed to Caitlin to be a most unlikely alliance. However, it was often hard to tell with Issoire, being such a private man. It didn't bode well that he had taken enough trouble to cross the River Caren from his home in the Western Territory to visit Borsa without paying his respects to the Queen Regent. It troubled her further that he may be implicated in the apparent plan to control the laws of Carentan without consulting the Royal Courts. She gave the freeholder her full attention.

"I have one last task for you," she said. The man paled under her scrutiny. "Make it known that I am very eager to hear your disputes, however trivial. My court is open to all. With this, you may consider your debt re-paid." The man bowed his head and backed quickly out of the Great Hall.

Caitlin turned to see a frown on Lorquin's face. "Well you said you wanted to hold court on my behalf, dear Chancellor. I think you may have plenty of opportunity now."

"Your Highness. About the Baron..." Caitlin held up her hand to silence Lorquin. She saw and ignored the spark of irritation that flared up then quickly faded in his eyes.

"If you mean Issoire, I have that in hand. I think the time has come to begin negotiations with our neighbouring countries. Call a meeting of my council, Chancellor, we have much to discuss."

Chapter Ten

Caitlin stood outside the conference room, smoothed the creases in her emerald green gown, took a deep breath then smoothed the creases of anxiety from her face. Reiner had always favoured this room which served both as an outer chamber to their living quarters and as a discussion room for the royal advisers. She strode towards the entrance doors before opening them inward. The royal guards stepped into position behind her and the doors thudded as they closed. All heads rose at her entrance and the conversation ceased as though a veil had been thrown across the room and its occupants. The large round table served to facilitate discussion and around it sat her retinue of staff, which included Seneschal Martan, Chancellor Lorquin and Warmaster Alaric.

Caitlin nodded and took her seat facing the window, which revealed the distant cliffs of the Helm; symbolic, she always thought, of the impenetrability of Castle Helmstedt. The men rose out of courtesy as she took her seat, before returning to their original positions. Sunlight spilt across the table and lit up the creased parchment rolled out and held down by a large grey flat stone in each corner. The room had a musty smell to it, like old scrolls. On the parchment was a detailed map of the Western Isles split into realms with a variety of markings added over the years to indicate various alliances and battles of times past. It was a favourite game of Reiner's to bring out the little wooden figurines that represented his armies and that of their enemies, to discuss strategic advancement with the Warmaster and their advisers. Caitlin had always sat in on their meetings, absorbing their tactics and watching as the political shape of the landscape of the Western Isles changed and evolved into what was represented on the ancient scroll spread out in front of them.

"Your Highness." Alaric Beothys, the Warmaster, was broad in stature and a formidable force to be reckoned with on the battlefield. His dark, long hair was tied roughly back and his clothes always had a rough and ready look. Must have been all that time he spent training the castle's defensive guard. Characteristic of a Northerner, his expression was stern and he had a dour outlook on life, largely shaped by an arduous childhood having been raised in a mining family in the foothills of the great Helm mountain range. Anyone surviving that kind of upbringing deserved respect, Caitlin thought.

"Chancellor Lorquin has briefed us of the royal intention to operate a wider remit in the courts system. However, my presence here can only mean one thing to me."

A fleeting look of irritation crossed the Warmaster's face and she ignored it.

"Alaric. I appreciate your concern, but let me reassure you that we are not about to launch into battle with our nearest neighbours." The Warmaster's shoulders sagged and she wondered if it was from relief or disappointment. "Please understand that I honour my husband's wish to have you involved in every step, political or strategic."

All eyes were fixed on Caitlin and the room collectively held its breath. Now she had their attention. "With the Barons attempting to control the courts system and the current civil unrest, I feel that the time is right to build an alliance. An alliance through marriage." She caught the Chancellor's eye and he smiled.

Caitlin took a measured look at Warmaster Alaric. He had been with House Andolin for most of his adult life and had served Reiner with unswerving loyalty, a loyalty that had always been extended to Caitlin. His strength was in strategic defence and battle tactics, so when it came to political discussions his input could be crucial.

"An alliance, your highness?" Nils broke her silent appraisal and Caitlin turned to address the rest of the room.

"As I said, an alliance through marriage." The advisers around the table nodded their approval, led as was often the case, by the Chancellor who was usually over enthusiastic about the Queen Regent's words – especially in company. Caitlin sometimes imagined him bursting into spontaneous applause. However, when the moment required it, Lorquin was not afraid to tell her when something was about to go horribly wrong. In this case, Caitlin was pleased to witness a comfortable level of support from her advisers. She glanced at Alaric and noted his face was grim. Something was bothering him about the whole idea and Caitlin was curious. She tried to catch his eye, but his gaze was steadfast and fixed at a point in the centre of the map on the table in front of them. He gently shook his head, as though shrugging off a crazy thought, then leaned forward to inspect the map of the Western Isles a little more closely.

"And the map, your Highness? I take it we are not here to plan a march into Vermondie?" Alaric scrutinised Caitlin. His look was challenging, but not enough to stir her defences. She met his eye with unrivalled composure and dignity.

"No, my dear Alaric. We are not about to march into Vermondie. However, the map is here for us to discuss a possible neighbour who might gain mutual benefits from marrying into the Andolin dynasty. Perhaps a royal wedding is just what this realm needs to bring back some stability. We all know how much the commoners love a celebration. Let us give them one to remember."

"Are we to assume that you have already discussed this matter with your eldest daughter, your highness?" Alaric asked in a tone that was polite and yet searching. Caitlin paused, judging the impact of her next words.

"Gentlemen," she said with her eyes on Alaric. "It was always my late husband's wish that Roda be married into a wealthy family to cement our alliances. However, on this occasion, it will be Nerys who is to be betrothed." Silence hung in the air. She thought there might have been some disagreement, Nerys being so young, but her advisers launched no complaint. Caitlin held her breath for a second and glanced at Alaric. She had expected to see disbelief in his eyes but instead was greeted with what could only be described as relief. Now she knew. The Warmaster had a softness growing for her eldest daughter, Roda. She should have felt heartened by this revelation; however, she regretted that she was only delaying the moment of bitterness for Alaric, as Roda had always been promised to another.

The Chancellor looked pleased with himself, but then the Chancellor already knew what Caitlin had in mind. The other advisers were a little sceptical.

"Your Highness," Nils said. "Her young age does make things a little complicated, don't you think?"

"Not at all Seneschal. We shall have an announcement, which will stir everyone up and get them looking forward to a betrothal ceremony, which will follow a few months later. Then we shall begin arrangements, which will take us up to the end of next winter, by which time, Nerys will be of age."

"Has Nerys been made aware of your plans?" Nils said.

"No, not yet. Nerys is far too young and flighty to know what is good for her. Besides, as long as we find someone rich and good-looking, Nerys will be absolutely delighted. It has always been her dream to marry into a royal family."

Nils nodded his agreement, although Caitlin could sense that he felt a little uneasy about it. Alaric, however, seemed eager to commence proceedings.

"Then we shall discuss the best possible place to begin negotiations," Alaric said as he began to study the markings on the map. Caitlin leant forward to look at all the markings that obviously meant something to Alaric.

The meeting progressed as well as Caitlin could have hoped. Serving staff came and went with refreshments, as the sun began its descent towards the horizon. The afternoon gave way into evening, the staff came and lit the wall candles and flickering shadows crept up the walls. The map retained its pride of place as the centre piece and the discussions narrowed to two possibilities; Malvas and Sarlat.

"King Phillipe Rudelle of Malvas has a son, doesn't he?" Lorquin said, hopefully. Caitlin could see that the advisers were tiring of the discussion, but she was determined to get the right match before negotiations could begin. To form an unstable alliance would possibly have a more damaging effect on foreign relations than no alliance at all.

"He does." Caitlin tapped the Malvas region of the map thoughtfully.

"Your Highness," Alaric said. "I have grave misgivings about an alliance with Malvas."

"Based on what, Warmaster?"

"On religious grounds, your Highness. Malvas has a long history of being in bed with the Priesthood, if you'll pardon the expression. The Archbishop of the Church of One God, Abiel Morda, has long had his eyes fixed on Carentan. Any alliance with Malvas could give him the foothold he has been waiting for."

"The Priesthood lack power in Carentan – it would be very hard for the Archbishop to displace the belief in the ancient deities. Although, I do acknowledge that Morda's ambition to create a Holy Church Authority may one day be strong enough to challenge us." Caitlin looked around the table and most seemed to be in agreement. "However, this is not a decision that we can take lightly. If we take on Malvas, we take on Morda and I will not tolerate his white clad, so called,

'Immaculate Knights' running amok in Carentan."

Caitlin fixed her gaze on Alaric. The silence was measured but decisive.

"What about Sarlat?" Nils said.

Caitlin scanned the room. There was no immediate negative feedback, but the expression on most faces was nothing if not wary. The Sarlatians were renowned throughout the Western Isles for their tricky and sometimes downright dishonest dealings. 'As honourable as a Sarlat' was the bitter jest used to describe a suspected dishonest person. In the same vein, 'when you have shaken hands with a Sarlatian, don't bother counting your fingers, just make sure you still have a hand.'

"Sarlat is a distinct possibility then," said Caitlin, taking the silence to mean agreement. She smiled briefly as the eyes widened around the table.

"Sarlat is also rife with believers of the One God," Alaric said hastily.

"Ah ha. True, but that was not your first thought or misgiving, Alaric, was it?" Caitlin watched his face flush under the chagrin of being exposed. She laughed. "We all know how circumspect people are when dealing with Sarlat, but I have met Alvar Correze, the King of Sarlat, and both he and his daughter, Fiamina, are very agreeable people." Caitlin paused to gauge the impact of her words, but her audience still looked unconvinced. "Besides, the Priesthood has far less power in Sarlat than in Malvas."

"Your Highness," Nils said. "Despite the many other considerations, Sarlat would be the most obvious choice in terms of political alliances. We all know that for many years, the risk of Sarlat joining forces with Tordre and Vermondie has loomed in the distance, threatening the very stability of Carentan. An alliance with Sarlat would put an end to speculation."

"They would turn and stab you in the back as soon as look at you." Alaric said. "And besides, the King has a daughter, but no son."

"We don't have to look at a direct descendent from the royal family. A rich and powerful baron would equally provide us with the foothold we need," Nils said.

"I can't see the Princess settling for anything less than a prince," Alaric said.

"Nerys has no choice in the matter." Caitlin was getting irritated with all the petty negativity surrounding both Sarlat and Malvas. "The Princess will do as she is told. Perhaps, Alaric, since you have made your disagreement quite plain, you have an alternative in mind?"

Alaric looked back to the map and all heads around the table returned in silent scrutiny to the scribbled political notes that had built up a picture of the Western Isles over the years. His short stubby fingers traced around the borders of Carentan, passing Sarlat to the west, Malvas to the north, Vermondie to the south and coming at last to rest on the small border between Carentan and Tordre to the south-west.

"Tordre," he said. "No religious alliances. Politically, situated right in the middle of the unofficial triumvirate of nations working against Carentan. Without Tordre, there is no way that Sarlat and Vermondie can move against us. In addition, the capital city of T'sar is situated in the north, here." Alaric stabbed a finger on the map and all eyes followed his movement. "Right beside the estuary leading to the river Caren. An ideal spot from which to gain advantage, should the other two nations decide to invade."

Caitlin smiled and nodded. Ever the strategist, Warmaster Alaric had his moments of sheer genius. She looked around the table and saw enlightenment in the eyes of her advisers.

"The Tordreans are a peaceable nation," Caitlin said. "Indeed, they are probably the least of our worries in any conspiracy against Carentan. An alliance here would not put paid to the clandestine negotiations between Sarlat and Vermondie, but it would certainly drive a wedge between them." She nodded her approval. "However, they have an unusual system of succession to the throne, which may or may not work to our advantage. According to my closest eyes and ears in Tordre, upon the death of the current Monarch, the succeeding ruler, be they male or female, is chosen by an arcane combination of votes and acclamation."

"Your Highness, the current ruler, King Morra Dreiden, has no offspring and is not expected to die off any time soon. I understand he is quite a young man," Nils said. "If we were to begin negotiations in Tordre, might we think about setting our sights no lower than the king himself?"

"Do we know if he is looking for a queen?" Caitlin said. There was an excited buzz of conversation around the table and she looked to Alaric who appeared satisfied that his suggestion had caused so much excitement. "It would not guarantee her or any children as successors to the throne, but it would cement our relationship with Tordre in the short term." Caitlin waved a hand to silence the room and all eyes once more fell to her for guidance. "Nils, we shall work on a letter to be dispatched at once. I will need your assistance with a cipher as I fear this is one letter that may not find a direct route to its recipient."

"House Borsa, I presume?" Alaric looked grim. Caitlin nodded.

"We must always presume that our correspondence is going to be intercepted. However, I have an idea that may throw him off track."

"The ciphers?" Nils rose and bowed briefly. "I shall return."

At his departure, the room buzzed with light conversation as the meeting dissolved into idle chat and expectation of events to come.

Chapter Eleven

On a good day, the reflected sunlight would cast an ethereal shimmer across Lake Mariac, but on that particular day the sky was overcast and the surface of the water murky and fathomless. It was not very often that Gereinte was granted permission to ride with the Queen's Guard beyond the Outer Gate and even less often that his sister, Alliane, was allowed to accompany him.

It took Gereinte's breath away whenever he looked towards the precipitous cliffs on the castle's northern side. Every other side of Castle Helmstedt was bound by Lake Mariac, where they now stopped to allow the horses some water. Alliane trotted her chestnut pony alongside Gereinte's palomino mare and together they walked the animals to the water's edge and allowed their heads to drop down and take a drink. The smell of horses, stagnant water and fern permeated the air.

"How is the training, dear brother?" Alliane said with barely concealed mischief.

"The training is fine, dear sister. How is the subterfuge?" Gereinte said.

"I think Nerys suspects something."

"Well, you never could keep a secret from Nerys."

"I didn't tell her a thing," Alliane said.

"Ally... you don't need to. When will you learn?"

"Well, it just annoys me. She is always poking her nose into things."

"Perhaps we should tell her – she'll find out soon enough and tell mother." Gereinte was convinced

72

that the Queen already knew what was going on. He had a fair idea of who reported to whom and although it probably suited both him and the Queen to pretend, it would not be the best idea in terms of winning the hearts and minds of the nation, if his sister were to go shouting about his whereabouts.

"I'll talk to her when we get back," Alliane said. Gereinte could feel her discomfort. He knew only too well how Ally longed for independence from her twin and loved to hold a secret that Nerys did not share.

With the horses sufficiently watered, the scouting party continued along their route. They were accompanied by the Queen's Guard arrayed in their purple colours, two personal guards – largely to watch the backs of the royal children – and five royal advisers. The advisers acted as both a protective measure and an educational opportunity for Gereinte, but it was often Alliane who took advantage of their vast political and historical knowledge.

The plan was to follow the outer edge of the lake until they could go no further, stopped by the cliffs of the helm, then make their way back on the inner edge towards the Outer Gate drawbridge.

The royal advisers closed their net around the Andolin children and Gereinte cast a sideways glance at Alliane who was smiling at his discomfort. Unlike his sister, who loved attention, he dreamt of being able to ride off alone towards the forest in search of an adventure. He wondered what would happen if one day he to set off in search of adventure dressed as a squire. How long would it take the royal entourage to come running after him?

Perhaps he might test that theory... but not until he had exhausted his interest in playing at being a squire. In a few weeks' time, there would be an opportunity for Gereinte to accompany Fulk on a ranger patrol out in the forest. After much cajoling as Fulk's squire, Gereinte had managed to persuade him of the benefits he might gain from such an experience. Fulk remained dubious, insisting that the forest rangers did a completely different kind of work to that of the knights, but in the end Gereinte had won him over.

When Gereinte had first turned up at the training ground to replace Fulk's original squire, there had been not a flicker of recognition in his eyes when Fulk looked him up and down. Gereinte had wondered then at the simplicity of both his plan and his knight. It had all gone far more smoothly than he had expected. Almost as though the entire castle was 'playing along'. Well, he would find out, one way or another. And if it turned out that he had been 'allowed' to play the fool, then he could certainly stir up some action and have everyone dancing to his tune, if only for a little while.

Chapter Twelve

There was definitely something strange going on. She couldn't quite put her finger on it, but Nerys knew when Alliane was hiding something. She hoped it wasn't another one of her hare-brained plans to protect Gereinte from the world of rough and tumble that seemed to preoccupy every boy of that age, royal prince or not. As far as Nerys was concerned, the only person Gereinte needed protecting from was himself. Still, she didn't want Ally landing herself in unnecessary trouble for the sake of a boyish whim. Another thing that bothered her was that Alliane had suddenly taken an interest in the boys at the training ground. It wasn't at all like her.

The chamber was quiet. Celie bustled about with blankets and was seeing to the bed linen. Josselin was asleep and his nursemaid, Isla, could be heard singing a soft and soulful lullaby to the baby. As far as Nerys knew, Alliane was outside watching the boys train. Gereinte would be next door studying. Lately, he had become very attentive to his studies. Normally he would be looking for every excuse to get outside. Perhaps he had begun at last to take his situation seriously; one day soon, he would be the king. Perhaps he had begun to understand the burden that was attached to that responsibility. It was just unfortunate that someone had had to beat him within a whisker of his life before he would see some sense.

Nerys started for the door. Perhaps the new responsible Ger could shed some light on their sister's erratic behaviour. A few weeks ago, he had stated quite clearly that he did not want to be disturbed during these three hours, but Nerys felt that her concern for Alliane outweighed the possible distraction to his studies. The guard outside the door shifted his weight, then settled back down when Nerys crossed the corridor. She knocked lightly on Gereinte's door and heard a muffled response, which sounded like 'go away', but she couldn't be too sure, and so gently pushed the door open.

Gereinte was sat behind his large oak table, back to the door and head buried in a pile of books. He did not look up as Nerys entered the room and closed the door behind her. Something about the way he kept his head down and did not respond to her entering the room didn't seem right to Nerys.

"Ger..?" Nerys said. Gereinte coughed and almost forced the words out of his mouth.

"Can't talk, right now." More muffled coughing, followed by a lot of fumbling around with books and pages, almost as though he had been interrupted in the middle of doing something bad and just realised that he was supposed to be studying.

"Ger, I need to talk to you. It's about Alliane." Instead of responding with curiosity about his sister, which Nerys might have expected, Ger was behaving very strangely. He pulled at his clothing, re-arranging himself as though he had a chill and pulled his hat down around his ears. It was most bizarre. He remained seated, facing away from the door. Well. Nerys had just about had enough of this. She strode towards her brother, expecting to elicit a reaction.

"Gereinte… the least you could do is turn and face-" she took a sideways glance at Gereinte's

76

face. "What in the world have you done to your..." Nerys's hands flew to her face and she stifled a scream as the person whom she thought was Gereinte leapt up from his seat and started waving his hands about.

Her first thought was 'someone has murdered or kidnapped my brother and replaced him with this strange boy'. But clearly this boy did not look like the murdering type, so it dawned on Nerys that her original instinct – that Gereinte and Alliane were behaving out of character – was more likely. And judging by the way that the Gereinte-imposter was leaping about, waving his hands and making shush noises, further confirmed her worst suspicions; that Alliane had colluded with Gereinte and that they were both up to no good.

"Who are you?" Nerys said. The boy had begun to calm down; now that he was satisfied Nerys was not going to scream down the tower.

"Devlin, my Princess." He stopped leaping from one foot to the other, bowed his head down and averted his eyes. Nerys felt suddenly as though she was back in control of the situation. She was the Princess, he was the imposter and she was going to get some answers out of him.

"Devlin? Devlin who and what are you doing in Prince Gereinte's quarters?" He peered up at her and gave that dark sultry look that Ger was so good at. He tried ineffectively to hide his smile.

"I'm not allowed to say, my Princess." His big brown eyes caught her gaze, and then looked away. Nerys' heart began to thump steadily in her chest. No one had ever called her 'my Princess' before. It was always, your Highness or just Princess. It had a kind of familiarity to it that bordered on audacious. He was an extraordinary looking young man, now that she had been able to get a closer look. He did look a lot like Gereinte; noble features, slight of build, but with hidden strengths. This Devlin had a moody playfulness that Nerys found instantly attractive. Nerys had the distinct feeling that he was not going to just give her the information she needed.

"I see," she said. She had seen her mother use this approach with commoners before. Don't let them think they had won any kind of advantage from the outset. "Well, if you are not going to tell me what I want to know, then I shall have to call the guards in and have you removed." At which Nerys turned smartly on her heels and strode towards the door.

"My princess... I implore you," Devlin said.

Nerys stopped before she reached the door, smiled to herself before fixing a stern look to her face and turning to face Devlin.

"Well?" she said.

"I'll tell you what you want to know. But first, I would like you to tell me something," Devlin said. Nerys was flabbergasted.

"You do not bargain with-"

"Hear me out, my Princess. I wish to know if you are betrothed?"

"I.." The words stuck in her mouth. "I.." All thought and reason flew out the window. Nerys was torn between feeling outraged and flattered. Her instinct told her to turn and leave the room immediately, but something kept her there, some unknown curiosity about this boy. It bothered her. It

78

bothered her a good deal that this young man was even here, let alone taking such a studied interest in her.

"No..," she said cautiously. "Not yet." Devlin's eyes twinkled and he grinned mischievously. He came a little closer, bent down on one knee and took hold of Nerys's hand. A warm feeling spread throughout her body as his skin touched hers and she shivered involuntarily despite the heat of the moment.

"Then may I ask if you will marry me?" Devlin looked earnest. Nerys could not believe what was happening.

"I... don't be ridiculous. I have to marry a prince."

"I am a prince. Look," Devlin smoothed a hand down the front of his tunic.

"But, that is just..."

The door burst open and the real Gereinte came tumbling in, closely followed by Alliane. Nerys turned and gasped, as though she were the one who had been up to no good. Devlin rose to his feet and for an instant, Gereinte looked confused.

"Oh don't mind her," Alliane said. "She's most likely got everything she wants to know out of him by now."

Nerys turned back to Devlin, her face a cloud of anger. "It was all a ruse, wasn't it?"

"I... no, please. I'll explain everything," Devlin faltered under her gaze.

"Don't bother. I think I can work out what is going on here." She turned to face Gereinte. "How long did you think this would go on before someone found out your stupid little plan?"

79

"Nerys, no one needs to know. This way, I get to go out, practice my fighting skills and all under the protection of the Queen's Knights," Gereinte said. Nerys looked from Gereinte to Devlin, then back to Gereinte, then smiled slowly. She felt a little of her anger ebb around the edges.

"It is a good likeness. You could have trusted me, you know. I thought Ally… oh, I don't know what I thought." Nerys looked back at Devlin and frowned. "That wasn't funny."

"What wasn't funny?" Alliane said.

Devlin lowered himself to one knee again. "My Princess, I meant every word." Nerys saw Gereinte and Alliane exchange glances and Alliane raised her eyes to the heavens and sighed. Nerys ignored Devlin and swept past Gereinte and Alliane, grabbing Alliane's hand on her way towards the door. "Come on Ally, we have things to talk about. We'll leave the boys to their fun and games."

Nerys closed the door of the chambers behind herself and her sister. She leaned her back against the door and let her head tilt back. She had never been quite so taken with a young man as she was with Devlin; he was… different. Confident, far too confident and she must not let him think he had got to her.

Alliane was looking at her with a raised eyebrow. Nerys knew that look and Alliane had this annoying habit of giving her that look at the one moment in time when she least needed it. Alliane almost always knew what Nerys was thinking.

"Please… don't tell me you've fallen for that idiot?" Alliane said. Nerys gave herself a mental shake and stood up straight. She strode across to the window and looked out over the castle grounds.

"Don't be ridiculous, he is just a squire playing at being a prince."

"You have, haven't you?" Alliane stood with her hands on her hips. Nerys hated it when she did that.

"What has it got to do with you anyhow?" Nerys said. "At least I have an interest in men, unlike you who just wants to be one of them. I can't see any prince worth his title taking a second glance at you, all scruffed up and muddy after playing at being a ranger."

"Nerys, Just listen to yourself. You couldn't marry one of those boys even if you wanted to. They are beneath you – don't even waste time thinking about it."

"Who said anything about marriage? I just like him, that's all. Besides, I think a woman should marry for love not money," Nery said.

"I thought your lifelong ambition was to marry a prince and cement an important political alliance?" Alliane said with a sneer.

"Oh, bother all of that nonsense," Nerys said, not quite convincing herself.

"With that attitude, you might as well marry a stable boy," Alliane said.

"Why don't you just run along and find a big dumb knight to manipulate instead of annoying me?" Nerys said.

Alliane fumed. "Oh, go and jump out the window, Nerys."

"Maybe I will, then you'll be sorry."

"I don't think so."

"No?"

"No."

"That's good then."

"Good."

"Good."

Both girls folded their arms across their chests and turned their backs to each other. Nerys contemplated the window, then thought better of it, for risk of spoiling her gown. She looked over her shoulder and glared at Alliane's back. Alliane's shoulders began to jig up and down and for a moment she thought she was crying and then realised that she was actually laughing. How could she? After all that... but despite her anger, Nerys started to giggle in spite of everything and Alliane swung around at the sound and threw her arms around her sister.

"I'm sorry, Nerys. I would be sorry if you jumped out the window. Your face was a picture." Nerys returned her sister's hug.

"Why didn't you tell me about Gereinte's plan? I feel like you two don't trust me or something," Nerys said.

"I was about to tell you. In fact I was just coming to find you, but unfortunately you found Devlin first."

"Oh, yes. He is kind of sweet though."

"He's still an idiot," Alliane said. Nerys glared at her. "So we'll agree to disagree on that. Besides, he won't be around for much longer. Ger is going on a ranger patrol in the next couple of weeks, after which he has agreed to call a halt on the whole thing." Nerys felt her heart flutter.

"But, why?"

"Well, you'll have to speak to him about that, but I think he is getting restless again. This prank was a welcome distraction, but now it is starting to bore him. You know what he is like, always looking for the opportunity to stir things up. That's how he always ends up getting into trouble," Alliane said. Nerys knew that this was true, but it troubled her to admit it.

"If he is to be king, he is going to have to learn to curb his inquisitive nature," Nerys said.

"I think you're wrong. It may get him in to trouble now, but in years to come it will help. He can think about things from all different angles," Alliane said. Nerys looked sceptically at her sister.

"You've been talking to Nils again, haven't you?" Nery said.

"He makes a lot of sense, you know. You should try talking to the adults sometimes, it might improve your outlook on life."

Nerys pulled a sour face at Alliane. "Well, let's just hope Ger doesn't get himself killed before he has a chance to use his superior thinking skills."

Chapter Thirteen

Fulk was looking out of the window across the grounds of Castle Borsa, when he saw the messenger arrive. It was one of Reynald's spies. He knew them all now, which ones worked at Helmstedt, which ones were with the Clergy and all the others dotted around and about the various Baronial palaces in Carentan. This one was the postal messenger. He worked at Helmstedt and intercepted all communications from the Queen and her advisers. The messenger skidded to a halt at the stables and dismounted in such a hurry that Fulk thought he might fall flat on his face in the muddy courtyard. He threw the reins at the stable boy, then marched up to the house.

This would be interesting. No doubt Reynald would require Fulk's presence, along with the House Seneschal, who did all the deciphering. Absolutely nothing of any importance went out from Castle Helmstedt without a cipher. Quite simply, the Queen knew all of Reynald's little tricks. Fulk knew that whatever the letter contained, Reynald would never get to the bottom of the truth, as the Queen used codes from every book written to hide her true intent. However, Reynald could never admit that he didn't know what she was up to, even if it were the complete opposite. His pride would never let him admit that the Queen had outwitted him.

Fulk put on his formal tunic and traced his steps towards the meeting room, where Reynald was sat poring over maps of the Western Isles with his Chief Armsman. Reynald was barking orders and servants were running about this way and that, rounding up his officials and advisers. He spotted Fulk hovering near the door and beckoned him in. Fulk entered, confused by the unusual activity.

"A message. From the castle," Reynald said. "For the god's sake, man – get the Seneschal." A servant scurried off at top speed looking like a startled hare. One or two officials took their seats around the table and servants brought refreshments. Fulk took his place at the table as they all awaited the man who purportedly deciphered the Queen's letters. Although, he had been known to get it spectacularly wrong on occasion. Like the time that Reynald had sent all of his troops out to supposedly support the Queen's Guard from an imminent invasion from the West by Sarlat. As it happened, all they found was an escort of forest rangers, bringing King Alvar and his retinue safely through the Forest of Dreams on a friendly visit to Castle Helmstedt. Fulk had been by Borsa's side when they had circled the party demanding to know the meaning of this unprecedented visit. Borsa's embarrassment had been quickly smoothed over by a story of extra safeguards to protect the Queen Regent and her visitors, but it all fell flat when he realised that she had the best in Carentan already in attendance. The forest rangers, who knew the territory better than anyone and the Queen's guard, who were renowned throughout the Western Isles for their fighting prowess. Reynald had been outnumbered, outmanoeuvred and outwitted.

A thin weaselling man appeared at the doorway, carrying two large weathered books. He hesitated before entering the room. Fulk wondered at how the current Seneschal had survived here with all the bullying and punishing behaviour. But Reynald could not manage without his expertise in the written word. Despite his sometimes-skewed attempts at deciphering, he kept a tight rein on the household budget. Which was exactly how Reynald liked it.

"Come, come – dear god, man, we've been waiting half a day for you."

The Seneschal flinched and placed the two books in the centre of the table. "Ah. The Almanac of Medicine and the Book of the Past, good choice, good choice." Reynald nodded his approval. Fulk smiled to himself. If he had all the almanacs ever written, they would never clearly decipher the Queen Regent's message. Fulk knew this, but said nothing. Let Reynald play his games and pretend that his sister Caitlin, wasn't really steering him on exactly the course she wished. The Seneschal carefully scribed the words in the letter onto a piece of parchment, then started to flick through the almanac looking for matches.

Hours later, Reynald sat back in his seat with a sigh of satisfaction. He

looked around the table at his advisers and the Seneschal who was sweating profusely over a copy of Abiel Morda's Herbal.

"So… we are to have a royal engagement. Fitting, in such a climate. Let us not see if we can throw a few barriers along the way. Are you sure it is with Sarlat that they begin negotiations?" Reynald pinned the Seneschal down with his gaze. The Seneschal wilted under his scrutiny.

"P…p…p… positive, my Lord," the Seneschal

said, sounding anything but.

"So this letter to King Dreiden of Tordre is a hoax, to throw us off track? Hmm. Interesting. Sarlat would be the obvious choice, so why would my dear sister think that we might consider the ridiculous notion of pairing with Tordre? Tordre has always looked towards Carentan with secret admiration. They pose the least threat. Coupled with which, their political system does not guarantee a royal bloodline." The advisers nodded in appreciation of Reynald's logical conclusion. "Prepare an envoy to go to Sarlat on my behalf. We shall begin some negotiations of our own. We may even supersede the Queen's best laid plans." Borsa chuckled and dismissed his retinue of staff. Before Fulk had a chance to escape, Reynald placed a hand on his shoulder.

"There are some things we need to discuss, Fulk." Fulk sank back down into his chair and resigned himself to the inevitable scrutiny of Reynald's plans. "All is set, yes?"

"We ride out in one week's time, my Lord."

"Good, good." Reynald produced a tightly rolled scroll from inside his jacket and unrolled it. Fulk recognised the map of the Forest of Dreams and its immediate surroundings. "There is a path, just here, that leads to a section which is secluded and cannot be seen for miles. That is where the outlaws will wait. It is unfortunate that there will be other casualties, but we need to make it look like an accidental death. After all, no one really knows it is the Prince who is riding out with you. As far as anyone else is concerned, it is just your squire. I would just love to see the look on my sister's face when she discovers she has been deceived on all counts."

Fulk was silent. He had told Reynald as much as he knew. He had his own suspicions about how little or how much the Queen knew; he even thought that the Prince himself was probably more aware of what was really going on than he let on. He knew the Forest inside out. He also knew that the rangers they were riding with were not likely to let outlaws into the Forest; that was the whole point of the patrols.

"How will you get your men past the ranger patrols?" Fulk said.

"Ah. Eyes and ears, my boy. Eyes and ears." He clapped a hand on Fulk's shoulder and left him to worry about what that meant. "All you have to do is lead the boy to his end. Although I want this done properly, you cannot be seen to side with the outlaws; I still need your eyes and ears at Helmstedt. Their motive is robbery and some of the brigands will engage you in combat. Do what you need to in order to make it realistic. These men are expendable. You are not."

"What of the Princess?" Fulk said, deliberately changing the subject. A big ugly smile filled Reynald's face.

"I believe she has already met our lad and that she has taken the bait. I think we could yet scupper the Queen's plans for a happy engagement, even though at the end of the day, Princess Nerys will have to do the Queen's bidding, I am sure that her headstrong nature will make the path much rockier for all intended." Fulk remained impassive, though a sickly feeling stirred in his gut at what Reynald might be doing to the innocent young girl. It was one thing playing at outlaws in the forest with grown men, but this was messing with a young girl's mind on cusp of her changing into a young woman.

"We do it right this time," Reynald said. "You have seen what happens when you send a boy in to do a man's job. Well let us make sure the Prince has a taste of what it is like to be a man before he dies."

"What of the baby?" Fulk said, again changing the subject from mildly uncomfortable to unbearable if his thoughts lingered too long on the Reynald's plans. Plans that were set to destroy the Andolin dynasty in one fell swoop. Reynald justified his actions by reassuring himself that he was the one who had been wronged; that his true place in the hierarchy of Carentan rulers had been usurped. But even with this, Fulk could plainly see, he was having difficulty in vindicating himself.

"All is set. I have sent word. The job will be done amidst the chaos of what is about to unfurl in the Forest."

Chapter Fourteen

"Why do you look so glum?" Nerys said as she entered Gereinte's living quarters and went over to talk to Devlin. Since their first encounter and now that Nerys had got over the mistaken identity crisis, she and Devlin had found lots in common to talk about. There was something dangerously exciting about meeting like this, with an older boy and one with whom she shared her brother's secret. Devlin stood up, reached out and took both of Nerys's hands. His touch felt warm and reassuring.

"Tomorrow will be my last day here. Gereinte is riding out with the forest rangers, after which he has agreed that we will return to our former duties; he to being Prince of Carentan and I to being just a squire. I have come to enjoy the comforts of being prince for a while, even if I am holed up in the royal quarters." Nerys squeezed his hands in hers.

"Is it just playing at being prince that you will miss?" She said. He smiled and his whole face lit up.

"Most of all, I will miss our little meetings. But I feel we are living on borrowed time." He made puppy dog eyes at her and Nerys felt like her insides were full of butterflies. She let out a long sigh and he pulled her closer.

"This is never going to work," Nerys said. "The Queen would not allow it. I have to marry a real prince."

"If you marry me, then I will be a prince." Devlin said, with a glint in his eye. Nerys thought about this for a moment and could see the logic behind it, however misguided. For the first time in their growing relationship, she began to harbour a hope. A hope that one day she might indeed be allowed to marry for love, rather than duty. Devlin reached down and cupped her face in his hands. She was lost. Lost in his eyes and the sweet scent of his breath as he lingered close to her lips. The touch of his lips on hers sent shivers through her body and his kiss enveloped her in a warm shroud, awakening the young woman in her. He pulled away suddenly and looked at her, a fierce longing reflected in his eyes.

"We can still meet. It will be our secret," Devlin said. Hope blossomed inside Nerys.

"Yes. We can and we will," Nerys said. He wrapped his arms around her fragile frame and drew her close to his chest. She breathed in his musky scent, closed her eyes and willed the future to allow them to be together.

***

As Delyth cast an eye out of the window and across the castle grounds, she saw the big knight, Fulk, on his horse ride out with his squire. She pondered for a moment on the significance of what she saw. The knight was wearing the colours of a forest ranger. The boy glanced oddly over his shoulder. The good breed of pony the boy rode – far superior for a mere squire. The way the boy's hair sat far too neatly upon his head. Delyth had been trained to assess at a single glance the meaning of a set of circumstances, however seemingly trivial. Whatever was to happen that day, this family had the curse of a wealthy man on its back.

The chambers were quiet; unnaturally so. The quiet before the storm. It was true to say that immediately preceding an event of great magnitude, there was always an unearthly stillness, like nature holding its breath.

Josselin started to cry and Delyth released her hold, suddenly realising that she had been squeezing the child to her chest. The baby craned his body away from her, as though he sensed that something was not quite right. She took him to his feeding chair and gave him the concoction she had prepared earlier. He devoured the feed like his last supper and Delyth waited and watched as his eyes began to grow heavy and was waiting to catch his little body as it slumped in the chair. She wrapped him in swaddling clothes and hid him in a sling beneath her garments, over which she carried the panniers she was expected to use in order to collect supplies from the village. One last check of the rooms, to make sure that all evidence of her short stay at the castle had been eliminated, then she left at exactly the same time she did each day of the week.

Outside the door, the guard nodded at her and she politely dipped her head in acknowledgement. Celie would return very soon to find a bundle of baby clothes in place of Josselin, at which point the alarm would be raised. She had precious little time to get into the forest and disappear before the Queen's Guard would come after her. She knew that as long as she made it to the forest, they would never find her and they would never again see Josselin. That was the deal. The child must die and his little finger would be sent to her client as proof.

***

It was a usual morning. Gereinte and Devlin made their switch, as Devlin took up his post for the last time and Gereinte put on his squire disguise for his final foray into the forest as a squire to a Queen's Knight. He turned to leave his chambers and the boy, Devlin, winked at him in a far too familiar way that made his hackles rise with inexplicable alarm. There was something about that boy which didn't sit right. It also had not gone without notice that Nerys had been spending an unusual amount of time in his company of late.

Gereinte put aside his misgivings. It was probably just paranoia. He was starting to get like his mother, thinking that everyone was out to get him. Besides, today's adventure was far more appealing to think about. His first challenge was how to lose the royal spies that he knew would be following them every step of the way.

At the stables, Fulk was already mounted and waiting. He wore the traditional green and browns of the forest rangers and the sight of him towering above the world on his huge warhorse brought back flashes of memory from the time he had nearly died at the hands of Fulk's former squire. Gereinte had never quite been sure whether the knight's presence had been fortuitous or a foreboding. Over the weeks, he had come to trust Fulk, despite initial misgivings.

Gereinte mounted his Palomino, which looked like a pony alongside the knight's steed and they set off at a walk towards the Inner Gate. The gate was drawn back when they reached it and the inner walls were lined with the Castle Guard. No one came in or out of the inner ward without everyone in the Castle knowing. It was a comforting thought when it came to defence, but less comforting for

93

Gereinte's ever growing impatience for independence. They headed away now at a trot and although still within the middle ward of the castle, it felt like they were on common ground. The plain stretched ahead of them, circled in the distance by the woods, which surrounded the far end of the grounds and obscured the view of the forbidding walls. It struck Gereinte as odd that even with such a presence, he had managed to race unseen into the woods. He remembered what Nils had drummed into all of them from a young age; never to fully trust your staff, for powerful people have eyes and ears everywhere. Let the flimsy squires come after him now; he felt stronger and fitter than ever before. He had had several growth spurts over the last few months which, coupled with the rigorous sword training and daily duties, had developed his muscles. He still had a slim, lithe stature but now with an underlying strength.

They made it to the Middle Gate without being stopped by any royal advisers and Gereinte wondered whether they would make it into the forest without attracting the retinue of guards that usually popped up whenever he took off anywhere.

They passed through into the Outer Ward without incident and crossed the bridge to the far side of the Outer Gate and just as he took a deep breath of freedom, Gereinte sensed the movement behind them. He glanced briefly over his shoulder and recognised the purple colours of the Queen's Guard, settling into a steady pace at enough of a respectable distance to maintain objectivity. He let out a sigh. This only served to confirm his suspicions; he may have fooled Fulk and a host of other castle staff, but the Queen Regent was always one step ahead. It angered him that he had been played for a fool. But it was not in his nature to let it upset him. He would get even. There would be opportunity enough to lose the Queen's Guard once in the forest. And there was one thing that he had on his side today; the forest rangers.

Chapter Fifteen

Despite the camouflage of the trees, Gereinte could still see the steady retinue of purple following in their wake. He glanced at Fulk, who smiled and shook his head wearily. He knew. Of course he did; Fulk was a Knight of the Queen's Guard himself.

"Why didn't you say something?" Gereinte said. Fulk shrugged and remained silent. "Can we lose them?"

For a while, they continued at a leisurely pace, as Fulk remained silent. Perhaps today would be a day of reckoning. If Fulk were acting on behalf of the Queen for the Prince's safety then he would not allow Gereinte to wander into uncharted territory. On the other hand, how would he know that the Queen had not orchestrated some bizarre cover up to make it look like she had given him free rein?

Once they had turned a bend and momentarily lost sight of the purple clad pursuers, Gereinte took a sharp left up a long since disused forest path leading back upon themselves. Fulk was quick to follow and caught up with him.

"Your Highness. I do not recommend this course of action. There are things in this forest that are better left undiscovered. Staying to the path will ensure a safe passage," Fulk said.

"I cannot and will not be followed in every breath of my life by guards intent on dragging me back to the castle at the first sign of danger." Gereinte cracked his reins and took off at a canter up a steep slope, coming to a sharp stop at a point overlooking the path they had just trodden. He could see the purple of the Queen's Guard as they walked their mounts steadily up the pathway and past Gereinte's exit point from the track. "That was easy enough. They are not even looking at the tracks on the ground. Did they not expect us to take a diversion?" He looked at Fulk, who returned his gaze with a stony look.

"No."

"Ah. So you were supposed to keep me on the path?" Gereinte said. Fulk nodded once. "And they don't have a tracker in the party?"

"I am the tracker for the Queen's Guard." Fulk said. Gereinte burst out laughing.

"Oh, that is too perfect. Come on, let's get lost in the forest."

Fulk shook his head. "There will be no getting lost in the forest today, your Highness. I know these lands like the back of my hand."

Gereinte smiled to himself. Even better, he thought. Even better.

For a while they followed the tracks of the Queen's Guard, until the wash of purple that streaked through the forest greens became a distant blur and it was evident that they had returned to the castle. Gereinte pictured the Queen Regent's face as her retinue of soldiers admitted that they had lost track of the Prince Royal in the Forest of Dreams.

"I want to see the furthest reaches of this land before we return tonight." Gereinte gave an authoritative tone to his voice in the hope it might impact on Fulk's demeanour. Fulk stared impassively ahead, with no response to his liege. "Tell me about the Forest, Fulk. What is it that people fear?"

"Brigands, wildlife, kidnappers."

"Kidnappers?"

"Have you not heard the stories of how and why the forest rangers began?" Fulk said.

Gereinte thought for a moment, as an image of his father crossed his mind, telling stories of the dangers in the forest and his plans of securing the castle perimeter for the future King of Carentan. At the time, Gereinte barely recognised the fact that he might be that king, but enjoyed the story telling and the closeness of his father, nonetheless.

"I remember something. Something my father once told me."

"He was a good man, your father. This area used to be rife with strangers, looking to capture a Carentan princess." Fulk's voice wavered with a mixture of pride and revulsion. "That was until King Reiner set up the border patrols."

"Why did you become a forest ranger?"

Fulk stopped his horse for a moment to allow Gereinte to pass ahead of him so he could bring up the rear. Gereinte wondered for a moment at this manoeuvre; he had a very sudden and odd feeling of being watched, although he could see nothing to verify his instinct.

"A man who has the power to control his environment is a man who has the power to control his destiny," Fulk said, without further explanation. Gereinte wasn't sure if he felt safer with Fulk at his back or taking the lead, but as the man said, he knew the forest like the back of his hand so the best Gereinte could do was to learn to trust this strange and circumspect man and hope that his intuition was right about Fulk's loyalty.

They rode in silence for a time, Gereinte

familiarising himself once more with the sounds and smells of the forest. The scent of fresh earth and foliage had never really left him once he had experienced what it was like to have his face buried in the undergrowth.

"To be a true Ranger, you must live and breath the Forest, understand its nature," Fulk said, as though reading Gereinte's mind. The sticky scent of sap from the trees was strong and Fulk stopped briefly to examine a deep welt in the wood. Gereinte looked over his shoulder and watched him pass a hand over the bark, then rub his fingers beneath his nose. Gereinte looked at the forest floor - the evidence of a recent scuffle was obvious, even to his untrained eye.

"Stay close to me, your Highness," Fulk said. Gereinte looked around, but all seemed quiet, but for the occasional rustle from the indigenous wildlife. He looked up into the trees as though expecting to see brigands leap from the branches to attack, but there was nothing there. Despite that, he still had an uneasy feeling that someone or something was watching them as they moved through the undergrowth. He slowed down to allow Fulk to catch up, trying to look as though he knew what he was doing and not that he felt safer in the company of the awesome knight. Fulk looked across at him and Gereinte thought he saw a flicker of amusement in his eyes, but it was hard to tell with Fulk.

"What was it like to become a knight?" Gereinte said.

It was a good few minutes before Fulk spoke; his words thoughtful and measured.

"You ask a lot of questions, your Highness. Sometimes, I am not sure if I can do them justice."

"A measured response, Sir Fulk. When I was just a squire, you might not have hesitated before regaling me with your stories."

"A squire has a different standing, your Highness," Fulk said.

"But you always knew that I was more than just a squire."

"That is not the point, your Highness. You thought I thought you were just a squire and that is how you expected to be treated. Everything has changed now."

"Everything has changed but nothing is different. How quaint. How very typical of the Queen Regent." Gereinte searched for signs that Fulk was under the influence of mother's command, but the great man remained impassive. Perhaps, after all, he was Borsa's man.

They rode on in silence and Gereinte wondered if he had pushed Fulk too far now. Perhaps in a little while he would just sling him over the back of his war horse and carry him home to his mother. Or would he carry him straight into the arms of his enemy, waiting in the wings to overthrow the name of Andolin in favour of House Borsa?

"If you had continued to play your game of being squire, you might have found out for yourself what it really means to be a knight," Fulk said.

Gereinte snorted. "You mean if I hadn't realised that everyone else was just playing along with me? And besides, I'm sure my mother would not have let it get that far." He was thoughtful for a moment as they shifted their mounts into single file to pass through a narrowing of the pathway. The branches of the trees appeared to be reaching down towards them, as though shielding them from something evil in the sky. He had never dared go this far into the forest before and felt sure that if his mother knew, she would have sent more than just one man to accompany him, even if that man was the most feared warrior in the entire Queen's Guard.

Gereinte looked up again into the forest canopy and stopped for an instant to stare in wonder at how it appeared to be moving along with them. Fulk either did not notice or was used to the tricks that the wind and light could play on leaves in the trees. Perhaps he was imagining that they appeared thicker and greener than before.

"How much do you know about the formal arming of a knight?" Fulk said, still staring at the path ahead. Gereinte snapped his head back to look at Fulk.

The Aboubement. He had read about it. "I know what has been documented in text, but little about what it is really like. After you've been through all that dressing ceremony, do they really leave you in the Temple of Gods all night?"

Fulk chuckled. "Dressing ceremony? Your peers strip you down, bathe you as a symbol of purification, then dress you in a white tunic to represent purity, a purple mantle to represent the colours of House Andolin, then black hose and shoes to symbolise death and the earth in which we all eventually lie. It was nothing like I have ever experienced before. I come from a Northern family. We do not stand on ceremony."

"And in the morning, did you have to pray?"

"I prayed all night to the gods, lying before the temple altar and in the morning made my confession to the high priestess. I found it surprisingly liberating," Fulk said.

"Liberating?"

Fulk sighed. "In the village where I was brought up, we were taught that there was one god, not many."

"I see. So then you began to feel a sense of belonging?" Gereinte did not get a response, but felt a little closer to understanding Fulk's words.

"It was like the end of an era and the dawn of a new life for me. Receiving the accolade from your father, King Reiner, is something I shall never forget. That is how it was for me. That is how it is for me. I shall live or die by the four injunctions I received on that day," Fulk said.

Gereinte had also read about the injunctions, but for some reason, he needed at that moment in time to hear them from Fulk's lips.

"Injunctions?" He said.

"Never make a deal with a traitor; never give evil counsel to a lady and always treat her with respect, defending her against all; observe fasts and abstinences and to pray every day to the temple gods." Fulk's utter conviction silenced Gereinte's enquiring mind.

Chapter Sixteen

The Forest rustled its leaves and hid its secrets among the trees. The horses plodded forward, accepting that they were going somewhere, wherever somewhere was. Gereinte mused on what Fulk had said. It was no big secret what you had to go through to become a knight. It was more the way he had said it; with such sincerity that it left no doubt in Gereinte's mind that Fulk really believed that he lived by these rules. And yet, can he really be that misguided not to see where the allegiances of his own Lord and master, Baron Borsa lay? Gereinte knew that his mother had good reason not to trust her own brother, but if Fulk really believed what he was saying and knew about Borsa's wrong dealings, then what was he doing, guiding the Prince Royal through probably the most underused and secluded part of the Forest of Dreams to who knew where?

Realisation hit him full force and Gereinte stopped, his mare side-stepping as he tugged the reins. Fulk appeared not to notice and the great warhorse continued its course. Gereinte's heart pounded and he felt sick with adrenalin. He whirled his palomino around and bolted in the opposite direction.

Fortunately, having the smaller horse worked to his advantage. He glanced over his shoulder and saw the knight struggle to turn with any speed on such a narrow path. He turned back to the path and cantered as fast as he dared without a backward glance. He got about two hundred yards before the forest erupted around him.

Two riders, brandishing broadswords, cut his exit off ahead and forced Gereinte off the path and into the undergrowth. The branches of the trees scraped his cheeks as his palomino struggled to maintain its speed on the uneven forest floor. He glanced either side and it seemed like the trees were running with him. In the distance he heard shouts; men barking orders and he could hear the thundering of horses getting closer. The two men who had burst onto the path in front of him were careening towards him in a direct line at a distance of about two hundred yards. A glance to his left saw four more men on horses, one of which looked to be the right size and build of Fulk. The men wore black tunics and scruffy scarves wrapped around their heads. They were either brigands or wanted him to believe they were. He couldn't tell if Fulk were leading them or chasing them, but either way, all parties were about to meet in a clearing not one hundred yards ahead.

Gereinte burst into the light as his assailants cut off his exit once again. Fulk's warhorse thundered into the clearing at a fraction of a second behind the others and Gereinte watched as he threw something long, thin and silvery into the air as if launching a spear. Then Gereinte realised, as the brigands turned on him that he was sat atop his horse weaponless. He turned the horse just in time and reached up to catch the hilt of the long sword thrown by Fulk, as the leading man ran in to attack.

The brigand used two hands to launch an attack with his broadsword. It was a killing blow, but one that relied more on luck than speed. Gereinte parried quickly and the force of that blow reverberated down his sword arm. He switched hands and thrust his sword low, beneath the ribs of the man whose speed was hampered by the size of his sword. The man's eyes opened wide as he slid from Gereinte's sword and slumped over the back of his horse. Time appeared to slow down, and for an instant stand still, as Gereinte studied the fine quality of the horse beneath the man. He could see a finer layer of clothing masked by the black tunic below and wondered at the ease with which the man had died.

An earth-shattering scream broke across his thoughts and plunged him back into the fray as he sidestepped an attack from the next man before he could mull over what he had just witnessed. This next one was more determined than the first and was swinging his sword in an arc with almost disdainful neglect for swordsmanship. Over the man's shoulder, Gereinte could see Fulk running his sword cleanly through a third brigand, then suddenly from the trees burst a wave of men on horseback, all dressed in the same black robes. Gereinte was holding off his attacker only by virtue of his speed and agility. He knew if the broadsword caught him or he had to take the full force of a parry with his long sword, neither he nor his weapon could withstand the force. He dodged the attacks, he feinted with his sword and weaved around so much that his opponent was becoming frustrated. Each attack the brigand launched, was harder, stronger, but slower and slower. Speed was Gereinte's only advantage. A new force of men surrounded the ongoing battle, he could only think about the here and now and not getting cut by the maniac swinging a broadsword in front of him. Then the man stopped dead in his attack, his horse skittering beneath him and his eyes rolled up behind his lids. The tip of a sword was protruding from his chest and Gereinte had just enough time to sidestep before the man tumbled in front of him. Fulk stood in front of Gereinte, blood dripping from his wounds, sweat pouring from his brow.

The remaining men began to circle the two of them. Man and boy. Warrior and prince. The band of brigands evidently thought that the game was over, as they took their time to eye up their prey before the final moments of conquest. Gereinte wanted to shout. He wanted to cry out, but he knew it would be useless. There was no one around. That was the whole point of coming out here. But someone must have known. He gave Fulk a sideways glance, still wondering. His heart hammered to escape his chest and his lungs burned with the exertion.

"But I thought…"

"I know," said Fulk, his breathing laboured. "It is what you were supposed to think."

Before Gereinte had a chance to absorb this information, something else caught his eye. Behind the black clad brigands, the trees were moving. Ever so slowly, as though they didn't want anyone to notice, the clearing was getting smaller and smaller until, as he focussed carefully, Gereinte could make out hundreds of faces in amongst the trees. The forest was alive.

One of the men on horseback took a step forward and the group parted to let him through. He withdrew a long sword; clearly a fine weapon that chimed as he freed it from its scabbard.

106

"We can do this the easy way, or the hard way," he said, pointing the tip of his sword towards Gereinte. There was long drawn out whistle on the wind. "All we want is the b-" Followed by a dull thud.

The brigand's words stopped dead as he slumped forward in the saddle, the shaft of an arrow protruding from his back.

There was a split second's silence as everyone looked at the dead man before the forest erupted. Hundreds of green clad rangers poured into the clearing and started attacking the brigands. There were so many. How had they kept so well hidden? Many more were hiding in the trees and launching arrows from their vantage point. Fulk leapt into the thick of it, protecting Gereinte's back as another brigand engaged him in battle. Before the man had even drawn his sword, an arrow sliced through his exposed neck and the man screamed as blood spurted from the wound.

Gereinte turned and faced another man, just managing to withstand the force of a killing attack. His arm was aching with the pain of parry after parry and he narrowly missed being split in two by the massive sword before ducking in and under with a thrust to the man's exposed chest. The brigand went down like a sack of potatoes and Gereinte withdrew his sword, turning to look for Fulk. He was nowhere to be seen and Gereinte began to panic, even though it was clear that the rangers had the advantage over the brigands. What if Fulk had fallen to one of those murderous dogs? Before he had time to contemplate the next line of attack, a sharp pain bit into his side and he fell with a thud to the ground, clutching at an arrow shaft protruding from his midriff. As he went down, something large and heavy hit him on the back of the head. The pain hit him square behind the eyes like his skull being split in two. Lights danced behind his eyelids and he sank back into the ground. Then the view of the forest clearing and the ongoing battle dissolved, as a curtain of black drew him into unconsciousness.

Chapter Seventeen

Caitlin was standing alone, looking out of the window in her chambers when Nils brought the news. She had watched patiently as her guards returned from the forest without Gereinte. She had continued to watch from her vantage point that overlooked the courtyard, as her royal advisers ran to and fro arguing with one another over the minor detail of who was to bring news to the Queen Regent. It seemed to get even more chaotic and unnecessary when several bodyguards and even one of the children's nursemaids had got involved in the discussion. More scuttling to and fro, more frenzied discussion and yet there she stood, alone in her chambers, waiting for the inevitable news.

So it was not surprising that Nils had been the one chosen to be the bearer of bad tidings.

"Your Highness," he said. Caitlin remained facing away, looking out of the window and allowed him to speak to her back. "I have some very grave news for you." Caitlin said nothing and did not turn her head. Nils paused and the silence stretched between them. She heard him sigh with the burden. "The Prince Royal has disappeared."

Caitlin dropped her head and looked down at the floor, smiling to herself. She took a deep breath to compose herself before turning to face the Seneschal.

"But that is not all... the baby, Josselin, has gone from his crib." Caitlin's head shot up and she swung around to face Nils.

"What?"

The Seneschal's face was pale. He wrung his

hands repeatedly before responding.

"His nursemaid left for the village over two hours ago, as she usually does, leaving the babe to sleep. She has not returned and Josselin's crib was found empty."

Caitlin stared at Nils, uncomprehending. She felt sick, panicky. This was all wrong. It was meant to be Gereinte. How could Josselin be gone too? Where had he gone? Why?

"Round up everyone who has come into contact with Josselin in the last two days. I want to question everyone in the Great Hall. On the hour. Go." Nils stood looking at her with a strange expression on his face. Caitlin could kick herself for not realising – it was the shock of hearing about Josselin. "I want the Queen's Guard there too. All of them. I want to know Gereinte's exact movements for the last day – who he was with, for how long and why." Nils still stood staring at her, as though she had just grown two heads. "Move!"

Nils jumped into action, bowing as he took his leave scurrying backwards out of her chamber.

The door shut behind him and Caitlin stared at it for a moment before crumpling to the floor in a heap. She sobbed quietly, not wanting to attract attention to her weakness. She must be strong. Strong enough to endure this for Gereinte's sake. Strong enough to launch a nationwide search for her baby boy. Someone must know something.

She hardly noticed the door open and close softly. Before she realised that her mother had entered the room, the older woman was kneeling beside her and folding her arms around her. Caitlin and Audan hugged each other with a desperation

110

and fear that only a mother could understand. She feared for Gereinte and hoped that one day he would forgive her for what she had done. She was desperate for the safe return of her baby boy, the last in the line of Andolins; it had not been easy to bring Josselin into this world knowing that he would never see his father. To have him snatched from under her nose like this was unthinkable. How? Had she been too wrapped up in Gereinte to care about the rest of her children? Her sudden intake of breath caused Audan to release her hold on Caitlin.

"The girls... my gods, the girls. Are they all right? I must go to them at once." Caitlin tried to get up, but Audan held her down for a brief moment. They locked eyes and Caitlin searched her mother's grey gaze. Despite the attempt at reassurance, there was fear in her eyes.

"They are fine for now, my dear," Audan said. "You must remain strong for them – they rely on you. You know how they adore their brothers. Take a moment to compose yourself before you visit their quarters."

Caitlin could see the sense in her mother's concern. She took a deep breath before rising to her feet. She helped Audan up and they embraced once more before releasing each other. Audan cupped her daughter's face in both hands and smiled with all the apparent reassurance that Caitlin was lacking.

"It will be well. You'll see. We will find out it was all a mistake and Isla will return with Josselin wondering what all the fuss is about." Audan had convinced herself, but Caitlin still felt a sick sense of dread creeping down her spine. "Gereinte is safe now and out of harm's way. But do not forget that only a handful of people know the truth. You must try to be convincing about his disappearance." Caitlin nodded, despite feeling anything but convinced about Gereinte's safety.

She turned away. "Send for Ladys, please. I will refresh myself before the meeting in the Great Hall. Then I will visit the girls." Audan nodded once and left the room. Caitlin stood still for a few minutes staring at the closed door, before her tears began once again to tumble down her cheeks.

"My boys," she whispered. "My baby boys."

***

Sir Denzl Charrock stood before Reynald in the meeting room of his castle residence. Charrock was a tall and lanky fellow, who looked awkward carrying a sword. When Reynald had first taken him on, he had misgivings about the man's fighting prowess, despite his skill as a knight and his enthusiasm to swear fealty to House Borsa. However, he had other skills that had proved useful under the circumstances. It was a shame his idiot son had not proved equally useful. The only thing the young Squire Charrock had done of any use to prove his worth was to act as a convenient scapegoat when the plan to dispose of the Prince went wrong. Reynald grunted aloud at his thoughts and Sir Denzl flinched. Despite the knight's height, he had not the thickset Northern stature of Reynald and his fighting spirit remained relegated to creeping about in the dark making deals with dangerous people in the underworld of the Western Isles.

"So," Reynald said. Charrock flinched again, as

112

though he feared the presence of his master. "What news do you bring?"

"It is done, my Lord. The youngest one is dead." He looked pleased with himself, but Reynald was not convinced.

"And, you can be sure of this, Sir Denzl?"

"Absolutely, my Lord." Denzl reached into his pocket and produced a large dirty looking length of cloth. He placed the cloth on the table in front of Reynald.

"And?" Reynald said. He had already had enough of this game.

"It is the little finger of the Prince's left hand." Denzl had a twisted smile on his face, but still made no attempt to unwrap the package.

"So what?" Reynald said. "What does it prove? It could be that of any child."

"Josselin had a birth mark on the little finger of his left hand."

Reynald scanned the face of his knight for a moment, then he remembered. It was true. He recalled seeing it himself and wondering at the large blackened spot, thinking it a sign of bad luck for the child. How true that proved to be. He flipped over the edge of the cloth and there lay the little stub, bloodied and torn from its owner, barely the size of the tiniest of earth worms. He took his knife from its sheath and used the tip to turn the finger. The underside was as black as the day the child had popped into the world. There were folklore stories of a black spot being the sign of death. Reynald stared at it for a long moment before putting away the knife and wrapping the finger back in its cloth.

"Get rid of it. You have done well and you will

be rewarded for your loyalty." He noted Denzl letting out a long sigh of relief and hated the man all the more. "What of the Prince Royal – have you heard any news yet?"

"Word has been sent out that the Prince was ambushed in the forest of dreams by a band of brigands. Some are saying that he is badly injured, others that he died in the attack and there is also rumour being spread that he has been abducted. No word as yet from Castle Helmstedt."

Reynald grunted. "I don't expect to hear the truth from Castle Helmstedt. I guess we will have to await the return of Sir Fulk to find out the truth. But it is good to hear that the bitch's pups have been put out of their misery." Reynald laughed, then seeing Denzl mirror his mirth, he clapped the knight on the back in a friendly fashion. Denzl stumbled with the force of Reynald's touch, which made Reynald roar with even more laughter. It felt good to be on the winning side for a change.

After a good few moments, Reynald looked up to find himself being studied from the doorway by Fulk.

"Ah, my good man. Please, bring me more good news. The King is dead, eh? Long live the King!" Reynald punched the air with his fist and Denzl instinctively ducked, though the fist was nowhere near him. Fulk watched this display impassively, then entered the room and bowed.

"My Lord. The Prince Royal has disappeared," Fulk said.

Reynald stopped laughing and frowned.

"How did this happen? That was not part of the plan."

"I was fighting alongside him one moment, as we planned and turned to find him gone the next. It was all I could do to keep myself alive, as I note that your men were not briefed on who was fighting for whom." Fulk remained dour, his expression serious and unforgiving. Reynald was not interested in the trivialities of the fight. His mind was fixed on the strange disappearance of the Prince Royal. Perhaps he really had been killed and Castle Helmstedt was covering it up. Or maybe he was lying injured somewhere, awaiting death. Death. He must be dead or badly injured; those men were professionals and their brief was to finish off the Prince. He would consult his spy network and find out if the Prince was really dead.

Chapter Eighteen

The pain in his head was intense and forced open Gereinte's eyes. He shut them again and squeezed tight against the torrent of stars that danced on the insides of his lids. He reached up to feel his head but some kind of resistance weighed down his hand. He tried again and found that he could just about touch his head but his wrists still felt heavy and cumbersome. There was an almighty lump on the back of his head, which had been bandaged. He tried lifting his head, but the pain was too much, so he sank back down onto the hard bedding and slipped back into unconsciousness.

His eyes flew open with urgency as he rolled his body to one side and heaved over the side of the pallet. He emptied the contents of his stomach, which consisted mostly of liquid and bile onto the floor. His eyes watered with the effort, as he laid hanging with his head facing down towards the floor. Someone had the foresight to put a container beside the pallet and he was now looking down at a pool of his own vomit miraculously contained in a wooden bucket. The floor was also made of wood and it was swaying. No. It was Gereinte who was swaying. Or was it the bed? He shook his head. Perhaps it was the dizziness from the clout to the back of his head. The air was thick with the salt of seawater and the grimy scent of too many people living in one place.

A deep voice chuckled from somewhere across the room. Gereinte squinted towards the sound and saw a pair of feet dangling from a bunk. The feet were attached to a pair of thick legs, like tree trunks

116

and as his gaze continued upwards, Gereinte took in the stocky build of a middle-aged man with a long dark drooping moustache.

"You get used to it eventually," the man said in a heavily accented version of Etanese. The last thing Gereinte remembered was being in the middle of a fight in the Forest of Dreams. Then an arrow sliced into his side and someone or something had hit him over the head. "Takes some longer than others, but the sickness will pass, believe me, lad." Gereinte strained to pick up the lilt in the man's voice. It sounded like a patois indigenous to Skyeland. If his History lessons were accurate, the language spoken there was a mixture of Etanese and Jarvik, the main language of Klagenstill, which lay at the most Northern point of the Western Isles.

Gereinte stared at the man. If he truly was in or near to Skyeland, then he was most certainly a long way from home. The voice and attitude of the man speaking was neither ill disposed nor friendly towards him, so Gereinte kept his own counsel until he knew where he stood. But it did not bode well when he lifted his head and realised that he was being held in shackles to the bunk.

"Wh... where am I?" He tried speaking in Etanese, but with a common accent. The man looked him up and down as though appraising a piece of merchandise.

"Aboard the Skyelady brig, lad. That's where." The man smiled. It wasn't a warm smile, neither was it a malicious smile. It was as though he had just remembered a funny joke but did not see fit to share. Gereinte tried lifting his head again, but an iron collar was restricting it. A lump started to swell in his throat and he fought back tears of frustration.

"I can't be... I'm not... it's impossible. I'm from Carentan. Slavery is banned."

"You'll not be in Carentan now, lad." The man nodded his head towards a porthole between two bunks and Gereinte strained his neck to catch a glimpse of the view. He could see the bright blue sky and a line of masts, behind which lay a dock and a row of mismatched buildings in the distance. It was the boat that was swaying gently beneath his bunk. He let his head drop back with the strain and turned towards his captor, trying to keep a hold on his emotions as the tears swelled behind his eyes. "That's Sarne, out there," the man said. "I paid a Sarlat slave trader a goodly sum for a cabin boy yesterday and you were delivered to me last night. What's your name?"

Gereinte stared at his captor, hesitating. Someone, somehow had set him up. Was it Fulk? Did Borsa want him out of the way so much that he would sell him as a slave? No, that didn't make any sense – why not just have him killed? Or was that what the plan had been, before someone clobbered him over the head and dragged him halfway across the Western Isles? He recalled the black clad brigands who had jumped them in the forest. They had fought with the intention to kill. Fulk had watched his back as the two of them defended their lives before the forest exploded with rangers and arrows were flying across the wind hitting their targets with ease. Perhaps, someone had tried to protect him, by taking him far away from the conflicts in Carentan. Had his death been faked? What was his mother thinking at that moment – that

118

he had disappeared, or died in battle? Perhaps it had all gone wrong. Perhaps he was meant to be taken to a safe house, but never arrived. He had been captured and sold into slavery and no one knew who or where he was. So many questions... so many what ifs. One thing he did know for sure... if it was all a mistake and he revealed his true identity, he could be placing his life in even greater danger. Who would believe him anyway? It was too bizarre a story. He met the man's measured gaze.

"Griff," Gereinte said, plucking the name from memory of one of the pageboys at Castle Helmstedt. "My name is Griff." The man seemed amused, though it was hard to tell beneath that long dark moustache, but his eyes held a twinkle of mirth.

"Well, Griff," he said. "I am Haro Dal, Captain of the Skyelady. This is a Coustiller brig and like everyone else aboard, you'll have to earn your keep."

Coustiller. Gereinte had heard that name before somewhere and as vague as his memory was at that precise moment, he felt sure it had something to do with pirates. Wary as ever, he lifted his hand and rattled the chains that held him fast to his bunk.

"Rest now, lad. Once at sea, you will be taken out of the shackles. That is to make sure you don't jump ship before we sail. You will be sent for." Haro Dal jumped down from the bunk and left by the cabin door.

When he had left, Gereinte hoisted himself up as far as his restraints would allow and pressed his face to the barred window above his bunk. His eyes were level with the deck of the ship and all he could see were feet moving about accompanied by the bellow of incomprehensible orders. A thin pinched face popped out of nowhere and Gereinte jumped back. The man grinned and Gereinte shuddered, trying to recall where he had seen those dark ringed eyes and slight features; a Vermondien. Gereinte swallowed back the lump in his throat. Slavery was a widely practiced custom in Vermondie, much to the disgust of their Tordrean and Carentan neighbours.

The Vermondien sprang up and continued about his business. Despite his headache and the gut-wrenching sickness that still threatened to engulf him, Gereinte was fascinated to watch the crew, bustling about and the orders being barked by someone out of his view. He had sailed a few times before on ships and was surprised by an eagerness to get out on deck and see for himself where he was and what was going on. For what seemed like hours, he fought the need for sleep with a longing to see the sea and breathe its scent of freedom. But the throbbing in his head forced him back down to lie still and close his eyes in the hope that someone soon would come and get him. He feared more being left alone to vegetate in that bunk than being put to work with the crew. He slipped eventually into sleep.

Chapter Nineteen

He slept fitfully and dreamt of Castle Helmstedt. The stone walls were dark and forbidding as he ran from one end of the western wall to the other looking for something. He was not sure what he was looking for or why he felt such a fierce sense of urgency. It was dark outside as he mounted the steps leading up to the highest lookout point where the castle guard would be keeping watch. But there was no one there. The castle walls were empty of their keepers. He looked out towards the West, but could see nothing beyond the middle gate. There was an unearthly silence stretching for miles into the forest. A sickness stirred in his gut with pounding of his heart. He looked down at his clothes; he was in full battle gear, with a sword at his belt.

He circled the wall trying to clear his mind and think like a king. Then he heard the distant clang of a bell; a call to action. He tried to remember where he was and why, but the clang-clang of the bell stifled all thought. The back of his head throbbed. He ran round and round, circling the walls of the keep, looking for something. Looking for answers. And all the time the bell went clang-clang. His head felt as if it were about to explode. He clutched his hands to his ears to try and muffle the noise and deaden the pain. As suddenly as it began, the bell stopped. He released his hands and held his breath, looking out to the forest for some answers. Then the inner walls erupted as fighters poured over into the inner circle brandishing weapons and torches of fire.

These were not soldiers or knights, but ordinary people, dressed as commoners, waving weapons and throwing their torches at the castle keep. Gereinte stared. These were his people. His kingdom, setting fire to his castle, trying to burn him alive. What had happened? Why had they rebelled against him? Where were his troops? The fire licked up the side of the keep and rushed in to meet him. He had been betrayed, by his own people and condemned to be roasted alive in his own home. The fire took its hold and his skin prickled with the heat, which intensified with every second. His whole body was like a furnace as he dropped to his knees. He was in chains and there was nowhere to go.

***

He was blind. His eyelids opened but a black shroud seeped around the edges of his vision. There were voices in the background, shadows moving above him. Two people talking with that distinctive accent of Skyeland.

"He's burning up. Get them chains off him now."

"Aye, Captain. Shall I send for Mr Jabir, Sir?"

"Aye, quick as you like now Fenner, an' ask Cook if he has anything to help the fever. Damn it. I shouldna' left the lad like this."

Again, he heard a distant clang-clang and Gereinte raised his head a little as he remembered where he was.

"Now don't you be worrying about that lad. It's the change of watch, tha's all. You'll get used to the bells as quick as you get used the sickness." Haro Dal's voice. Gereinte let his head drop and winced in pain. His body felt lighter now that the chains had gone. The sickness still stirred and his skin was slick with sweat. The air smelt different, cleaner and yet still with the salty scent of the sea.

Another man entered and strode to Gereinte's side. His vision began to clear and he could make out the hazy features of a man, very different to the Coustillers. He had a naturally darker skin and his build was slight compared to the stockiness of Haro Dal and the other man called Fenner. In stark contrast, his head was completely bald and he had a small gold ring through his left ear. He didn't look like a sailor or even a slave. He wore a long brown robe, like that of the religious monks of the One God. But this man had a kindness behind his eyes, despite the fact that Haro Dal was barking orders to him as though he were no more than muck on his boot.

The man put a palm to Gereinte's forehead and looked into his eyes with concern and a keen understanding. Gereinte trusted him. He was someone who, for whatever reason, appeared to be in a similar predicament himself. The man spoke briefly to Fenner, who rushed off again and Gereinte tried in vain to catch the words, but they escaped without him being able to place the strange man.

Fenner returned and handed a bowl to the man, who squeezed out something green, wet and leafy and placed it on Gereinte's forehead. He then turned to Haro Dal and said something quietly so that not even Fenner who was closest to him would have been able to make it out. Haro looked at Gereinte, then back at the man and nodded.

"I leave you in the capable hands of Jabir ed-Din,

lad. He will see to your wounds and your fever. It may be days yet before you get to see the sea. Don't be too hasty to leave your bunk, I need you fit and well for the work I have in mind for you."

Gereinte's heart sank as the Captain left, closely followed by Fenner. He was left with the man named Jabir and a thousand questions playing on his mind. The boat swayed gently, though the feeling of movement was different to before. He stole a glance out of the porthole, but could see nothing but the dark skies of night.

"We are at sea now. You must rest while I tend to your wounds. Does it hurt anywhere else, other than your head?" For the first time Gereinte heard the man's voice, but could not place his accent. He spoke fluent Etanese, but not like a commoner – more like one of the ruling classes. What was a man like Jabir doing aboard a pirate ship off the coast of Sarlat? Gereinte shook his head, hardly daring himself to speak. Jabir rolled him over and inspected his torso. As he peeled back the bedcovers, a sharp pain bit into his side and he looked down at long raw gash. Then he remembered the arrow that had caught him before the thump on the head. Jabir set about cleaning and dressing it with a poultice of green and brown leaves which stung a little, but had a soothing effect.

"Who are you?" Gereinte said whilst Jabir worked. Jabir paused for a long while before answering and if Gereinte had not already heard him speak fluent Etanese, he might have thought the man had not understood his question.

"Jabir ed-Din," was his only reply. It was an eastern name. That much he knew.

124

"Tell me about this ship," Gereinte said, trying a different tack. "Am I really a slave? Are you too? Who are these Coustillers – are they pirates? Is my life in danger?"

"It will be if you don't let me deal with your wounds," Jabir said. But he was smiling as he said it and he shook his head.

After some time, another Coustiller entered, recognisable by his build and droopy moustache, though this one had a cook's apron on. The Cook laid down a tray of hot broth and a plate of bread. For the first time since waking up on this ship, Gereinte felt the rumblings of hunger gnawing at his insides.

Jabir ed-Din sat and watched him in silence as Gereinte carefully sipped the broth, mopping it up with the soft brown bread chunks. The man looked curiously serene, sitting on the floorboards cross-legged with his hands gently cupped together in his lap. Gereinte began to feel the edges of his hunger dissipate as the food tamed the hot and cold flushes of the fever. He felt better.

"So," Gereinte said, wondering why Jabir was still sat there watching him. "When do I get to see the rest of the ship?" Jabir smiled faintly and took his time to answer.

"Have you forgotten already, the Captain's warning not to be too hasty to rise? Life aboard the Skyelady is not going to be so easy. Rest now and you will have plenty of time to get to know the ship."

Gereinte lay his head back, tired and weary. He thought about his home and the family he had left. What would they be feeling now? Would he ever see his sisters and his baby brother again? With a pang of misery and anxiety, he pushed away the thought and turned his head toward the man who now appeared to be the only person who cared whether he lived or died.

"Tell me about the Coustillers," he said. After a long pause, Jabir opened his mouth. Gereinte was not used to having to wait so long for an answer and wanted to prompt the man to speak, but he was not in any position to command anything of anyone. Besides, he needed above all to build the trust of at least one person aboard this vessel.

"The Coustillers are honourable folk, who live mostly at sea-"

"Huh," Gereinte said. "Honourable folk don't take slaves." Jabir frowned at his words, but declined to comment. Had he upset the man? Perhaps he was not after all another slave. Gereinte regretted his outburst – he should be more careful in his choice of words.

"As I said," Jabir said. "They live mainly at sea but come into port to trade and provision their ships."

"There are more ships of Coustillers?"

"Indeed, they are a sea-faring tribe, descendants of the original inhabitants of Skyeland, which is the southernmost and largest island in the Island Ring."

"Originally settled by migrant Kelts of the Green Island, yes I know that... you are starting to sound like my history professor."

Jabir's eyes glinted in the moonlight with a keen intelligence that belied his apparent status.

"I think you and I may have some secrets in common, young Griff. Perhaps it would be well for us to keep this education to ourselves for now. Until our situation becomes, shall I say... a little more stable?"

Gereinte cursed himself at his stupidity. He had just revealed his status by reference to his education to this man who could be anyone for all he knew.

"As you no doubt already know, Skyelanders intermarried with the people who eventually became the Gaullians and Malvatians."

"They used to steal girls from the mainland. That's why my... King Reiner set up the ranger patrols."

"Indeed." Jabir paused and raised an eyebrow. Gereinte got the message. It was going to be tough not being able to talk openly about his life, but it was better to get used to it now. "The economy of the Skyelanders was based mainly on fishing supplemented by some hardy crops such as oats and rye."

Gereinte wondered why, when he had only asked a simple question, he had been furnished with an entire lesson in the history of Skyeland.

"The Skyelanders were a stocky race combining the dark hair and blue eyes of their Kelt ancestors with the hazel eyes and darker complexion of the Gaullians. Although you and I both abhor slavery, these people have a strong sense of personal honour."

Gereinte pulled a sour face. "Where did the name Coustiller come from?"

Jabir paused for a long while. So long that Gereinte was beginning to think he was punishing him for his impatience.

"I will tell you in good time. But you must hear

the story, for it only makes sense if you know the history." Gereinte resigned himself to hearing the entire story and wondered if by some strange quirk of fate, this man had been sent to stop him from going slowly mad at the hands of his pirate captors. "At some time during the 50 Year War between the northern and southern clans of Klagenstill, the fortunes of Skyeland changed dramatically." Jabir continued with his story and Gereinte lay back to listen and piece together what he already knew from his lessons at Castle Helmstedt.

"At a key moment in the war, one of the more dominant north Klagen clan chiefs came to the view that he needed a more disciplined and better trained force of warriors to complement his itinerant bands of roving fighters. With unusual intelligence and insight, he realised that his traditional clansmen were, by temperament, incapable of becoming the force he needed and that he therefore had to go outside his country to find the raw manpower required. Thus, he descended upon Skyeland with a large force of warriors and proceeded to impress every able-bodied man he could find into his army.

The clan chief's eastern military advisors and trainers rapidly moulded the Skyelanders into a tough, competent, light infantry brigade. In the ensuing battles and skirmishes, the tough Skyelanders achieved an enviable reputation for the savage efficiency with which they used sword and dagger in close combat. The dagger, Cultellus, or more commonly, Coustel, seemed to be their weapon of choice and thus they adopted the name Coustillers.

A few years later, the 50 Year War ended with

the Treaty of Tennengaul, and the clan chief suddenly found himself with a large number of expensive troops for whom he had no particular use. He thus declared them to be free men and, generously, offered them passage back to their homeland.

Shortly after the Coustillers had settled down back in their island, two pirate ships sailed into the main harbour of Skyeland confident of achieving their usual ends of rape and pillage in the absence of, they believed, all the able-bodied men. The ensuing conflict was brief, sanguinary and in the case of most of the pirates, terminal.

Now owning two sailing vessels, the Coustillers decided to go into the cargo transport business. Within a few years they had established a fleet of ships and a reputation as honest traders who delivered, as far as possible, on time and were, most importantly, ferociously resistant to pirate attacks." Jabir smiled.

"So they are not pirates, then?" Gereinte said.

"Apparently not."

Gereinte tumbled this new information around his head for a while before sitting up suddenly in his bunk, which he regretted as the dizziness returned to his head and his stomach began to heave again. Despite this, he made an attempt at swinging his legs over the side of the bunk.

"We cannot be slaves then. We must be able to leave, we must at least try."

"I think you should stay put for now. These are not men to be trifled with. These are men who are stronger and much fiercer than any pirate sailing the seas. The pirates steer clear of the Coustillers. Their

129

reputation precedes them." Jabir stood and guided Gereinte back into his bunk. Gereinte had neither the energy nor the wit to argue with the man and let himself be settled back down.

"We must now look out for each other, young Griff. There is hard work ahead of us both and we must embrace it as our destiny. For now, you must sleep. Take it from me, you will need all the rest you can get, for you will be yearning for your bunk in the days ahead." At that, Jabir left Gereinte to mull over his story about the Coustillers.

Chapter Twenty

The insistent clang of the bell woke him from a dreamless sleep. Gereinte felt his energy restored and was eager to see the rest of the ship. There was a rustle of movement in the bunk above him, then a head swung down and stared at him. Gereinte flinched as a man snarled at him. He was lighter in complexion than the Coustillers, yet had dark hair and black eyes. He looked very much like a Sarlatian, from an upside-down kind of viewpoint.

The man's face disappeared and two seconds later he swung himself down and landed with a thud. He was short, though not as stocky as the Coustillers and his accent confirmed Gereinte's suspicions - Etanese, spoken with a haughty kind of authority that only the Sarlatians managed to pull off.

"Come on then. I'm to take you to Fenner, the Boatswain. Rest time is over." He chuckled and Gereinte distrusted the man.

"This here is the forecastle where the crew sleep and that there is my bunk." The Sarlatian nodded his head towards the bunk above the one in which Gereinte had been sleeping. "That there is Fenner's bunk," he indicated another set of bunks one on top of the other which ran across the other side of the forecastle. "And the one below that belongs to Jabir ed-Din. Strange fellow that. Hardly says a word. He spends all his time meditating and scribbling notes on scrolls and maps. Hasn't been here long, can't understand why the Captain brought him aboard." Gereinte was wondering the same thing. The Sarlatian took Gereinte forward to the far end of the forecastle where he showed him two more bunks, one belonging to the First Officer, Kaysin Dal and the other to the Vermondien, whose name was Rastiffe.

"I would steer clear of Rasti, if I was you. Rasti don't like slaves. The last one we had on board got tied up in the rigging and accidentally hung himself. Course Rasti always said he had nothing to do with it, but he did taunt the boy." The Sarlatian grinned at Gereinte who stared back impassively.

Up one level was the Captain's quarters, alongside the galley, where the Cook looked up from preparing breakfast and gave Gereinte a cheery wave. Gereinte smiled back and the Sarlatian merely snarled.

"More crew's quarters down there," said the Sarlatian, clearly fed up with playing tour guide. "I'm sure Fenner will show you the rest." At this he sloped off and left Gereinte standing on deck, all alone. The sky was dull and cloudy, as the sun had just begun to rise, dispelling the twilight. The sea was calm and Gereinte stood in awe of the measured activity going on to keep such a vessel afloat. Seabirds screeched overhead.

Fenner bounced into view with a huge grin on his face.

"Well, well, Griff, me lad. Welcome aboard. Sorry it was touch and go to start with, but here we are now. All well and rested. Have you eaten your breakfast yet? Get yerself a brew and a bite before the duties of the day begin and I'll show you what's what."

Somewhat confused by the jovial nature of the Coustiller compared to the gravity of the Sarlatian and measured control of Jabir ed-Din, Gereinte let himself be led back to the galley. Cook was waiting with cups of hot steaming liquid, which tasted much like a watered-down version of the broth he had been given the day before and slabs of hard bread, which softened in the mouth when eaten with the broth. Despite its blandness, Gereinte felt better for eating. Fenner watched him all the time, which unnerved Gereinte.

The Coustillers seemed fascinated by the appearance of Gereinte, as though having a slave boy aboard was a novelty. The only crew members that showed open disdain were the Vermondien, Rastiffe, and the Sarlatian.

"Take no notice of those two," Fenner said. "They're just jealous of all the attention you're getting."

"Can I ask a question?" Gereinte said trying to sound common enough to be a slave. Fenner nodded enthusiastically. "Am I really a slave?" Fenner thought about this question for a moment before responding.

"We prefer to think of you as an honoured crew member." He nodded with satisfaction, pleased with this definition of slavery. Gereinte frowned.

"And Jabir ed-Din?"

"Well, let's just say that he too is an honoured crew member." Fenner gave him a quick wink. "But between you and me, I wouldn't let on to the rest of the crew." Gereinte looked up and saw the Vermondien scowling at him. Fenner followed his gaze. "Don't worry 'bout him. I'll sort him out. Now then. What do you know about ships?"

Gereinte had sailed several times before on ships

133

similar to the Skyelady and was reasonably familiar with the equipment and tackle. He shrugged at Fenner, then looked about him.

"Not much really." But he noticed and was puzzled by a number of stout vertical posts attached to both the port and starboard guard rails. They all had a metal bracket which appeared to be able to rotate and pivot attached to the tops of the posts. They reminded him of the fortifications of Castle Helmstedt. "Arbalests," he whispered to himself.

"What was that?" Fenner said.

"Oh, er, nothing...just remembering." Remembering his war-tutor's lectures on the use of the huge crossbows, which could send a heavy bolt with force and accuracy into targets up to 500 yards away. Considering the number of arbalest stations and the powerful, muscular Coustillers around him, Gereinte began to have some idea how the Coustillers had gained such a fearsome reputation. On the outside, they seemed quite boisterous and friendly, but there was no doubt that there lurked an inner strength that you wouldn't want to take issue with.

"Well," said Fenner, bringing Gereinte back to the here and now. "This is a brig and we have two square rigged masts, fore and aft. The main mast is the taller one aft." Gereinte strained his neck to look at the large red flag with black crossed daggers flying high atop the main mast. Fenner followed his line of sight and chuckled.

"As I was saying, the big sail there is the mains'l and above that is the main tops'l. Above that again is the main t'gallant sail. We don't have a royal 'cause the Captain don't believe in em. The small fore-and-aft sail behind the mains'l is the boommains'l. You see the spars attached to the yards?" Gereinte nodded. "These can extend the yards so we can hoist studding sails for fair or light winds.

The foremast there holds a fores'l, fore tops'l and fore t'gallant sail. You can see that between the fore mast and the bowsprit are the fore stays'l, jib and flying jib. Those piles of cordage over there are the running rigging."

"I'll never remember all that," Gereinte said.

"You'll do fine, lad. We like brigs 'cause they are nimble and fast, even though they need a big crew. But big crews come in handy sometimes eh? Skyelady can just about touch twelve knots. However she is on the large side for a brig; nearly a hundred and eighty feet and close on five hundred tons."

Gereinte let his jaw hang open and just stared at Fenner like a dumb struck common boy. He watched the crew as they moved through the rigging with the ease of seasoned sailors.

"We'll have you learning the ropes before too long, lad. But not before that head of yours is fully recovered." Fenner guided Gereinte back towards the galley to continue where the Sarlatian had left off.

"There is the deckhouse forward which houses the galley, cook's berth, the crew quarters including the bunkhouse you are sharing with the Master Navigator Jabir ed-Din, amongst others."

"Master Navigator?"

"Things are not always what they seem, young Griff. That you will learn to accept aboard the

135

Skyelady." That was all the explanation Fenner was going to give. Gereinte followed him back down past the galley and into the Captain's quarters, where Haro Dal stood talking to another Coustiller. Upon their entrance, he turned and gave an open gesture with his arms.

"Our Carentan. Welcome aboard the Skyelady. This here is my nephew and First Officer, Kaysin Dal." Haro gestured toward the other Coustiller, who nodded his head at Gereinte, then grinned beneath his long droopy moustache.

"Quite a survivor, I understand from my Uncle. We'll make a sailor of you yet. Any problems, you just come and talk to me, we'll sort things out," Kaysin said.

"Well, I'm sure Fenner has a list of duties for you to attend to, so we'll see you on deck and good luck holding on to your breakfast, lad." Haro Dal laughed and Gereinte gave him a vacant look.

Fenner took Gereinte on deck and handed him a broom.

"The deck gets scrubbed once a day. 'Tis a three-man job; two to scrub, one to douse water. You'll be joining Rastiffe and Genno over there." Gereinte looked up and saw a cheery Coustiller wave and throw a bucket of water across deck. The scowling Vermondien started scrubbing with another broom. Tentatively, Gereinte imitated Rastiffe's movements. Happy that he had got the idea, Fenner disappeared shouting orders to the Coustillers who were flitting about overhead.

As the sun drew up, several crew members stripped to their waists, displaying their taut lean muscles. Gereinte kept his tunic on, but began to

136

regret his modesty as the sweat ran in rivulets down his neck and back. Back and forth he scrubbed and each time he finished a section, Rastiffe would throw some more water down and make him do that bit all over again. He was subtle about how he did it, so that Genno only got the impression that the boy was merely thorough. Gereinte did not complain, he just continued to scrub. He scrubbed harder and longer as the Vermondien began to apportion his own share of the work to Gereinte as well.

By lunchtime, all one hundred and eighty feet of deck had been covered and some bits of it more than once. But Gereinte would not utter a single complaint. Despite this, he thought his back would break with the strain of continual movement. It was evident that the Coustillers were used to such manual work, but he, fresh out of his sick bed with a mere squire's training. He stopped scrubbing at last and wiped the sweat from his brow. His hands were red raw from the continual grip on the broom and beginning to blister.

"It's no wonder the last slave hung himself," Gereinte muttered.

"What was that?" Rastiffe said, snatching away the broom and replacing it with a bucket. Gereinte looked at the bucket, then glanced over his shoulder at Genno who was making his way to the galley. The smell of cooked meat rose up to his nostrils and Gereinte's stomach began to rumble in complaint. "Oh no. Not yet, my lad. Not yet for you. I'll have my pound of Carentan flesh before the supper bell rings."

Supper? What happened to lunch? The bucket

137

contained water and a swab.

"Take this and clean all the paintwork. Start with the rails aft of the vessel, and then work down to the cabins. That should keep you busy." Rastiffe laughed and left Gereinte to it.

It was actually a relief for his sore hands to douse them in the water and a kind change for his aching back to be able to stand upright for a few hours. Gereinte took to the task with renewed vigour and the kind of 'I'll show you' attitude that had often got him into trouble in the past. Whenever his weary limbs began to complain, he reminded himself of the time he was nearly beaten to death and had looked his captors defiantly in the eye, facing certain death. He longed to make his father proud. Despite having missed lunch, he made good headway and he moved eventually down a level towards the cabins. He earned a few troubled glances from the Coustillers, but still, no one said anything to him and he kept his own counsel and got on with the work.

The sun descended toward the horizon, the supper bell had rung and Gereinte had one side of the upper cabin left to do.

"You may as well finish up in here, as there'll be no time in the morning, boy." The Sarlatian stepped into Gereinte's path blocking his exit toward the galley. "When you've done that you can come back and clean our cabin." Gereinte stared at the man, gritted his teeth and set to work.

An hour later, the cabins were done. Gereinte wrung out the swab, rinsed the bucket and returned it to the deckhouse forward. He rinsed his own hands and face before going to the galley, hoping

138

that there was still some food.

The Cook took one look at him and produced a platter of hot meats, vegetables and bread with a cup of broth. Gereinte sagged into a seat and ate as though it were his last meal. He watched from a distance as the Coustillers relaxed by playing at knife fighting and dancing to the tune of a fiddle. As he ate, they gave him his peace but once it was evident that he was finished, they dragged Gereinte into their little circle.

He watched Genno and another crew member circling each other, with their knives out at the ready. Genno's cousin, Bayant nudged Gereinte and whispered in his ear.

"Yer in for a treat here. Our Genno is the best aboard the Skyelady." The two Coustillers dodged and weaved about one another making quick flicking movements with their wrists. Before he had even had a chance to unpick their technique, Genno had stepped in on the inside of his opponent's thrust and flicked the other's knife clear of the circle. A cheer went up and not a drop of blood was spilt. "You need good reflexes for this game, young Griff. Do you have good reflexes?"

"I... no, not really." But before Gereinte had a chance to argue, the Coustillers had started up a chant.

"Car-en-tan, Car-en-tan, Car-en-tan." He was pushed into the middle of a circle with a wooden knife thrust into his sore and shaking hand. He looked down at the battered practice weapon and sighed. At least it wasn't a real knife – he had to be thankful for that at least.

His opponent was much bigger and stronger.

139

Although weary, Gereinte had to use his nimbleness as an evasive tactic. He managed to avoid several thrusts forward without any due harm, but his lack of skill with the knife was his eventual undoing. Before too long, his sidesteps were countered and with one deft manoeuvre, he was disarmed and left for the kill. A massive cheer erupted and several of the Coustillers were shaking their heads and tutting at Gereinte's apparent lack of expertise with the knife.

It surprised him how gentle and controlled the Coustillers were when fighting each other; there was a mutual respect among them that Gereinte saw as a rarity among fighting men. He recalled the bruises and pain that he endured during a single session of sword fighting as a squire. As he faded back to the outside of the circle, he noticed Bayant nod at his brother Genno and gesture furtively at Gereinte.

A few more bouts ensued. Some, like Gereinte, used the wooden practice knives, leaving the experts like Genno to use the real blades. But still, not a drop of blood was shed. Once the Coustillers had satisfied their desire for sport, they took up the floor for a round of jigs accompanied by the fiddle. Gereinte sat back and watched, enjoying the scene but too exhausted to dance. He managed to sneak off before too long, but not without passing the Cook, who stopped him.

"You'll be with me the 'morrow, lad. Squared with the Captain, so I expect you up sharp at six bells, before the crew swap for breakfast."

"Aye, sir," Gereinte said with some measure of relief.

140

He sank into his bunk and lay thinking for a moment. If he was going to survive beyond a few weeks, he was going to have to work out a strategy that enabled him to keep his head above water without losing sight of who he really was and the life that was waiting for him back in Carentan. If there was a life waiting for him.

Chapter Twenty-One

On the sixth bell, Gereinte's eyes flew open. Whilst he had lain, half comatose during the first few days of his internment aboard the Skyelady, he had memorised the order of the bells and begun to use them as a structure to his existence. The hardest thing to get used to was the fact that the number of bells didn't actually correspond to the number of the hour. There was one bell for each half hour of the four-hour watch; eight bells in all. So you would hear a strike of bells every half hour. Eight bells for breakfast and change of the night watch, who take breakfast, then sleep until noon. The sixth bell meant time to get up and attend to his duties before breakfast.

He swung his legs out of the bunk and grimaced at the aches in his back and down his legs and arms. He felt like he had taken several bouts with Fulk on a good day and only just lived to tell the tale. He took a quick splash of water, before joining the Cook in the galley.

"Ah. Good, lad. One of your duties will be to help out here when required, so I thought – and the Captain agreed – that you would spend some time here today, watching me and helping out. That should keep you out of trouble's way for a time, eh?" Gereinte nodded. He hardly needed to speculate what the Cook meant by trouble.

It was a welcome break from the duties of the previous day and Gereinte learnt a lot about food preparation in a confined space. He was used to watching the castle kitchen staff in a kitchen five times the size of that on the Skyelady.

When eight bells rang, the deck hands came in for breakfast, which consisted of fried meats, bread and pickles.

"What is this, Cook," Rastiffe said, staring at Gereinte. "Stealing away our staff and only on his second day of work?" The Cook merely waved a hand in dismissal.

"If you want to eat, my son, I need some help too. Our young Carentan will be sharing his time between us all. So don't you be getting any ideas about keeping him all to yerself."

The Vermondien sloped off and sat in a corner, where he was joined by the Sarlatian. Several Coustillers came in who raised the atmosphere with a run down of the previous evening's activities. They soon forgot about the fact that Gereinte was not theirs for the day and ignored him.

Once the morning crew and the night team had taken their fill, Cook produced an enormous plate, which he piled high with food and placed it in front of Gereinte. He looked at the offering, then back at the Cook, not sure whether to accept this or what the protocol was for a slave to accept gifts beyond his status.

"Tuck into that lad, that'll grow the inches on yer," Cook said with a hearty laugh. "You're going to need to build some muscle strength to survive work 'board the Skyelady."

The Cook did not exaggerate. The days were long and the work was hard. As the months passed, Gereinte rapidly developed into a responsible crew member who was given a job and trusted to get on with it with a minimum of fuss. He became something of a jack-of-all-trades, being involved in anything from scrubbing decks to helping Cook in the galley. Once he had overcome his initial fears, he became as agile and adept aloft as any deckhand. He scampered through the rigging with whoops of joy and antics, which drew blistering remarks from the Captain without daunting his enthusiasm in the least.

The healthy open-air life and strenuous exercise was quickly developing the sinews and muscles of his lean frame at a phenomenal rate.

The evenings were always an enjoyable time for Gereinte, as the Coustillers took a great liking to him, nurturing his fighting prowess and encouraging participation in their games and rituals. Genno and Bayant took it upon themselves to teach him the art of knife fighting and they appeared amazed at the speed with which he learnt. Although lacking the physical upper body strength of the grown men, he soon became skilled due to his natural agility and keen reflexes.

The Coustillers were delighted to discover that Gereinte was an accomplished flautist and they managed to root out an old wooden instrument that had belonged to Genno's father's uncle and had been passed down, unfortunately without the knowledge or skill to be able to play it. Gereinte was silently thanking his mother for insisting he took lessons, as it was a useful tool to enable him to escape the humiliation of having to dance, which had never been his strength. He and the fiddle player provided a rollicking accompaniment for the Coustillers' jigs and hornpipes and every evening they insisted he play for their entertainment.

To his surprise, the Captain also insisted that

Gereinte spend at least one hour every day with Fenner learning the basics of seamanship including the mysteries of knots, bends, hitches and splices.

"The more you know, the more useful you will be," was the Captain's motto. He was also required to take lessons from Jabir ed-Din in navigation, history, geography and philosophy. Jabir had a great love for knowledge.

"Knowledge is like love. When you give freely to someone, your stock shows no loss, but your soul shows a gain." The easterner's eyes held a gravity and depth when he imparted his wisdom as though it were his calling in life.

"But the knowledge that you impart to me now – how is it useful on this ship? What use is the history of the Western Isles to a slave boy from Carentan?" Gereinte had long since abandoned his pretence of being a commoner in front of Jabir, but still trusted no one with his true identity. Jabir looked thoughtful and Gereinte waited patiently for his response.

"Even a slave boy might one day change the world."

"But how? What can I do to change the world? Why would I want to change the world?" Gereinte was getting frustrated now at not being able to just say what he thought or how he felt or even how he longed to see his family and Castle Helmstedt.

"Knowledge is power, given to the right person at the right time. Believe me, young Griff, there are changes afoot in the world. Major changes that will affect the Western Isles in years to come. What happens in the Kingdom of Carentan, is just a small stitch in the rich tapestry of this world. However, do not be fooled; unpick one stitch and the whole picture falls apart."

Gereinte was thoughtful for a moment. What was it that his father used to say to him? That Carentan was best placed, both geographically and politically to unite the Western Isles if ever there were a threat of invasion from overseas. There are changes afoot in the world. He felt a prickle of foreboding snake down his spine and he shivered.

"Master Jabir – do you think we will ever get off this boat?"

Jabir opened his mouth to speak, then paused. "That, my young friend, I cannot say. But if we ever do, would you not want to be as prepared as you can be for what may lie ahead?"

Gereinte could see the wisdom in that.

"But, if the opportunity arose, would you not want to escape?" Gereinte said.

Jabir raised an eyebrow. "The opportunity most certainly will arise, but maybe not today," he said.

"When it does, will you help me? Will you come with me?"

"Now, why would you want an old man like me with you?" Gereinte paused.

"Because, 'old man', if I were a king, you would be the person I would have at my side."

Jabir was silent, as he appeared to measure the weight of Gereinte's words. Then he smiled.

"If you were a king, I would happily serve at your side."

Gereinte felt a prickle of pride that made the hairs stand up on the back of his neck.

"What I don't understand," he said, "is why you are also a slave on this ship." A fact which seemed

146

to have no effect on the way he behaved or how he was treated by the rest of the crew. "Surely by now you have earned your freedom."

"The Captain has his reasons," Jabir said. And the matter was left there.

147

Chapter Twenty-Two

Caitlin looked out of the castle keep towards Lake Mariac and the surrounding villages. Every day, she paced the entire circumference of the inner castle walls, attracting dubious glances from her guards. She felt imprisoned in her own home, unable to step foot beyond the inner ward for fear that she might miss some vital piece of news or information from her spy network. So she paced, every day, against the better judgement of her advisers, like a caged tigress. It had taken its toll on her health, as her appetite waned and she had developed a wracking cough which did not want to shift. The castle medic gave her a draft to take, which eased it a little but still it persisted.

The Royal Court remained as popular as ever, now that word had got around that the Queen Regent would hear the woes of the commoners. As more and more people poured into Castle Helmstedt for a hearing, so the barons got more and more agitated as they tried in vain to rein in the control of their subjects through the local courts.

At a distance, Caitlin could see the sun glisten and reflect off the Lake and remembered not for the first time in hours, that she would never again see her baby son, Josselin. Despite her mother, Audan's comforting words that day, six months passed and the nursemaid, Isla, had not returned. Two days after Josselin's disappearance, Caitlin received a parcel by messenger, which contained a small black box. Attached to the parcel was a note, which read "All heirs to the throne of Carentan are dead. Relinquish your regency to the rightful heir and

King of Carentan. So say the common people." Inside the box was the horrific bloody stub of her baby's little finger. Caitlin shuddered and felt sickened even now when she recalled that day. She knew it belonged to her Josselin, as he had a birthmark, the shape of which was so unique, it left no question in her mind.

As she paced, she forced back the lump that caught in her throat. She coughed into her handkerchief, which drew concerned looks from her guards. Her health was not good, but she gained strength from the fact that she knew Gereinte was well and developing into a fine young man. Each day that passed drew her closer to the month's end, when she waited impatiently for letters from Jabir ed-Din.

At first, the word had gone out that the Prince Royal had disappeared. That, she could not help, as there were witnesses that saw him there one moment, then gone the next. She had felt the need to inform key staff at the castle that he was safe and been sent away on a tour of the Western Isles as part of his education. It was an important part of the deal, that Gereinte was led to believe that no one knew where he was or what had happened. In that way, he was open to influence and education at his own pace, which curbed his innate desire for rebellion. Oh, my dear son. So much like his father. Caitlin allowed herself the indulgence of imagining Reiner by her side; she so missed his commanding presence and strong sense of purpose, his arms around her felt so right, so safe. Her entire life now depended on getting Gereinte to a point where he could take Reiner's place. Then, she would know the country would be safe. It would be safe then for her to relax and to relinquish her regency. But until that time, she lived only to make it to the end of each month for news on her beloved boy.

She worried also about the girls. They were all so headstrong and commanding; not at all the right temperament for the life that they would be constrained to lead. Each one would be wed for political advantage, the first being Nerys. Caitlin sighed. Dear Nerys. Her head was full of fancy ideas of love and having children, but unfortunately not to the person who had been picked out for her. That was another mess that she was going to have to sort out. As for Alliane, the way she carried on chasing around with the forest rangers, it would be a wonder they would be able to find anyone to take her of their hands. Roda was easy. She had been promised to Baron Issoire a long time ago. In fact, not long after her eldest daughter had been born. That was something that had been cemented between Reiner and Issoire themselves.

Issoire was an interesting fellow. Despite his lack of open allegiance, Caitlin felt sure that Reiner would not have mis-placed his judgement when making a deal over his eldest daughter. Perhaps once it was out in the open, Issoire would be bound then to state his fidelity to the Andolin line. It concerned Caitlin that he was still making a show of negotiating with Baron Borsa; over what, she had no idea as yet. Borsa had a tight rein on his own household and was known to have spies at work within Castle Helmstedt itself. Perhaps that was why Issoire was waiting and not openly staking his claim. As with the rest of Carentan, speculation was rife about whether the Prince Regent really would return or whether in fact it was a conspiracy on the part of House Andolin to cover up his untimely demise. Issoire, it seemed, was merely sitting on the fence waiting to see which way to jump.

There were other rumours coming in every day of ambitious leaders from outside Carentan who had suddenly taken an interest in the internal affairs of the country. It had been reported that Phillipe Rudelle, King of Malvas was amassing troops on the border of Carentan and Malvas. Quite what he hoped to achieve at this early stage in the game was debatable, however, it was evident that the levels of civil unrest in Carentan had triggered other nations to review their political circumstances. Then, there was the Archbishop, Abiel Morda, who most certainly had a hand in the current movement in Malvas. Nothing would please the Church more than for the two nations to engage in a war. The opportunity for infiltration of the Church of the One God would certainly be facilitated by such action. The man was a fanatic.

On occasion, Caitlin's fevered pacing served a purpose, other than keeping an eye on her castle staff. Her best decisions were made whilst walking around the grounds of the castle. The time was right to announce the wedding of her daughter Nerys, to King Morra Dreiden of Tordre. Negotiations had gone well and the King was interested. It was only Nerys that was being difficult. But Nerys would have to comply; Caitlin had been patient enough. She wasn't going to like it, but it was her duty and that was that. Carentan needed some good news for a change. And it needed another nation to stand up in its defence and be counted amongst its supporters. Spurred by this decision, Caitlin hurried back down the stairs in search of the royal advisers and her seneschal, Nils.

Chapter Twenty-Three

In addition to history, geography and philosophy, Gereinte learnt a lot about his seafaring companions. Skyelady was a coastal trader and her main business was carrying cargo from one port to another in the Isles. Transport by road over long distances was difficult, hazardous and expensive due to the poor condition of the roads, the penal transit duties that many countries imposed and the menace of robber bands. Haro Dal was proud of his fine record for safe and timely delivery and he was almost always sure of getting business whichever port he came into. He had an established range of contacts utilising the existing network of trader agents who employed a very efficient courier pigeon communications system.

Skyelady was capable of transporting a wide variety of bulk goods, such as pulses, grains, barley and oats being exported mostly from the rich farmlands of Carentan to other countries in the Isles. She also carried higher value bulk cargo including iron ore, copper, bronze and even, to the crew's disgust, livestock such as horses, cows and pigs.

In addition to the coastal trade, Skyelady was renowned as one of the few seafaring ships in the Isles which had successfully accomplished longer voyages to the Green Island and across the Inner Sea to ports in the southern, eastern and northern lands. These feats were due in some part to the seamanship and courage of captain and crew, but was more recently because of the navigational skills of Jabir, who was capable of dead reckoning as well locating the ship's position from the stars.

"It's a bit like looking at the past to determine the future," said Jabir, as enigmatic as Gereinte had learnt to expect. The easterner put down a pile of maps and papers with circles and squiggles decorating every corner of available parchment. He waved an open hand across the pile, inviting Gereinte to challenge his knowledge and wisdom. Everything was an uphill struggle with this man. Although he had unofficially taken on the role of his teacher and mentor, he still didn't make anything easy for Gereinte. It was almost as though he teased him with just enough information to whet his appetite for more. Gereinte took the map off the top of the pile and studied the calculations scribbled alongside their current position. There was a line, which plotted back from where he guessed they probably were now, with approximate speed, distances and timing. The line then projected forward to a point which he guessed was where they were likely to be at any given time. Mathematical equations were scribbled in the margins across every sheet of paper and map in the pile in front of him.

"Where do the numbers come from?" Gereinte said.

"The crew feed them to me. We have a ship log to measure speed but I prefer using the traverse board, which records both speed and direction. Even the slowest of our crew members can use a traverse board." Jabir grunted as if he had made a joke and Gereinte found it hard to imagine that any of the Coustiller crew could be described as 'slow'.

"How do you keep track of all these numbers?" Gereinte shuffled through Jabir's notes. Jabir tapped the top of the pile with his fore finger and smiled. It irritated Gereinte and he wondered if the man got some kind of perverse enjoyment out of being so mysterious.

"If it's on here, it's in here," he said, then tapped his finger to his temple.

***

Gereinte was often to be found loitering about the Captain's cabin. Haro Dal had quickly established a routine of having Gereinte serve light refreshments during most of his trade negotiations. He maintained that 'Griff' was an excellent cook, thanks to his training with Cook in the galley and a useful pair of hands to run errands whilst the Captain was tied up with business. There was nothing that the Coustillers did that now surprised Gereinte. Despite his 'slave status', he appeared to be privy to every little piece of business and news happening aboard the Skyelady. The Captain maintained that the most useful of cabin boys were those that had a wide knowledge and understanding of trade and traders. Gereinte was unconvinced by this curious justification, but despite this remained attentive, as the business of trade was far more interesting than scrubbing decks. Haro Dal's guests on board the ship, for the most part ignored him.

The ship was moored in Sarne Harbour, after having delivered a cargo of iron ore. Haro Dal was entertaining a Sarlatian merchant named Jenrot who claimed to deal exclusively in precious stones, in particular, diamonds. As Gereinte made his way from the galley to the Captain's quarters, the jug of ale and tray of biscuits he carried nearly flew out of his hands as Morley stepped in front of him cutting

155

off his exit.

"There's decks to be scrubbed when the Captain's finished with you," he snarled. Gereinte merely nodded and the man moved reluctantly to let him pass. It had been a while since Rastiffe and Morley had interfered with orders. Perhaps he was feeling jealous that the cabin boy Griff had been allowed, even encouraged to be part of delicate negotiations with one of his countrymen.

Gereinte shook off his unease about Morley and slipped into the Captain's study, currently occupied by the Captain himself who sat opposite the merchant Jenrot. Jenrot cast a cursory glance at the cabin boy as Gereinte placed the ale and biscuits on the table and retreated into the shadows as instructed by Haro Dal.

Jenrot engaged in an elaborate dialogue with Haro Dal, using an archaic style of delivery. The Sarlatians were arrogant enough to believe they were the people closest to the legendary Etanese, who were the original settlers in the Western Isles. According to Jabir ed-Din, there were at least 15 individual languages spoken in the Isles, a large number of which were used in the highly fragmented, tribal dominated countries of the north, Klagenstill and Tennegaul. Within the midland and southern countries of Sarlat, Carentan, Tordre and Vermondie, the most common language used was Etanese. The purity with which the Sarlatian merchant spoke the language was about as close as he could get to the original Etans. However, the reputation of the Sarlatian nationals was starkly divergent from the legendary honesty and probity of the long dead Etanese. Gereinte mulled this thought over as he listened to Jenrot speak.

"I do not trust the honesty or security of the cross-country caravans, which is why I have come to you, Sir. The reliability and integrity of the Coustillers is renowned across the Western Isles and beyond."

"Indeed, indeed." Haro Dal was nodding in agreement. They were such an easy race to please, the Coustillers. All you needed to do was slip in a few words of praise and they would roll over themselves to help you. That, of course, and the princely sum that Jenrot was offering for the transportation of his diamonds; no fool would take on that level of responsibility without due return. The diamonds were to be conveyed in a large container from Sarlat to the port of Killanin in northern Carentan. Gereinte supressed an ache of longing to see his homeland again and focused again on the merchant's words.

"This consignment is the greatest part of my fortune," Jenrot said. "I must be absolutely certain it arrives safely."

"Yessir. You can count on the Coustillers. We have not lost a single cargo yet, nor reneged on an agreement." Haro Dal was beaming with pride.

"There is one thing however," Jenrot said. "I cannot abide sea travel under any circumstances, I am sure you understand. I will go by road to Killanin and meet the Skyelady when she arrives." Gereinte noted how he had managed to keep down several kegs of ale and a plate of biscuits without too much trouble, with the ship swaying in its mooring.

"Understood, Sir. 'Tis not for all, travelling by

sea." The captain seemed to accept this without further explanation.

"Good. Let it be done, then." Jenrot rose and shook hands with the Captain who pumped the small and gaudily dressed merchant's hand with a little too much enthusiasm. "The container shall arrive at midday tomorrow."

Haro looked expectantly at Gereinte who held up four fingers, which he flashed twice to mean eight bells. The captain smiled and nodded at Jenrot, who looked over his shoulder and frowned at the cabin boy. Gereinte dropped his head and looked at the floor. At the exit, Jenrot turned as though remembering something and produced a document from somewhere beneath his robes.

"By the way, you will need this." He thrust the document into Haro's hands. "It is a certificate confirming the value of the consignment attested to under oath by an independent expert." The Captain glanced at the paper and his eyes widened. Apparently, he needed no further persuasion.

Gereinte stayed in the Captain's cabin until he returned from having escorted the Sarlatian merchant, Jenrot, off the ship. Haro Dal beamed at Gereinte, clearly pleased with the deal he had just made. When he saw the boy's expression, he frowned and took a seat.

"Well, lad. What is it?"

"I don't trust that man," Gereinte said.

"I don't see what could go wrong," Haro Dal said. "We take the diamonds on board, sail around to Killanin, deliver them to Jenrot and collect the other half of our fee." Gereinte was shaking his head.

"All right and good," he said. "And what happens at the other end when Jenrot examines his diamonds and finds, correctly, that they are all fake and worthless? You know who he is going to blame. You could lose your fleet and spend the rest of your life in jail."

Haro Dal smiled. "Ah yes. Clever lad. You spotted that possibility eh? But I have a certificate here that attests to the value of the diamonds."

"Certificates can be forged, Sir," Gereinte said. "And you don't know that the consignment to which that certificate refers is the one that will be delivered here." The Captain looked at the piece of paper in his hand, looked back at Gereinte, then rubbed his chin thoughtfully.

"Alas, that is true," he said at length. "So what would *you* do?"

"I would have a diamond merchant waiting here *before* the consignment is delivered. He would be responsible for opening the crate, examining the contents and certifying its true value," Gereinte said. Haro Dal stared at his cabin boy for a long moment before his face broke into a smile. Then, to Gereinte's bemusement, he began to laugh out loud with great hearty whoops, smacking his thigh in the process.

"Dear boy," he wiped tears of laughter from the corners of his eyes. "I knew there was a good reason to have you aboard. It will be done – I have a contact in Sarne who owes me a favour. Now then. You head off and take these things back to the galley. I'm sure Cook could do with a hand for lunch." Gereinte cleared away the empty platters and jugs, then left the Captain to make his

159

arrangements for the next day.

On his way back to the galley, he heard two of the Coustillers talking loudly to another group.

"…Carentan Princess. Rumour is on the streets, that a wealthy Carentan Baron has sent an envoy to negotiate with the King of Sarlat himself, Alvar Correze. There could be a royal wedding before the year is out."

Gereinte stopped suddenly and a jug toppled over with a crash onto one of the platters. The Coustillers looked up at the noise and saw Gereinte standing there with his mouth open. Excited by the news, they bounded down and encircled him.

"What do you think of that, our Carentan? A royal wedding… with Sarlat?" The Coustillers clapped their hands with joy. Gereinte knew how much they loved a celebration and this one would be a great excuse for going ashore to party. They looked a little nonplussed by Gereinte's frosty reaction. Morley, the Sarlat, was leaning against the aft rail glaring at them all with a stony expression. He didn't seem to think it was great news either.

Who was getting married? Surely not one of the twins, they were far too young. It could only be Roda. But why marry a Sarlatian? They were the last nation in the Isles that he would trust as political allies. What was the Queen Regent thinking? He wanted to know more, but daren't go ashore, especially if there really was an envoy from Carentan in the City. If he were caught in Sarlat, they might imprison him and use him as a bargaining tool. It was not unheard of in the Sarlat's muddied history of international relations. Technically, he was a prisoner aboard the Skyelady,

160

but he could think of far worse places to be held against his will.

The Coustillers grew tired of this game, once they realised that they were not going to get much joy from Griff. So they dispersed and returned to their duties, leaving Gereinte to mull over the news.

The next day, the consignment of diamonds arrived and Haro Dal was there to take delivery. Jenrot did not appear, but the Captain's expert opened the container, made a thorough investigation and pronounced the diamonds to be entirely fake. Neither Gereinte, nor the Captain were particularly surprised and for a small fee, the expert produced a certificate which attested to their true value.

Once the expert had left the ship, Captain Dal began delegating in preparation for their next voyage; to Killanin and to meet with the unscrupulous Jenrot who no doubt had some highfaluting plan, which awaited them there.

Chapter Twenty-Four

Some days into the voyage, Gereinte was on deck with Morley, when Fenner shouted "Jump aloft and take in the Square-s'l." Morley looked at Gereinte and grinned, but before he made a move to climb the rigging, Gereinte sprang up like a cat and was already past the sheer-pole before Fenner had time to object. He guessed the order had been aimed at Morley, but since the Sarlatian had given him ample rope to hang himself, Gereinte saw no reason not to oblige. Besides, he had become quite adept at furling the sails since coming on board. Gereinte stopped halfway up the topmast rigging at the cross-trees and looked out to sea. The ship swayed under the wind and he glanced back down to the deck, breathing deeply to overcome the giddiness. The deck looked so small. He could see the Coustillers milling about their duties and Fenner looking up into the rigging to watch what he was doing.

Out at sea, Gereinte saw a dolphin chasing flying fish. The fish were skimming above the water by several feet, just ahead of the dolphin, which looped in and out of the water, just missing its prey by inches. Sometimes he felt like those flying fish; always trying to be one step ahead and forever looking over a shoulder as though there were someone chasing him down.

Part of the reason he jumped at the chance to bring in the sail in front of Morley, was an attempt to show both the Coustillers and the Sarlatian that he was as good as any of them. In the months that he had been aboard the Skyelady, he had become adept at most of the duties. He had developed such a keen style of knife fighting using his natural agility that even the experts like Genno had difficulty in now defeating him. He knew that certain crew members were jealous; jealous of the attention he commanded from the rest of the crew, jealous of the apparently special treatment he got from the Captain and certainly jealous of the unmitigated amount of time he spent with the unusual eastern navigator-cum-scholar, Jabir ed-Din. He was aware that certain crew members were apt to remind him from time to time of his slave status on board the ship.

A gust of wind caused the ship to roll leeward which brought Gereinte firmly back into reality. He began pulling the canvas sail to windward, which cracked and slapped against itself in the wind. He gathered it in and rolled everything up neatly. He noted the Sarlatian watching him from the deck, probably hoping that he would miss a step and make a bad job of it or else slip and fall to deck. Fortunately for Gereinte, neither of those wishes came true and he returned to deck to be greeted by Fenner, who beamed and clapped him on the back.

"Good job, lad. Now then Morley, I've more for you to do aft," he said turning to the Sarlatian, who followed him.

Gereinte leaned against the taffrail and looked out once again to sea, watching the dolphin, which had been joined by its mates. He took a deep breath of salt air and enjoyed the rushing sound of water as the boat cut through the waves. The dolphins darted in and out of the water, criss-crossing in the wake of the ship, following the Coustiller vessel.

He had a disturbing feeling that he was being watched and turned his head just as his world exploded into pain and darkness. Something hard had struck him from behind. His legs gave way and before he had a chance to regain his footing, he was slipping headfirst over the taffrail. He plunged into the sea, the cold water bringing him partially to his senses. He held his breath as his body sank down and down, lungs bursting for air, but afraid to open his mouth for fear of breathing in the seawater. He began to despair that soon he would lose consciousness entirely and that would be the end of his life. A wasted opportunity to be the best he could be, finished at the bottom of the ocean off the Tordrean coastline. No one would know what happened to him; his family would never see him again and Carentan would continue its journey into an unknown and hostile future without its heir.

Gereinte's body hit something soft and for a moment he thought that he had reached the seabed. Then the soft thing he had hit began to move and nudge him upwards. There were two, either side of him, propelling him upwards at a gentle, yet urgent speed. He burst suddenly out of the water and took a precious lungful of air. Coughing and spluttering, he realised that he was being supported by two dolphins that were whisking him through the water chasing the Skyelady, which was sailing off in the distance, oblivious to Gereinte's misadventure. The dolphins cradled his body, keeping him just above the water, but still the spray from the ship's wake soaked his face, so he had to fight to keep the air coming into his lungs. The dolphins started up a shrill whistle and clicked loudly. As they drew closer, there was a great commotion on deck as they were spotted. It seemed that the entire crew on and off duty had gathered to help launch a single small rowing boat, with one Coustiller on board to rescue their Carentan cabin boy.

Once on board the rowing boat, the dolphins made a show of jumping in and out of the water, clicking and whistling, then retreated to join the rest of their school.

Hundreds of questions were fired at him all at once when he was finally dragged back onto the Skyelady. Gereinte coughed and spluttered for a while and eventually came up with a suitable story to tell the crew.

"I leaned too far over the taffrail, went overboard, then hit my head on a rudder." The Coustiller crew chided him and fussed over him and the Captain had a 'told you so' look on his face as he was always attempting to discourage Gereinte from some of his more acrobatic antics.

He was sent to his cabin to dry off and change, then filled with hot food that the Cook had been preparing and insisted on him having first sitting. Jabir ed-Din was seated in the galley and when Gereinte sat beside him, Jabir's expression was thoughtful.

"Is there something you want to tell me, young Griff?" he said. Gereinte filled his mouth full of potatoes and chewed before responding.

"There is. But this is something we must discuss with the Captain and his First Officer." Gereinte kept his voice low, as he was aware of the crew filtering in for their dinner. Jabir nodded, then rose and left Gereinte to finish his meal. He was not surprised, therefore, when later in the evening, he was called to the Captain's cabin, where he found

165

Haro Dal with Kaysin, Fenner and Jabir.

"It has not escaped notice that there are certain individuals on board that might rather see you at the bottom of the ocean, Griff." Haro Dal had a serious expression, which Gereinte found a little uncomfortable given the Coustillers customary buoyant nature. That aside, when a Coustiller was serious about something, you knew he must be serious. "Tell us what happened to you today."

Gereinte recounted his tale, starting with the moment that Fenner had given the order to pull in the sail. A few eyebrows were raised at the part the dolphins played in the rescue; the Coustillers revered the dolphins and felt honoured by their very presence. The fact that they had followed the Skyelady from Sarne Harbour and then rescued their cabin boy left the Captain and his crew slightly in awe of Griff.

Now that he had looked death in the face so many times and won, he was more determined than ever to make it back home and start to rebuild a nation that was teetering on the edge of self-destruction. He owed it to his father, his mother and most of all, to the ordinary people who lived their lives in the hope that someone would guide them and look after their interests. Well, he intended to be that someone.

Finally, Gereinte intimated the connection between his untimely visit to the ocean depths and the Sarlatian, Morley, who appeared to be goading him at every opportunity.

"Captain, I know it may be difficult to believe, but I sincerely hope that you understand I would not lie to you," he said.

Haro Dal looked at the others in the room. Kaysin and Fenner both raised their bushy eyebrows and Jabir merely smiled and nodded his head. Gereinte realised, too late, that he had fallen out of his cabin boy common usage of Etanese and back into the diction used by Prince Royal of Carentan. The Captain composed himself and adopted an earnest expression.

"We believe you, lad. But I don't think that there is any merit in making this knowledge available to the rest of the crew, that is until the would-be assassin can be identified."

"Agreed," Kaysin said. I say we bring in the Sarlatian for questioning. See where we go from there."

"I say, we all get some rest and bring him in at eight bells," Fenner said. "From the day we've had, I think we would all do well to sleep on it."

"Wise words, indeed, Boatswain. Till eight bells, it be then," Haro Dal said. "Lad, you must rest now, you are excused duties in the morning. Let us deal with what the Sarlatian has to say."

At that, the meeting dispersed and Gereinte fell thankfully into his bunk, lungs and body still sore from his wrestle with the sea. He slept and dreamt of home.

Chapter Twenty-Five

He awoke with a start. Had he missed the bells? For a moment, he lay still, wondering what day it was, where he was and what he had to do that day. But the cabin smelt of night; sleeping bodies, dark skies and nocturnal creatures. As his brain registered that he was lying in his bunk aboard the Skyelady, it also noted that something or someone had woken him from a deep sleep.

Someone else was in the cabin. He pricked his ears and slowly lifted his head. As his eyes became accustomed to the dark, he could make out a figure standing beside his bunk. It took a few moments to recognise Morley and seconds to realise that he was standing with his hands up in surrender. The Sarlatian then put his finger to his mouth with a sibilant shush.

Not really knowing why, but indulging a curious instinct, he followed Morley out of the cabin, shuffling his feet as his body began to wake up. The night watch was convening to exchange shifts and as Morley and Gereinte moved in the shadows, they could hear the voice of the Vermondien, Rastiffe, talking to the other crew members.

"You know, lads, you can always rely on a Vermondien to support you when all is done at sea. Let us shift now, I'll take a turn at the wheel."

"Ah, so Vermondie is the race of favour now, is it?" Morley said, stepping into the centre of the gathering. Gereinte stayed back in the shadows to listen and watch. Issuing a jovial challenge, Rastiffe took it and responded as such.

"Ah, my good friend. I think we understand one

another. What are you doing on deck at this time?"

The Coustillers watched, knowing that there were always fireworks where these two crew members were concerned and enjoying a jolly good wrangle, they expected nothing less than a late-night showdown.

"I think, thanks would be why I'm here tonight. My reputation precedes me. I stand to take blame for attempted murder and I wasn't even near the lad at the time," Morley said.

"As honourable as a Sarlat," Rastiffe said. "You would take the blame for something you didn't do to enhance your reputation as the ship's bad boy." Rastiffe began to clap his hands with a slow, purposeful rhythm. The Coustillers, still thinking they were playing some elaborate foreign game, began to mimic the Vermondien and took up the rhythmic beat of hand clapping.

"Of course," Morley said, "I have your reputation to live up to."

Rastiffe smiled a wicked grin and stopped clapping. The Coustillers stopped and the noise faded leaving a silence between them that stretched out to the furthest gull on the darkest shores.

"You have no reputation, Morley. Who was it that got rid of that last slave idiot that served aboard this good ship? Yes, me. With no help from you, I might add." At this, the Coustillers began to disperse and pretend that they weren't hearing what was being said but still keeping all ears open for any further developments. "And who was it this time that nearly got rid of that cocky slave filth that darkens our deck now?" There was a gasp of horror from the surrounding crew members. The hairs on the back of Gereinte's neck prickled. A murmur of disbelief came from the crew members. One or two were whispering to each other.

"Our Carentan... is he talking about our Carentan?"

Then, realising what he had just said, the Vermondie tried to back track.

"No, I... what I mean is..." But it was too late for him. Too many of the Coustillers had heard his words and Gereinte himself had heard what he had to say.

The following day, the Vermondie was held for questioning by the ship's captain, alongside the Sarlatian who continued to profess his innocence and even managed to dredge up a few witnesses who agreed that he was in the bows of the ship at the time of the attack on Griff.

In due course, Rastiffe was set off the ship along the Verton Delta, off the eastern coast of Vermondie, not far from his hometown. Morley was permitted to stay on board on the understanding that he would no longer harass the cabin boy, Griff, to which he agreed. Gereinte no longer suffered any untoward behaviour from the Sarlatian, as they continued their journey across the Verton Delta and onward towards the eastern coast of Carentan and the port of Killanin.

***

The remainder of the passage was blessed with fair winds and the Skyelady arrived in Killanin without further drama on board, save for the usual antics of the Coustillers. Haro Dal went ashore to seek out the local magistrate in order to explain their predicament.

Gereinte had been asked to keep an eye on the consignment of diamonds whilst the Captain was gone. He had been asked to attend to give his take on the story, but Gereinte had come up with the excuse that he was not feeling well enough to leave the ship at that moment. He feared more than anything else, being recognised in Carentan, though the port was far from his home. It wasn't that he didn't want to go home, it was just that he had a sense of commitment that up until the point when Haro Dal had asked him to accompany him, he had not realised was so strong. To be recognised now would mean a setback for the Captain and the plans he had so carefully laid down in order to settle with Jenrot.

As it was, the Captain returned in due course with the magistrate in tow. The magistrate was a slight fellow, with a friendly face and a typically sunny Carentan outlook on life. He looked at Gereinte, who braced himself for what might follow, but the man's gaze rested briefly on the boy before settling on the consignment of diamonds and the certificate that the Captain had thrust in his hands. Gereinte caught sight of his own reflection in the porthole and barely recognised himself; his hair had grown long and he had begun to develop a layer of thin wispy hair above his lip that had not been there when he had first arrived aboard the Skyelady.

"This is outrageous," the magistrate said, "that a Sarlatian would attempt to perpetrate such a crime on an honest Coustiller in Carentan."

The Captain looked pleased with himself as the magistrate huffed and puffed about Sarlatians; a national pastime for most Carentans. Between them, they carefully laid down a plan to catch Jenrot out when he arrived the next day to collect his diamonds.

As the magistrate was leaving the Skyelady, Gereinte hesitated for worry of being recognised, and then decided to risk it.

"My Lord... I'm from Carentan. Is there any news of the Prince Royal?"

The magistrate swung around and fixed his gaze on the cabin boy in front of him. He narrowed his eyes and Gereinte's heart began to thud.

"The Prince Royal is away on a grand tour," he said lifting his chin, then he turned to leave.

"And what of the Royal wedding?"

The magistrate turned and glared at him. "Not that it is of your concern boy, but the royal couple are to wed in the spring. The engagement celebrations commence as we speak." The magistrate again tried to leave, but Gereinte put a hand on his arm, to which he looked most perturbed. The magistrate looked around for the Captain, but Haro Dal was talking to his crew on the lower deck.

"Please, my Lord," Gereinte said, trying for a sympathetic ear. "I have a sister who works in the castle as a maid to the bride. I just wanted some news and I am worried that there are Sarlatians involved."

"Sarlatians?" The magistrate looked perplexed. "At the castle? I hardly think so. You must have your information wrong boy. Princess Nerys is betrothed to King Morra Dreiden of Tordre." At that, he snatched his arm away from Gereinte and stalked off the ship.

Gereinte stood for a moment, staring at the empty space where the magistrate had been. Then as the words began to sink in, he smiled. It made perfect sense when you thought clearly about it. The envoy sent to Sarlat had been a decoy, probably to confound House Andolin's enemies. The real engagement was with Tordre. He could almost hear his mother's voice explaining the strategic importance of such an alliance.

Then he thought of Nerys and how she had been so taken with the young man who had helped their little game of 'swap the squire'. What was his name? Devlin, that was it. Devlin. There had always been something about that lad, something Gereinte had not quite trusted. He could just picture Nerys' face when she was told the news that she was to be wed to a complete stranger from a foreign nation. Poor Nerys. He wished he had been there for her, even if only to smooth the way and ease her aching heart. Alliane would never have understood. Despite the fact that they were twins, Alliane had less in common with Nerys than he did.

He wondered how Roda was feeling; left out perhaps. Being the eldest, it should have been her turn first. How his heart ached to see his sisters again. They said he was on a Grand Tour, or so the public have been led to believe. He wondered what his family really thought; that he was dead? He missed his little brother too and hoping beyond all reason that Josselin remembered him if he ever made it back to Castle Helmstedt.

King Morra Dreiden of Tordre. Well, his sister could do far worse; she would be a Queen. She would outrank even her own mother. Gereinte tried

173

to recall what he knew of King Morra. He was a quiet and reflective man – that would get on Nerys' nerves, for a start. She was far too gregarious to put up with being stashed away in a castle with no one to see. Although, perhaps it would be a welcome distraction for the King. Perhaps he needed someone to be his socialite, so that he didn't need to worry about entertaining guests and organising functions. Nerys would be in her element if the relationship allowed her to be Queen of her own castle.

As far as he knew, Tordre had been waiting patiently for their King to take a bride and most people speculated about the fact that it had been five years with no sign of a betrothal. A Carentan king could not have got away with it for so long, as the position of heir to the throne always fell to the eldest son of the king. However in Tordre, they had a bizarre system of voting whereby the incumbent royals could get dismissed from post to make way for a new family that curried favour with the voting public. It was a calculated risk, putting Nerys into the fray, hoping to gain a political advantage for Carentan. However, knowing his sister, if she were committed to the idea she would more than woo the people of Tordre into accepting a Carentan princess as their Queen.

"Catching flies, our Carentan?" Kaysin said. Gereinte, snapped his mouth shut. "You'd best prepare yourself – all crew with any fighting ability are to be on deck at the next bell. We're expecting the return of the diamond merchant." The bells rang out on deck and Gereinte swung back past his cabin to collect his weapon. He concealed it beneath his tunic, hoping that he would not have to use it.

As predicted, Jenrot returned, accompanied by one of the magistrate's lawmen, whom he believed was acting as a witness for his own benefit. He looked confident and was dressed in robes of bright orange and yellow, which made Gereinte's stomach churn if he stared too long on the swaying ship. Jenrot was a short man with a pointed nose and eyes that were far too close together. Gereinte's mistrust had not abated since their last meeting, despite the drama of their voyage to Killanin.

Jenrot motioned the lawman to accompany him to the consignment, and asked one of the Coustillers to open it up in order to confirm the contents before handing over the second half of the fee to the Captain. He paused over the diamonds for a few minutes, took a sample in his hand, rolling it back and forth before holding it up to the light. The entire crew waited with bated breath as the diamond merchant inspected the stones.

"Good, then," Haro Dal said. "I shall have my men take the consignment immediately ashore for convenience and we shall exchange goods for payment of delivery, as agreed in Sarne." He made a motion and the Coustillers jumped to attention.

"Wait." Jenrot held up a hand. He was still inspecting the stones, with a long-drawn frown, creasing his brow. "I do believe these are fakes." He turned toward the lawman and started screeching in a high-pitched voice, as though he couldn't believe what was happening. "Robbery, robbery, I say. Arrest this man immediately," he pointed at Haro Dal. "He has replaced my dearest possessions with fakes. It was his intention all along to fool me into

175

parting with my good money and then to take my diamonds as well. I should be richly compensated for such criminal injustice. Arrest the man at once."

The Coustillers stood, hands at the ready to take up arms against the merchant, should he turn violent.

"I have been wronged... truly wronged."

The magistrate stepped out from a concealed spot behind the consignment and faced Jenrot. "Ah, just the man. I wish to claim full restitution for the wrongdoing of this diamond thief. I have here a certificate proving the value of my consignment before it left Sarne Bay."

The magistrate shook his head. "And I have here a certificate which shows the true value of this consignment before it left Sarne Bay." Jenrot's face dropped. "I am placing you under arrest for the attempted embezzlement of monies in connection with this worthless consignment of diamonds."

"But... but.."

"Save it for the courts, Sir. We have all the proof we need, but you can be assured, you will have a fair hearing."

At that, Jenrot was marched from the Skyelady ashore to be placed under arrest and sent to the local jail, there to contemplate at his leisure the iniquitous depths of the Coustiller mind whilst awaiting trial.

Gereinte sighed with relief. At least that was one less unscrupulous Sarlatian merchant relieved of his duties to the blessing of all those respectable dealers out there. He looked to the Captain, who had a wry smile on his face.

"We never did get to collect the second half of our fee," he said. Gereinte shook his head. Of course, there was sometimes a fine line between honesty and profit, as he realised that the Captain had in this case gained at least half the asking price and a consignment of fake jewels.

The Captain began shouting orders to his crew, who jumped into preparing the Skyelady for departure. Gereinte stared out at the port of Killanin, wondering what would have happened if he had jumped ship here and tried to get home alone. The Captain, as though reading his thoughts, clapped a hand on his shoulder.

"Don't be down, lad. We have plenty more adventures in store for you aboard the Skyelady. I will have my money's worth, before I release you from my service. Besides, what kind of life would a poor boy like you have to return to in Carentan? Best let the Coustillers look after you now, lad."

Gereinte had to swallow the lump forming in his throat. He longed to tell Haro Dal who he really was. Sometimes, he thought the Captain already knew, then other times he would say something like that and dash his hopes of ever getting off the ship. He sighed and turned back towards his duties, heart heavy with longing to see his homeland and family once more.

"To Tordre!" the Captain said. There was a loud cheer from the Coustillers. "I have it on good authority that the port of T'sar is the place to be as the country prepares to meet their future Queen."

Gereinte looked at the Captain who winked, his curly moustache hiding the remnants of a smile. So, to Tordre. He thought again of Nerys and hope crept over his skin.

Chapter Twenty-Six

Nerys had thought that her heart might break when the Queen Regent announced the news of her betrothal to King Morra Dreiden of Tordre. She had been within a whisker's breadth of eloping with Devlin. The very thought of him made her stomach knot inside and brought on a cold, cold sweat. So close to destroying everything dear to her. Imagine what it would have done to her family if she had gone ahead with that dirty weasel's plans. If it hadn't been for her nosy sister, bless her soul, Nerys could have been in hiding on the Green Island, renouncing her royalty and living a miserable life at the mercy of the very enemies that sought to bring down House Andolin.

The maids fussed with Nerys' appearance. She was sitting in the Royal chambers at King Morra's castle in T'sar. Through the melee that accompanied her to the castle she had caught a glimpse of the King, albeit briefly and even then she had been hurried along, as it was deemed bad luck for the King to see his future Queen before the betrothal ceremony.

He was taller than she expected and much younger. When the announcement was made, it was like a punch in the gut. She envisioned some elderly man who was doing this for political might. King Morra looked up at the moment she passed, caught her eye, and then looked away. His hair was fair in colour and tied loosely back to reveal a slender neck with milky white skin. It was hard to tell what his feelings or thoughts might be; his steely grey eyes revealed nothing to her at all.

Quite a different man than she had expected and quite different from that waste of space, Devlin, she had spent the last few months moping over. A wave of disgust washed over her. She was angry and embarrassed, but there was still an emptiness gnawing away inside of her. Of course, she had not believed Alliane when she first came running with news of Devlin's deceit.

They argued and Nerys had accused Alliane of being jealous and spiteful and trying to ruin her happiness. Alliane had accused Nerys, quite rightly, of being stupid and gullible. In the end, the two of them conspired to catch Devlin at one of his meetings with his contact. He turned on Nerys and tried to persuade her that nothing was going on. But it was too late. Nerys had heard with her own ears the conspiracy behind their relationship.

Now she felt alone. Alone and stupid. She wanted to bring Alliane with her to T'sar, but mother would not allow it. The Andolins were to travel separately to attend the ceremony and Caitlin would need additional attendants, owing to the fact that she was a little under the weather. So Nerys was there alone, to face her future. How she missed Gereinte. If he were there, he would know what to say to make her feel better. He would know how to ease her anxiety.

What if they didn't get on? What if he didn't like her? He had seemed so distant when she saw him earlier. They had locked eyes for only seconds and were silently appraising one another. She felt disappointed when he looked away, then remembered that it was deemed unlucky for the King to see his future consort before the betrothal

179

ceremony. Besides, after Devlin, she no longer trusted her feelings. Perhaps he was feeling anxious too. He had only others accounts of what the Carentan Princess was like. He was no doubt thinking, what if she is ugly? What if she doesn't like me?

Nerys was astounded by the attention she had generated on her journey through T'sar towards the castle. In some ways, she had hoped to have a tour of Tordre before the ceremony, but because of the travel arrangements, mother had thought it best to arrive fresh from the Carentan border for the ceremony, then to accept a formal tour with her future King the next day. But the people had come out in celebration to see her arrive. There were musicians and jugglers in the street and people were dressed in brightly coloured clothes, waving flags with both the Tordre and Carentan standards flying in the wind alongside each other.

For the first time, she began to realise the magnitude of such an alliance and despite the creeping unease that lay in the pit of her stomach, she began to claw back some of the dignity and royal duty she had grown up to embrace. It was the beginning of a new era for their two nations. Despite wanting to ride her pony, mother had insisted that she be carried in a litter, which had been opened up on her arrival, so that she could wave and smile at the onlookers. Nerys had felt strangely regal, sitting there and just a bit too imperious for her liking. She hoped the King would not see her arrive like this and was relieved to be able to walk into the castle before he set eyes on her. She made a mental note of insisting that she ride her pony when they took their tour.

The people of Tordre were friendly and reverent. They spoke a mixture of languages, both their native Langan and Etanese. It was fortunate for Nerys that interspersed with the unfamiliar guttural sounds of Langan, she could make out words and phrases of Etanese. It was as though the commoners on the street forgot for a moment she was a foreigner, then remembering, shouted in Etanese their words of welcome. She was touched by the display of regard from the Tordreans and their joyous enthusiasm lifted her spirits.

In a moment of complete madness, she thought she saw Gereinte in the crowds of people lining the streets. She sat up like a cat ready to pounce and stared out at the sea of faces, then relaxed back when she saw that it was just a sailor boy whose scraggy good looks vaguely resembled Gereinte. The hair was too long and he was far too grubby, though he did seem to stare somewhat at her. She glanced back again and saw him swept away by his seafaring companions, who seemed like a boisterous bunch.

Nerys looked at her reflection in the mirror. The maids had done well; her silky hair was curled into a long dark river which snaked down her back, intertwined with sparkling jewels that looked like the reflections of a million lights on the surface of a lake. Her gown was of sky blue, encrusted with silvery sequins. A white lacy veil topped the outfit, to hide her face until the moment that she was revealed to her King.

There was a loud rap on the chamber door which made her jump. The maids took a note from the messenger and returned to the side of the princess.

"The Royal family of Andolin have arrived," the maid said, in what Nerys thought was probably her best spoken Etanese. "They are settling now in the guest's quarters in preparation for the ceremony."

Nerys smiled and nodded. "Thank you," she said, feeling not quite as alone as she did before. She rose and stood in front of the window, looking out over a courtyard of frantic activity.

There was a pang in her heart that stung much deeper than any wounds inflicted by Devlin. Somewhere out there, both her brothers lay dead or lost. It was only by the luck of nature that her sister Alliane had discovered the truth about Devlin, otherwise Nerys might have been lost or dead too. This thought, however, gave her little comfort now. Perhaps she might never even know what happened to Josselin and Gereinte.

182

Chapter Twenty-Seven

Krajikk grunted at the assembled men of Klagenstill, as he ripped a leg from the cooked carcass of meat and proceeded to devour it in between great gulps of beer from the keg on the table. His enormous bulk took up half of the small dining room aboard the pirate ship, which was moored just off the coast of Tordre. He stopped, looked up and with cheeks bursting, barked in barely discernable Jarvik.

"Coustillers, you say? In T'sar?"

The assembled semi-barbaric crew of the pirate ship nodded enthusiastically at their chief. Krajikk was entertaining and making deals with a clan of slavers from Klagenstill for the rich pickings that were guaranteed in the port of T'sar during the week of royal celebrations. The crew was tough and physically formidable. The slavers were rugged and not seasoned fighters despite their physical resemblance to the pirate crew.

Krajikk chewed slowly, his blue eyes roving around the table, not settling. His pale skin and fair hair gave him a ghostly air, which he sometimes used to his advantage when engaging in acts of sex and violence, but not necessarily in that order, as it enabled him to frighten the little southern rabbits into submission.

Descended from successive generations of marauding raiders based in the Kingdom of the North, Klagenstill existed as a loose confederation of semi-autonomous clans, each having its own chief. The nation was ruled by the Chieftain of the clan of clans, who frequently disclaimed all knowledge and responsibility for the marauding Klagen war parties that sailed south, raping, looting and pillaging undefended coastal villages.

"By Odin," Krajikk said, slamming his fist into the table and causing cups and plates to jump. "The time has come for some real sport. Let the Jarv clans once again regain their reputation of being the most feared and indestructible forces this side of the Island Ring."

"Err... Chief," Arvij said. "Let us not forget our original deal?" The mighty Krajikk turned his icy gaze on the captain of the slave ship. He stared at him for a moment before breaking into a guffaw, which sprayed the table with masticated wild mutton.

"But of course, of course. You lead us to the prize and we will... how shall I put it? Secure your half of the deal. How does that sound?"

"Marvellous, marvellous," Arvij said, taking a gulp of beer. "But we would like some of the men to be physically intact, if you know what I mean. In our line of business, we don't profit much from damaged goods."

"Understood, I am sure. It will be a pleasure to keep a few back for your purse strings, my brother. Our approach must be one of stealth for the most part. The element of surprise will be their downfall and this is where we bow to your expertise." Krajikk continued to gnaw on his leg of meat and shoved the platter enough that it slid across the table to stop in front of Arvij. The captain of the slavers ripped a chunk of meat from the carcass and lifted a beer mug to the chief of the pirates.

"May the goddess, Sol shine her light on your

every journey, my good chief." An almighty cheer went up from around the table, followed by multiple fists being repeatedly banged on the wooden trestle to the timing of ritual grunts and whoops of joyous abandon.

***

Gereinte stood still in the crowd for a moment, jostled from either side by the commoners, eager to catch a glimpse of the Carentan Princess. Nerys was staring straight at him as though she knew it was him and all he wanted was to jump up and down and shout 'It's me, Gereinte. I'm here.' But he was frozen in the moment, like a startled fawn in a forest opening. His mouth went dry and his limbs limp. He saw her look, double back, stare at him in earnest, then the moment was gone and he was being swept away by the Coustillers who for some reason seemed eager to get back to the ship. Didn't Haro Dal promise them a stay in Tordre for the royal festivities?

Panic welled up in his chest and throat. His ears started ringing, as he was carried away from the town. He tried to dig his heels in and scramble back, but each time a burly Coustiller with a cheery grin thwarted his attempts. After several times, he broke free and ran back along the dusty track towards the crowds and the departing Princess. He was like a mad man who had escaped his slaver's leash. Looking over his shoulder, he saw the crew racing toward him at a speed he would hardly have thought possible of the sturdy sailors. He slowed his pace to a walk, then a shuffle before dropping to his knees in defeat.

As quickly as the panic had risen, it dissipated,

185

like a veil had been thrown over him. He stifled a sob, before rising to his feet to face his captors once more. Besides, who would believe that he was a prince, the way he looked? He doubted even his family would recognise him now. There was an instant when he thought Nerys had, but then she had dismissed it almost as quickly as the thought had occurred; he had seen it in her eyes.

Chapter Twenty-Eight

On board the Skyelady, Gereinte cast his weary eye over the harbour of T'sar, trying not to look as though he were sulking. The ship's longboat approached, carrying two passengers; was the reason for the sudden departure from Tordre? He looked around to see if anyone else had noticed the addition to the crew, but the only Coustillers in sight appeared to be monitoring him. He sighed. Not only had he managed to make himself look like an idiot mad man, but also he had betrayed the Captain's trust.

Jabir ed-Din was studying a map and looking out to sca. He turned to meet Gereinte's studious gaze. Jabir smiled and shook his head, before resuming his work. Gereinte going to have to work doubly hard to re-establish his credibility with Jabir as well. He would find a way to re-gain their trust and steer the course of his life back to Carentan where he belonged. Nerys was to be wed to a king she barely knew, who may not even speak the same language. Gereinte should be there in the spring to support her. Alliane would need him too, once Nerys was gone and what about Roda? Was she to be left holding the baby?

Jabir kept him well informed about the political situations in the Western Isles; he actually felt that Nerys's betrothal, although a bit sudden, was an astute manoeuvre for Carentan. Gereinte was becoming impatient, being given second-hand reports on a nation that he should be influencing himself. Perhaps a real grand tour would be one of the first things he would undertake on his return. In that way, he could really gauge firsthand how volatile the political situation really was and who his real allies were.

The longboat pulled alongside the Skyelady and Gereinte could get a better look at the passengers. Odd that Haro Dal had broken his rule of 'no passengers aboard' other than merchants associated with the cargo they carried. More to the point, the passengers looked female, unless he was very much mistaken. Female and young – well, at least one of them was young, probably about his age. The other was somewhat older from what he could see. Female and beautiful – whatever the age. For the first time in months he felt his heart quicken with anticipation, as they were escorted aboard the Skyelady.

As the ladies were hustled off deck towards the guest cabin, Gereinte was left with a vague feeling of recognition – especially for the younger of the two. He looked around him and could see the Coustillers gathering in tight circles; how they loved to gossip and the presence of women was a welcome distraction. Gereinte skulked close by, trying not to attract attention. He managed to glean that the young girl's name was Lady Iriline and the elder of the two was her maid, Marie, both from Sarlat. Apparently, both the passengers and a cargo of grain were to be carried to Holmport in the Green Island.

Then, it was all hands to deck, as the Skyelady prepared to sail out of the port of T'sar and Gereinte was preoccupied with the chores of being a sailor again. As they moved slowly out of the port, Gereinte saw another ship, much the same size as the Skyelady manoeuvre into position behind them. He thought he had seen the ship before; perhaps it had been there when they had anchored, but he couldn't swear by it. He watched as the black-sailed ship turned away from the Skyelady and settled into its own course.

Once they were well out to sea, the two women appeared on deck and he was able to get a closer look at them. He still had a strong sense that he knew the younger of the two from somewhere. She had a slight figure and a light brown complexion. Her eyes were dark and keenly observed the activity on board the Skyelady. The moment she stepped onto deck, all eyes swivelled in her direction and there was no mistaking that she was aware of this attention, though she pretended not to be. She ran slender fingers through her dark auburn hair and flicked a length of it over her shoulder; astutely aware of the effect it was having on the crew. Enrapt by this display of femininity, Gereinte put a piece of the puzzle into place. It was her attitude that gave her away; he had seen that supercilious smile once before. It was back in Carentan when he had first met her. He knew now why she looked so familiar. About three years ago, the Court of Alvar Correze paid a formal visit to the Andolins at Castle Helmstedt. Gereinte had a vivid memory of Princess Fiamina, a very pretty, but haughty young lady.

A few years older, maybe, but just as contemptuous as ever. Now what, in the name of the gods, was the heiress to the throne of Sarlat doing sneaking off to the Green Island in disguise?

As he approached them, Fiamina looked up at him, first in surprise, then down her nose in disgust.

189

He turned and pretended to be busy tidying up the cordage, but it was too late.

"Hey, you," she said. He acted as though he had not heard her, then she called again. "Hey. I'm talking to you." She took two steps forward and Gereinte looked up in feigned surprise. "Yes, it is you I wish to speak to. There are some things I am not happy about in my cabin. The floors are not clean enough and the bathing water is not warm enough. I want you to see to these things." She had spoken in perfect Etanese. He stared at her for a few moments before replying slowly in a broad Skye patois. He stood with his jaw hanging down, looking for all the world like the village idiot.

"Do I look like I speak some inbred island language?" she said. The Captain loomed up beside her.

"Lady Iriline," he said. "Please do not disturb the crew at their work. You have a maid for your own needs. If you require anything special, let me know and I will take care of it." Fiamina turned on her heel and marched away, head held high. Gereinte watched her stalk away and breathed a sigh of relief that she had not recognised him. He looked up at Haro Dal who gave him a sidelong glance.

"Do you know who that is?" Gereinte said in a low whisper. Haro Dal stood silent. "Well," he continued, "it is none of my business, but if something goes wrong, you should know that Alvar Correze is a bad man to have as an enemy."

"I don't know what you're talking about," Haro Dal said.

"No, Captain," Gereinte sighed, "of course you don't."

Haro Dal turned and marched away in almost a parody of the Princess. Gereinte dropped the cordage and took off in search of Jabir, hoping that he at least might be able to throw some light on the Princess's appearance.

Chapter Twenty-Nine

It was some days into their voyage before Gereinte managed to pin down Jabir. He was on his own in their cabin, poring over piles of old maps. For the last few days, Gereinte had kept his head down and got on with his chores, trying to ignore the supercilious stares from the Sarlatian Princess and the less than subtle attempts by the Captain to keep her out of his way. Every time he tried to speak to Jabir alone, the old man somehow managed to elude him.

Jabir looked up at Gereinte, smiled, then went back to studying the maps.

"I take it you noticed then?" he said without taking his eyes off the crumpled old parchment laid out on the floor.

"Noticed what? That the Heiress to the throne of Sarlat is hiding out on our ship? Or that we seem to be being followed by an unknown pirate vessel?"

"Ah. Good observations. I have taught you well, I see," Jabir said. "Now listen, what I have to tell you is in the strictest of confidence." Jabir looked up and held Gereinte's gaze, before continuing. "On the basis of seniority, experience and knowledge of these waters, Haro Dal was the obvious choice when King Alvar Correze of Sarlat needed the Coustillers to smuggle his daughter out of the Isles to Holmport where she would be safe with family and allies. The Coustiller ruling council readily agreed in the light of the considerable fee on offer and the very great favour Alvar would owe them. The reason for the subterfuge was that Alvar needed a little time to fix his temporary local difficulties.

Recently, several of his more intransigent barons had unexpectedly combined and managed to subvert some very senior officers in Sarlat's large and powerful navy. There was a small, but real possibility that the barons be tempted to seize the Princess Fiamina and hold her hostage until their demands had been met. She was unlikely to be in any personal danger, but in such situations, accidents could happen and Alvar was not going to take the slightest risk with his precious daughter's well being. Hence the clandestine journey to safety."

Gereinte stared at Jabir. "I see," he said. "And the pirate ship?" Jabir resumed the study of his maps and chuckled to himself.

"I think you will find more than a pirate vessel waiting on the horizon."

"What? How do you know?"

"Just stay calm, my friend. Everything will become apparent," Jabir said, running a finger across a small patch of islands south of Holmport, "just... about... now."

Gereinte heard a commotion on deck, frowned at Jabir, then scrambled to his feet. Jabir just sat in his spot, smiling and nodding to himself.

On deck, the first thing Gereinte noticed were the Coustillers running to and fro. Then the Princess passed him, too busy complaining about being hustled below decks to even notice Gereinte. Then the voice on lookout above, rising above the tumult on deck.

"Sails to the east on the starboard bow. At least five and coming up fast. They look like war galleys." All eyes looked east. Haro Dal began to swear and curse, unaware of Gereinte's presence. War galleys from the east could only mean one thing; the Sarlatian Navy coming out of Sarne. There was no way that the Captain could hope to outfight them; five war galleys meant close on a thousand armed men. The Skyelady could not outrun them; the winds were light, but even in the best of conditions, a hundred-oar galley would easily catch them. Haro Dal looked desperate, then Gereinte had a sudden flash of inspiration. He dashed back down into the cabin to find Jabir holding out a map for him. With barely a moment to wonder how he knew, Gereinte took the map and scrutinised it. He looked back at Jabir and grinned.

"Ingenious. They are not going to like it, though."

Jabir shrugged and went back to looking his maps.

On deck, Haro Dal was pacing up and down and cursing louder. Gereinte looked out to the west of the ship, then back at the map in his hand. Sure enough, there it was; a small rocky island about a mile west, just visible above the chop.

"Captain," he called. "I have an idea." Haro Dal looked at the boy and the map he was waving, then looked out to sea and spotted what it was that Gereinte was so interested in.

"You know, boy," he said, animated. "I'll never rue the day I took you on board." With all previous recriminations forgotten, he jostled Gereinte below deck into his own cabin, where they talked.

"I can swim well, as you know Captain, but will the rock be out of sight of the galleys?"

"It will be for the time being, but we must make

haste if this plan is to work. You may have to support the..." the Captain glanced at Gereinte. "Lady Iriline, if she is weak in the water. You must take her to the island and wait there until the Skyelady comes for you. Do you understand?" Gereinte nodded and followed the Captain, who was to break the news to the Princess.

Haro Dal rapped on the cabin door of the Lady Iriline and was invited inside by the Lady's maid. Once seated, the Princess attended to their concerns without the slightest sneer or downward glance. She listened in silence to the proposal and although a little pale, showed no sign of panic or hysteria. She grasped the importance of the Captain's words and the haughty aristocrat was replaced by a cool dispassionate stateswoman. She reminded Gereinte so much of his mother and sisters at that moment, that it left a pang in his heart.

"If you take this route, I cannot guarantee your safety, my Lady. The sea is relatively calm, Griff is a good swimmer and the rock is not too far. But as you well know, at sea..." The Captain grimaced. "There is an alternative, if you think the risk is too great. I could give you up to the Navy. I don't think your life would be in danger, although there is no guarantee of that either. However, I could not begin to forecast the political consequences. And on balance, I would prefer not to have to explain to your father how we lost you on route between T'sar and Holmport. But this has to be your decision."

The Princess looked coolly at the Captain, then settled her eyes on Gereinte, as though noticing him for the first time. Gereinte held her gaze as an equal; now was not the time to start playing the fool.

195

Fiamina took a sharp intake of breath and looked back at the Captain. Her eyes flashed with passion.

"I can swim well and I will not give in to my father's enemies."

"Good, good," the Captain said and turned towards Gereinte. "Griff, my boy, go find Kaysin and Fenner. Bring them up to speed, then find a heavy cloak and strap it with two full water bottles to your back." He turned and addressed the Princess's maid, Marie, who looked startled to be the centre of attention.

"Marie, dress the Lady for swimming. Then, remove every item of her clothes and belongings and hide them in my cabin. They won't search that," he said grimly. "When you have finished, strip down to your shift and get into my bed." Marie gasped and looked at the Princess, who nodded.

Gereinte followed the Captain up on deck and set about his duties. Kaysin helped with the water bottles and Fenner soon had a bunch of crewmen wandering casually up and down, effectively screening the action from the rapidly approaching galleys, but also hiding the rope ladder he had fixed on the port side amid ships.

Very soon, the Princess arrived on deck and Gereinte helped her down the ladder and into the sea. Despite the cold water, Fiamina did not complain and began making wide strokes away from the Skyelady in the direction of the island rock. Gereinte followed behind her, keeping her pace and watching out for any signs that she might be struggling. To his surprise, she swam with confidence and speed. The fast movement and exertion began to warm his body, despite the chill

196

of the water. Only once did the Princess look over her shoulder and he had a weird feeling that she was checking that he was not struggling with the effort.

It was high summer and the sun beamed down on them as they struggled to get a foothold on the rock edges of the island. The Princess slipped at one point, grazing her leg. Gereinte held onto her arm to support her as they both climbed out of the water and they all but crawled to the centre of the island. There was a slight depression, filled with sun dried moss and seaweed, towards which Gereinte steered the Princess. They slumped down, breathing heavily with the exertion.

The Princess looked at Gereinte and then at his hand, which held firm to her arm. He released his hold on her and averted his eyes, remembering who he was supposed to be. He glanced back at her and she was staring at him now, her hair dripping and shining in long dark tendrils down her back. She smiled and her face took on a whole new dimension, like the stars lighting up the sky at night. Then she started to laugh and her laugh was so infectious that Gereinte had to laugh too. They laughed together and he was not quite sure what they were laughing at; the ridiculous situation they found themselves in now, hiding from her father's enemies on a rock in the middle of sea? Or was it the fact that there they were, stuck on an island in their underclothes, dripping wet with nothing to do but admire each other in the cool light of the moment? Who knew, but it felt good.

The Princess calmed down and got up to have a look around. Gereinte grabbed her arm and pulled her down. She glared at him now.

197

"Princess, keep your head down. Do you want to give the game away?" He had spoken a little more sharply than intended, but the Princess did not look shocked, she just stared at him with a curious look on her face. He realised, somewhat belatedly, that he had spoken in Etanese, as one noble to another. She smiled and raised a finger to his lips. Her skin was milky white and wrinkled from the time spent in the water.

"Who are you?" she whispered. He took her hand in his and wrapped the cloak around the pair of them as they lay down, shivering, to watch the sun descend towards the horizon.

"I'm just a slave boy," he said, hoping that she would accept this. She sat up and looked at him again with a dubious expression on her face.

"A slave boy who speaks perfect Etanese and who seems to be treated as an equal by the Captain of the ship?"

She was certainly an observant young lady and he should not have underestimated her curiosity. He kept quiet, hoping that it would not be long before the Captain would send a boat for them. The Princess sighed and lay back, accepting that she was not going to get any more information out of him about the truth of his presence on the Skyelady.

"What do you think is happening on board the ship right now?" She said, changing the subject. Gereinte answered carefully.

"The officer in charge will most probably be interrogating the Captain, as we speak," he said.

"For what? I hardly think it is any of their business."

"They will want to know where the Skyelady is

198

heading and for what purpose. If only to eliminate the possibility that the Captain is working in alliance with their enemies."

"You mean my father?" Fiamina said.

"Quite possibly. The Captain will give appropriate replies in order to satisfy the lieutenant-commander and then the lieutenant-commander will order a search of the ship, much to the vehement protest of the Captain."

They lay in silence for a while, watching the skies and when the Princess shivered involuntarily, Gereinte pulled the cloak tighter around her and kept his own body close to hers in order to warm them both. They drank some water and as the sun began to set, their clothes had dried off enough to provide them with some warmth as the night began to draw in.

"What about Marie?" Fiamina said. "Will she be found out?"

Gereinte chuckled. "When they search the ship, the Naval officers will throw open the Captain's cabin door and there will be Marie, half naked in his bed."

The Princess drew her breath in sharply. "My goodness. Poor Marie. What will they think of her?"

"And what do you think Marie will do when she is discovered?" Gereinte said.

"She will probably scream rather loudly, I should think," Fiamina said.

"Precisely," Gereinte said, "and the Naval officers will shut the door quickly, give the Captain a sly nudge and a wink and be on their way."

Fiamina laughed and held her hand to her mouth, so Gereinte could only see the laughter in her eyes.

It was quite endearing. He could not help but join her. As the laughter faded, she turned towards him and said quite matter-of-factly.

"You are far too astute to be just a slave boy."

A long boat loomed out of the mists of dusk and the two fugitives were carried away to safety, Fiamina's father being none the wiser of their little adventure.

There was just one thing that troubled Gereinte as they moved swiftly away from Holmport, after having left the Princess safely in the hands of her relatives; the one pirate ship that had followed them since the port of T'sar had apparently multiplied into three.

Chapter Thirty

The three pirate ships disappeared as the Skyelady cruised back down the western coast away from Holmport and back towards Sarlat at a leisurely pace. Haro Dal intimated that there was more trade to be gained at Sarlat, now that he was in good regard with Alvar Correze, having delivered his daughter safely into the hands of family and allies. So it was that they sailed back towards the port where Gereinte's adventure had begun, ever aware of the menace of pirates in their wake.

Gereinte awoke one morning to see the Coustillers sharpening their knives with whetstone and their wits with merry banter. He darted over to the aft rail and far in the distance, he could make out two pirate ships following them. He went to find Fenner.

"Aye, lad. They are pirates and it looks like they mean business."

"But surely the Skyelady could outrun them without any trouble at all. Why have we slowed down?" What was the reasoning behind the crew's acceptance of this fight on the horizon.

"Well, my boy," Fenner said. "This is what we do... what we are good at; fighting off pirates. Way we look at it is that we are removing a menace from the seas." Gereinte stared at Fenner for a moment, then looked around at the crew who all wore expressions of tenacity and purpose. Then he looked back at Fenner who shrugged. "Think of the innocent villagers that we will liberate from the fate inflicted on so many others and before you say a word... I have seen it and it is deplorable."

Gereinte had no doubt that it was; he had heard the stories in detail from the crew. He left Fenner to his own chores and sought out Jabir, who was at the helm, helping the Captain to navigate the vessel clear of a lee shore.

"We're heading into a storm," Jabir said, pointing towards a cluster of grey looking clouds. "If we get caught too close to here, we'll be in trouble." He stabbed the map he was holding with his index finger, then went back to his discussion with the Captain and the Helmsman.

Gereinte was frustrated and wanted to interrupt them, but knew better than to distract the Captain. He glanced aft once more and could just see the topmasts of the two pirate ships on the horizon. Where had the third ship gone? He tried to dismiss the thought, but it kept popping unbidden into his mind. What if it was a trap and the third ship were waiting for them? Perhaps they were even now being driven towards it. But no, that was impossible. It could not have got ahead of them so fast. It was probably still in Holmport. Then again, they weren't exactly travelling fast and who is to say that there were only three ships anyway?

He strode back to the hatch amidships and went down into his cabin to retrieve his own knife. If there was going to be a fight, then he too needed to prepare. With an air of grim determination, he joined the Coustillers on deck to prepare not only his knife but his mind for the inevitable conflict. The Coustillers seemed to accept his presence with a proud kind of bearing that a brother might have. In silence, Gereinte grazed the knife in long slow strokes up and down the whetstone, thinking not only of the coming battle, but also about that third ship. After a while, the repetitive motion allowed him to free his mind and a plan began to take form. He smiled to himself and looked up at the fast-approaching sails. I'm ready, he thought. Do your worst.

As the Skyelady sailed towards the storm, the skies darkened and the rain descended, bringing with it an ocean swell. Fenner was shouting orders.

"Take in the jib-top sail," he said and was rewarded with a voice from above, repeating the order. Gereinte ran forward to help haul down the sails and began to climb the rigging. The ship pitched forward and he nearly lost his hold, as his hands were slipping with the rain that had begun to sheet down. He clung to the topmast shrouds while the sail flapped about in front of him, with the wind shrieking stronger and stronger. As the sea rose, the ship heeled over at an angle and Gereinte closed his eyes briefly as he clung to the mast, a sickness welling up in his stomach. It was not just the pirates they had to fight. He consoled himself with the thought that the pirate ships would also have to deal with the storm. They could only live to fight the day, if they survived the ravages of the sea.

Gereinte was determined not to let the sail get the better of him, so he waited, hanging on for dear life, until the ship rolled to windward, then as she pitched forwards the sail flapped back in his direction. He grasped it quickly and felt its vibration in his hands as he furled it in, looking to the other crew members who were bringing in the mainsail. He dropped to deck and ran to the aft rail, almost slipping on the pools of water on deck, to see where

203

they were in relation to the lee shore and the pirates. Sure enough, as he had predicted, they were being driven towards the shore and backed by the two pirate ships, the third being nowhere in sight.

***

Krajikk stood at the helm of the ship as the heavens opened upon them and the crew scrambled about pulling in sails and brushing down decks to rid them of the water that would make it impossible to load the ballistas. He allowed himself a brief smile as he watched the Coustiller ship slowly fade from view as it was driven further towards the shore by the storm. One thing they would not be expecting was a close quarter missile attack.

"Time is short," Krajikk bellowed above the roaring wind. The crewmen looked up, then continued rolling out the hidden weaponry onto the deck of the pirate ship. "May Odin bring this storm within our grasp just in time." He turned to his second in command. "Just enough spice to scare the devil out of them, before we board to take our sport."

"So be it," the Klagenstill pirate said, drawing his broadsword in anticipation. He looked at his reflection in the blade and nodded with satisfaction.

Krajikk grinned and slapped his second on the back, then turned away, looking towards the shore. The Coustiller ship had disappeared completely now and his crew made ready their ambush. The minute they rounded upon their prey, they would take the ship along broadside and launch their attack, forcing it to run aground, upon which, they would swarm aboard brandishing their armour in a fit of Klagenstill fervour.

The plan was a good one. Once they had had their fill, Arvij and his crew would appear from the opposite side of the shore, cornering the Coustillers and rounding up their numbers. Those that survived the missile onslaught and the skirmish would be captured to be traded as slaves. As he reckoned it, they outnumbered the Coustillers by about four to one, so even by the reputation of these so-called sea warriors, the odds were stacked in favour of Klagenstill. Plus, they had the element of surprise.

The ballistas rolled onto the deck as the worst of the storm began to subside.

***

The storm pushed the Skyelady to the point of no return. They were going to run aground off the lee shore without a doubt. As they dipped out of view of the pirate ships, Gereinte noticed a sudden change in mood and activity on board. The Coustillers dropped what they were doing and began preparing what looked like an elaborate and intricate network of lookout posts.

"The arbalests," Gereinte whispered. He smiled. Of course, he had forgotten about that. This gave the situation an entirely new dimension. He looked out to sea and could just about make out the tip of the mast of the leading pirate ship. They had precious little time before they were within fighting distance. The helmsman was doing his very best to keep the ship on an even keel under the fading storm, but they still felt the weight of her groan as Skyelady hit the seabed and came to a standstill just off the shore. Haro Dal ordered the anchor to be dropped to stabilise their position and the crew continued to set up their posts in readiness for the inevitable onslaught of the pirate ships.

Gereinte could not help glancing behind the Skyelady to the opposite side of the shore. He noticed that Jabir had returned to the deck to size up the situation and while the attention of the crew was otherwise engaged, he took the opportunity at last to take Jabir to one side. They talked in hushed voices, while the crew made ready their defence mechanisms and the Captain threw orders above the noise of the fading storm. It turned out that Jabir had also noticed the absence of the third ship, which hardly surprised Gereinte, as the navigator rarely missed what was going on around him. Jabir listened to Gereinte's plan, nodding and smiling.

The two of them took the opportunity to roll out a rope ladder down the port side of the ship and drop silently into the chilly water. The sea was still fiercely lapping at the ship as they ducked into the water and let the waves carry them ashore. Confident that they had not been seen, they took for the cover of the trees that lined the beach, the newer waves covering their tracks almost as fast as they made them.

How effortless it had been. For nearly a year, he had been a prisoner aboard the Skyelady and now... he was free. It would be easy to just walk away and find refuge in the nearest town or village, leaving the Coustillers to battle away with the pirates. But something held him back. He couldn't explain, but he felt loyalty towards this crew of burly seafaring warriors. They had trusted him on numerous occasions not to run away, or cause a stir, when he could quite easily have created merry hell. And yet, right from the start, he had been afforded what can only be described as, superior status on board. How had that happened?

As he sat next to Jabir, he began to look at his situation in a whole new light. There was so much about Jabir that he didn't really know, many unanswered questions.

Jabir looked around at Gereinte and frowned under his scrutiny. The older man nodded towards the beach and Gereinte turned his attention back to the battle about to unfold.

Chapter Thirty-One

Krajikk held his arm aloft, palm facing toward the helm. The crew waited for the command as the two ships passed over the horizon and the Coustiller's brig came into view. It was obvious from the position of the ship that they had already run aground. Krajikk smiled to himself. Good. They were going nowhere. Nowhere to run, nowhere to hide. Little did they know that they were now at the mercy of the Bears. From that angle, they would not be able to see the ballistas that were being loaded, until the last moment. It was perfect. Everything was in order, the weapons ready and the crew of the Coustiller ship, according to his lookout, were still desperately flitting about, furling in sails and scrubbing the deck of water, without an inkling of thought towards what was coming their way.

Krajikk held his breath in anticipation. This was the moment he liked best. The silence on board, as every crewman was still, awaiting the signal. Moments away from either death or victory. Always victory in the case of the Bears. The ships sailed on, gaining on the Coustillers with every second. The only sound was the faint and distant howling of the wind, the sea birds squawking above and the rush of the water as the ships cut through the wake.

When it looked like the two ships were on course to plough into the side of the Coustiller brig, Krajikk bellowed at the top of his voice.

"Come about!"

At which the helmsman wrenched the wheel around, as the crew pulled hard to release the sails and anchor the ship's position. Krajikk looked over his shoulder to note that the second ship was following suit a split second behind them. Both pirate ships came around full in the wind bringing them alongside the Coustiller vessel, in position for a direct attack.

"Fire!" Krajikk roared.

He dropped his hand, slicing the air with his arm. Delighted battle cries filled the air, as the pirates launched their attack.

He was expecting to hear the ballistas fire, but the air was filled with a faint whistling noise, followed by several thuds. The battle cries of his men faded on the wind to be replaced by an odd gurgling noise and several screams. Horrified at how badly they could have misjudged their opponents, he swung around to look at his crew. The first to go down were those firing the ballistas who had not even been able to get one shot off. Crewmen lay slumped on deck, crossbow bolts protruding from their throats, some groaning over a midriff shot. He glanced at his sister ship which looked like a ghost ship, bereft of crew.

"Ahrggg!" Krajikk bellowed his rage at the enemy ship, but all he found was a number of crossbow bolts levelled at his chest. He put his hands in the air, as though in surrender, hoping that his back up crew beneath deck had heard the mayhem and decided to take action. He heard the whistle on the air and had just enough time to say "Oh, shit," before he felt the thud of the bolt hit his chest. He slumped to the deck.

***

Gereinte watched from their vantage point on the beach, as the Coustillers loaded up their weapons, administered with precision and skill. The Skyelady had been built with these weapons in mind as they fitted into perfectly designed posts, arranged at specific battle points on the ship. Once the pirate ships came into view, the Coustillers swivelled their arbalests out of view, so that for all the pirates knew, they were attacking an unarmed vessel. He wished he could have been close enough to see the look on the pirate captain's face as he realised his mistake.

They watched the pirate ships coast on towards the Skyelady, then turn about at the last moment in readiness for an attack, their weapons clearly displayed on deck, an easy target for anyone with a good eye for shooting and a powerful enough bow.

The pirates crumpled before they knew what had hit them. They didn't even have enough time to release one missile, before the crossbow bolts hit home. It was fitting that the pirate captain was given a few precious moments to consider what an ass he was before being released from his miserable existence. Haro Dal joined his crew members on deck and for a moment, there was no movement on board the pirate ships.

"Is that it?" Gereinte said.

"Shh," Jabir nodded towards the ships, "it's not over yet."

The decks of the two pirate ships suddenly erupted with more crew members, who appeared from the bowels of the ships. The pirates roared their rage and waved their weapons threateningly at the Coustiller ship. There were many more pirates than could be reasonably dispatched at one time, so the Coustillers just picked off a few who looked like they might take up the ballistas again. For a moment, the pirates looked stunned as they saw a few of their crew mates meet the same fate as those already lying dead beside the unused weaponry. Without proper leadership, they soon appeared lost. After all, they had expected to come on deck to find some able-bodied seamen to have a proper fight with.

The Coustillers stopped firing their bows and the pirates looked momentarily confused. A slow tide of Coustillers seeped onto the deck of the pirate ship. They climbed spiderlike over the aft rails and took the pirates by surprise from behind. Some pirates didn't have time to realise what was going on and just sank to the deck, with the blood of a neck wound adding to the sanguine pool. Others turned to fight, but didn't last long at the hands of the Coustillers and their skill with the dagger.

Gereinte was so absorbed by the sight of the remaining pirates dropping one by one, that he didn't notice until it was too late, the arrival of the third ship, which had anchored up behind the Skyelady. It appeared that the Coustillers had not noticed either. Before the Coustillers on board the pirate ships had finished dispatching the pirate crew, the remaining crew on board the Skyelady had been captured and outnumbered by the crew of the third ship. A surge of panic welled in Gereinte's chest and he made to stand up, but found Jabir's hand restraining his movement with firm authority.

"But, we must do something..." Gereinte said. Jabir nodded.

"Look," he gestured towards the crowd being shepherded from the Skyelady onto the beach.

"They have our Captain."

"Why don't they just attack them?"

"Because, while the Captain's life is in danger, they won't compromise his safety. What this new crew don't realise though, is that the Coustiller numbers are depleted because half the crew is on board the pirate ships."

They watched as the remaining crew from the Skyelady were lined up on the beach, some few hundred yards from where Gereinte and Jabir crouched hidden. Haro Dal had surrendered to the knifepoint of a tall, rough looking northerner who looked like a smaller version of the captain of the pirate ship. It raised hairs on the back of Gereinte's neck. This was something he did on a daily basis, as part of his living. Haro Dal was just another unfortunate victim of his trade. Gereinte looked at Jabir who nodded and smiled.

"He is a slaver. Wouldn't be at all surprised if you'll find a pile of innocent people, children included, locked up in his cargo hold, en route to a market."

Gereinte's stomach stirred and a wave of nausea washed over him.

"We can't let this happen." He slid his throwing knives out from their hidden sheaths, but again, Jabir held him back.

"You won't hit anything from this distance. We must wait until the right moment, then strike."

There were about eight Coustillers, including Haro Dal, lined up on the beach. The Slaver's crew were starting to string them together with ropes tied to their wrists and ankles. Gereinte doubted that the rope would hold a Coustiller who didn't want to be

212

held for too long. All they needed was a distraction. Enough to free the Captain, so that the rest of the crew had a window of opportunity to launch their opposition.

He studied Jabir; he was older than Gereinte, still quite fit, but not as fast. "I'll do it," he said. Jabir frowned at him.

"Do what?"

"We need a distraction; enough to free Haro Dal, so the others can attack." Gereinte looked at Jabir, willing him to accept his offer and hoping that he had the speed and skill to pull it off. Jabir studied him for a moment, before shaking his head.

"No. I can't let you do it. It is too dangerous."

"And you are too slow," Gereinte said.

Jabir's expression was grim. Time was running out. If they were to make use of the moment, it had to be now. He nodded curtly and before he could change his mind, Gereinte was on his feet.

Chapter Thirty-Two

Arvij was pleased with himself. Things had not looked too good when they had dropped anchor just behind the target ship and he had watched while the Captain of the Klagenstill pirate ships had been split in two by a crossbow bolt. Then, by fortune, he realised that most of the Coustiller crew had boarded the pirate ships in order to dispatch the reminder of the Klagenstill, which presented him with the very opportunity he was looking for. All had not been lost after all. As long as he held fast to their captain, they would do as he said. And, by the same fortune, he had an entire crew with which to trade. It was unfortunate, of course, that his Klagenstill brethren had met an untimely end, but he was not one to turn down an opportunity when the odds were stacked in his favour.

"Make sure you tie that good and tight," he said to his crew. Once they were at sea and this lot were ensconced in his cargo hold with the rest he had picked up over the last few days, he could dispatch the captain without fear of reprisal. He glanced towards the pirate ships which looked eerily calm. The apparent mayhem on board of a few moments ago had stopped and if you looked closely, you could just make out a mound of bodies littering main decks. He wondered if it was worth trying to salvage some of the remains. The markets he traded at sometimes had a desire for exotic foreign artefacts like clothes, jewels, furs. Some even traded in exotic meats – who could tell what they were buying? Nice lump of northern bear. A flicker of movement caught Arvij's eye.

He turned. But turned too late. He released his hold on the captain of the Coustillers. Big mistake. He raised his hand to release his knife. But it didn't even have time to leave his hand.

It happened in a blur. There was, what looked like a sandstorm, racing toward him. A thin, lithe spirit, with a mean and vengeful expression. Before Arvij had even lifted his hand, he saw the weapon released from the hand of the boy flying towards him. He saw it all as if moving slower than reality. With every footfall, the boy was enveloped in a swirl of sand making it impossible to see clearly what was happening. The only thing he could focus on was the grim determination in his every movement.

He saw the moment the knife left the boy's grip. He marvelled at the skill with which the throw was executed. He saw the knife spinning on a trajectory towards him. He took a deep breath, knowing that the knife would hit its target, but being unable to do anything to stop it or protect himself. He was rooted to the spot as the knife sunk deep into his exposed neck and a fountain of blood spurted in an arc, despoiling the otherwise clean, sandy beach.

***

The slaver sank to his knees, staring in disbelief at Gereinte, then his body rocked forward and he fell headfirst into the sand.

The beach erupted into mayhem as the Coustillers, suddenly free from their makeshift shackles, made light work of the slaver's crew. Gereinte retrieved his knife from the dead man and launched into the fray, taking a surprised pirate slaver from behind with a thrust to the midriff. The

215

remaining crew from the Skyelady swarmed the beach, overwhelming the slaver crew, most of whom had lost the will to fight once they realised that the odds were stacked against them. Some, who were no more than slaves themselves, held up their hands in surrender and were duly herded back to their ship.

Gereinte stepped back for moment, looking for Jabir, when a slaver driven mad by the moment ran at him screaming and brandishing a short sword. Before he had a chance to launch his weapon, the slaver came to a sudden halt, a knife protruding from his neck. Gereinte looked to his left and saw Jabir striding towards him. The navigator calmly retrieved his knife and nodded at Gereinte.

"Not bad for a slow old man, eh?"

Gereinte laughed and they watched a sanguine calm settle like a veil over the chaos.

The Coustillers rounded up the slavers that had surrendered and released the prisoners from their ship. Haro Dal was delegating tasks to his crew in order to clean up the shores and dispatch the dead to their watery grave. He turned to face Gereinte and Jabir.

"We'll be ready to sail within the hour. You have earned your freedom. I can no more keep you here than I ever could. We are a humble race and have truly been honoured by your presence aboard the Skyelady." Haro Dal looked pained to say it, as though he wanted to keep them both for a bit longer. He turned to Gereinte. "For what you did today, we will forever hold you in high regard. You are a true king, if ever I knew one." Gereinte looked at Jabir, unsure of whether Haro was just talking randomly

216

or if he knew something. Jabir just smiled.

For the first time he noticed that the crew of the Skyelady had stopped their work and were listening to their captain. When they felt he had said his bit, there was an almighty cheer from the Coustillers, who surrounded him and lifted him into the air with the chant 'Car-en-tan. Car-en-tan.'

When he was finally released back to the ground, Gereinte was flushed with embarrassment. He looked around him at the familiar faces, looked to Jabir, then finally came to rest his gaze upon Haro Dal.

"Captain, you have always treated me with the respect that even some kings don't deserve. I thank you for that." He looked around again at the surroundings. "Freedom is something that is not to be underestimated. However, much as I appreciate the gesture – I really don't know where I am. Would a safe passage be out of the question?"

Haro Dal threw back his head and roared with laughter. "Next stop... Carentan." With that the crew descended into whoops of joy.

Chapter Thirty-Three

Alliane was leading her pony to the stables when she heard a commotion in the courtyard. The smell of hay and horses was familiar and reminded her of the days when she, Nerys and Gereinte would come into the stables to help brush down their mares. Nerys had taken her pony with her to Tordre, but Ger's palomino whickered softly as she entered. The absence of Nerys and Ger was too much to bear, so she handed the reins to the stable boy, unable to bring herself to stay alone in there.

"What's all that noise out there?" she said to the boy as he walked her pony to the stable beside the palomino, which swished its long white tail. The stableboy shrugged.

"Don't know, your Highness. Heard there were two strangers sighted on horseback approaching the outer gate. 'Spect that's the Queen's Guard returning to report."

Alliane frowned. They didn't get many unexpected visitors; Castle Helmstedt was not the kind of place you just happened to be passing. She had just returned from a scout about with the rangers, much to mother's irritation, but they had not come across any messengers or tradesmen. Her curiosity was piqued and she made her way back into the courtyard. The cobbled entrance to the inner keep was three rows thick with a crowd of people; kitchen staff, guardsmen, nobles and children – all chattering and clamouring for a look. The only things that got that much attention were a royal visit or the travelling entertainers. Her heart began to thump steadily in her chest. Alliane squeezed her lithe body through the gaps to get a look herself.

In the distance, two ragged strangers rode at a leisurely pace towards the inner circle. One old man, completely bald and one younger man with long hair and a beard. And bringing up the rear was the Queen's Guard. Surely it shouldn't take all ten of them to escort two scruffy merchants to the castle? Fulk was there too, riding a little closer to the younger man than was altogether appropriate.

The children were whispering stories of mummers come to give a show, the kitchen folk were hoping for an herbalist to enhance their dishes, the stable staff were hoping that the visitors were not so lowly that they wanted to bed down amongst the horses.

The two men chatted in amiable companionship as they dismounted and walked their mounts up to the gate. The Queen's Guard stood rigid on horseback, as though attending to the Queen Regent herself. Alliane maneuvered herself to the outer throng of people. At length someone recognised her and a space opened up which enabled her to get to the front of the pack. She stood forward, straining to see what would happen next. Then the two strangers were given passage into the inner court and started to walk towards her for all the world as if they were royalty themselves. What was it that Nerys had told her on the day of her betrothal? That she had seen a ragged looking boy with long hair and a beard that looked just like Gereinte. Then her heart jumped up into her throat. Almost dizzy with sickness, she ran and ran.

She bowled into the young man, almost knocking him off his feet.

219

"Ger… Ger!" He wrapped his arms around her and she sobbed into his chest. He smelt of oil and grime and too many days on horseback, but she didn't care. His chest was jerking up and down and she looked up at him. He wiped a tear from his eye and started to laugh, holding her at arm's length.

"You haven't changed one bit," he said. She mock punched him on the arm. "Oww. What was that for?"

"Don't you ever go away again," she said. And he laughed some more, shook his head and continued to hug her.

"Little sis. How I've missed you," he said.

***

The joy of his return to Castle Helmstedt was marred by the devastating news of the kidnap and assassination of his brother Josselin. The weeks unfurled into months during which time Gereinte continually admonished himself for not being there to support the family. The fact that it had happened the same day as his own incarceration aboard the Skyelady made it harder still to bear. His own suffering in those early days upon the Skyelady seemed trivial by comparison.

Gereinte was soon overwhelmed by the attention lavished on him by his sisters, mother and grandmother and his return became the subject of idle gossip across Carentan for many months to come. There were some, it could be said, who viewed his miraculous escape once again from the jaws of death as an inauspicious omen. Most of the people in Carentan had only joy in their hearts for the safe return of their Crown Prince, which also put paid to the numerous rumours that surrounded his

220

disappearance. He learned also of his mother's involvement in the episode, which had at first infuriated him. The lack of trust had wounded his pride, but in time he became more reconciled to the necessity of the subterfuge.

His education continued with the addition of his friend and scholar, Jabir, to the castle academics. It did not surprise Gereinte to learn that the easterner had been in on the secret and was a former friend and ally of his father. The only other person who knew the truth of his circumstances had been Haro Dal. It took him some time before he was able to fully forgive his mother and see the wisdom of her decision.

The political situation in Carentan settled down after Gereinte's return as the nation once again began to have faith in the Regency and Gereinte was able to learn and train within the relative safety of Castle Helmstedt. And yet, he longed to return to the sea and to believe, at least for a short while, that he was no different from anyone else in the world.

Gereinte let himself be swept along with the preparations made by his mother for a real grand tour. Once he realised the extent to which arrangements had been finalised, he thought it only counter productive to be difficult, so decided to make the most of the opportunity to get out of Carentan for a while. He was to travel incognito, as the Count Merlac, with a party comprising of Carentan dignitaries and personal guards from the forest rangers. When the six of them reached Kallanin, a messenger was sent to intercept them at the port. To Gereinte's surprise and delight, he was told that they would be travelling aboard the

221

Skyelady, which due to weather conditions, was not expected to dock for at another three or four days.

Kallanin was a city in the north of Carentan with a busy port that provided most of the export traffic for its natural resources such as, meat, leather and wool. Being also so close to the River Caren, it enabled passengers to access almost any part of the Western Isles. It was a city full of travellers, tradesmen and local businesses. It was where anyone who wanted to make money from their wares headed because that was where you were most likely to find your buyers. The streets were lined with market stalls, buyers, traders, children and thieves alike. The air was thick with the scent of cooked meat, spices and the grime of the city.

Gereinte looked to his companions who flanked him either side; Darien Issoire, to his left, was a few years older than himself, a noble by birth and a dangerous look in his slate grey eyes that made anyone think twice before engaging his attention. His tousled black hair gave him a rugged look. He had inherited his brother, Chanac Issoire's air of mystery, though Darien was perhaps more generous and open in manner with a cheeky charm that mesmerised the ladies. Gereinte had known him as a boy growing up, so had seen his personality shape through the eyes of a child and remembered those days of childhood abandon outside the courts as they whiled away the time that the grown-ups spent discussing politics and important things. Darien had always been most accommodating when it came to implementing the next crazy plan that Gereinte came up with. Childhood to Gereinte had always been one long mystery and one thing he loved to do was solve a mystery. Maybe politics wasn't that different after all.

To his right was Etienne Martan, son of the seneschal to House Andolin. Short of having the eyes and ears of the entire Western Isles at your disposal, Etienne was the next best thing. He knew just about everything about spy networks and was one of the most useful people to have around you when a problem needed solving. He also had striking good looks, with sandy coloured short hair and azure eyes. So when the three companions trotted through the city of Kallanin looking for an inn or somewhere to pass the next few days, it was not surprising to see the female heads turn and stare.

No one would dare approach the party, of course, what with the two forest rangers bringing up the rear and the group headed up by Kemal ed-Din, one of the most renowned master swordsmen of the time. Kemal was not at all like his cousin, Jabir. Gereinte could not imagine getting a conversation about the political future of Carentan out of Kemal. He had a scar across his left cheek, made no less prominent by his olive skin and served only to give his face a rough and ready look; enough to make even the most determined of brigands think twice. They had been only three days on the road, but already, Gereinte's arms screamed in protest against the exercises Kemal had insisted form part of their daily routine. Gereinte was adamant that Etienne and Darien also take advantage of the opportunity to learn from this new master and the three of them secretly agreed that they were going to have to come up with some diversions if they were to make it to the end of this trip with their bodies intact.

223

Gereinte spotted an inn at the end of a dusty track called the Journey's End.

"Well, what do you think?" he said.

"Wishful thinking," Etienne said, with a wry grin.

"Aye, but it's as good a place as any to start an adventure." Darien winked at Gereinte.

"Good. That's decided then," Gereinte said. "A little light entertainment before we are on our way. Be warned, though. Once we do meet with Haro Dal and his crew, it will be all the entertainment you will need to last you this next six months."

Allard and Bolt glanced at each other, wondering what mischief the three lads were planning for the journey. Both had been present at the mayhem that had exploded in the Forest of Dreams shortly before Gereinte's capture and knew only too well how the Prince's undaunted self-confidence could lead him to paths better left unexplored. Kemal just grunted and pulled his reins in the direction of the inn. The rest of the party followed.

Chapter Thirty-Four

Ensconced in front of a roaring fire, having been fed a king's fare of venison stew followed by suet pudding, Gereinte and his companions proceeded to sample the inn's finest ale. The innkeeper glanced from time to time at Kemal, who propped up the bar from a vantage point over the other side of the room. The innkeeper was a cheery stout fellow, though he seemed a little skittish around the dark easterner in the corner and the burly forest rangers who had claimed stake to the table by the door. Gereinte had noticed the odd customer peer around the entrance door, take one look at the rangers then disappear back into the night street. Neither did it escape the notice of the innkeeper that the public rooms seemed rather empty of customers that evening. Yet he fussed and chatted to Gereinte and his party as though they were the only customers who mattered. Though he had no idea who they were, the innkeeper treated them as royalty and Gereinte made a mental note to compensate him for any loss of business due to their presence.

"So what does a traveller do for entertainment in these parts?" Darien said. The innkeeper topped up their tankards once more and laughed.

"Most will be looking for just a good night's rest before they be on their way, Sire. 'Tis a traveller's town. The locals make their homes in the surrounding villages."

"And what of the locals, how do they survive in these parts?" Gereinte was hoping to glean as much from his travels about the commoners, as his mother intended him to learn about the nobles.

"Ah, now, let me see," the innkeeper said, rubbing his beard. "Obviously, there is the work at the docks, loading and offloading. Many come into town for that. There are the markets, where locals will trade their bread, meat and trinkets, such as travellers like to buy. There are farmlands further out and of course the smithy at Cannan - now there's a story to be told."

"Oh?" Gereinte said. Darien and Etienne leaned in closer. "I do love a good story."

"Well now. Jael - that be his name, you see - Jael is a master swordsmith."

"I have heard of this man," Darien said. "He is the most renowned and expensive swordsmith in the entire Western Isles."

"Aye, well therein lies the truth of the matter," the innkeeper said nodding.

"You see, only the very rich and famous can afford to buy a Jael sword. Just one sword can take years to craft, as he heats the metal and folds it, then beats and folds it, then heats it again. Not only that," the innkeeper leaned in close, then looked over his shoulder, "some say there is magic in his touch and that each sword is crafted with its owner in mind. Them that wields a Jael sword, is said to have been chosen. Not even the money guarantees the buyer a true Jael sword."

The hairs on the back of Gereinte's neck prickled.

"Course, he does make all manner of other things at his smithy and I hear that his very able assistant has been living with him for the last few years, taking some of the mundane work away, so he can concentrate on his finer items." The innkeeper

226

paused to take in the effect of his words and to replenish the empty tankards. Gereinte looked at Darien, who looked at Etienne. The two companions smiled and shook their heads at Gereinte, second-guessing his thoughts.

"I must have a Jael sword," Gereinte said. "If we go and see him tomorrow, then perhaps by the time we pass through this city on our return, it may even be ready."

"Aye," the innkeeper said. "If your journey is a year or more, that may even be so. Only hope you have the fortune to back your desire."

"That is something you might be well to consider first, Count Merlac," Etienne said.

"As always, my friend, your first concern is the finance. That is why, indeed, that you were chosen for this trip." Gereinte looked to the innkeeper, whose eyes had bulged at the knowledge that he was in the esteemed company of a Count. "Very well. We shall visit this man, Jael, and commission him to forge me a weapon for my return. That way together, Etienne, we have the entire journey to work out how we are going to pay for it."

"That's not quite what I had in mind." Etienne frowned.

"Good. That's settled. We shall leave tomorrow, after sleeping off the effects of this marvellous ale," Gereinte said. Flattered by his words, the innkeeper fussed and worked around the party, re-filling their tankards as need demanded.

Etienne, seeing that his attempted pitch for restraint was being ignored, offered his services to stay behind and keep watch for the Skyelady.

***

Gereinte, Darien, Kemal and the two forest rangers set out the following morning on horseback to find the famous smithy of Jael in the village of Cannan. They followed the coastline track out of the city, travelling north according to the innkeeper's directions. There was little traffic on the way, save for an obnoxious noble on horseback flanked on either side by his lackeys.

"Well. What do you make of that?" Darien said, as the nobleman flew past emitting a growl of impatience, which was echoed by his henchmen.

"He is obviously in too much of a hurry," Gereinte said. "His day will surely end in sorrow. If not for him, then for someone else." The two rangers looked at each other and shrugged.

"It will surely end in sorrow for him, if I catch up with his sorry arse." Kemal said.

"No need for that." Gereinte cast a worried glance at the master swordsman. "Time is on our side today. Let's just focus on the purpose of our trip." Nothing was going to distract Gereinte from commissioning his sword.

They reached the village of Cannan just before lunch time and stopped by a small brook to water the horses and take a bite to eat before commencing the search for the local smithy. In the distance, Gereinte could see the sunlight shimmer from the surface of Lake Mariac, beyond which lay the very distant but distinct turrets of Castle Helmstedt.

"Looks like we haven't gone that far at all," Darien said, following Gereinte's gaze.

"There was a time when I thought I would never see that again," Gereinte said.

"We can only hope," Darien said, "that Carentan

can wait for your return before the leeches move in on the regency." Gereinte grimaced.

"The barons know their place. As long as my mother maintains the status quo, there should be no problems. It is when I take the crown that I expect the troubles to begin."

Darien nodded and smiled.

"Anyway," Gereinte said, shaking free of tomorrow's concerns. "Let's be off in search of this talented man who can make me a sword."

After enquiring of several people in the village, the party of five was finally directed towards a modest little house with an adjoining workshop. Outside the workshop, there were three horses tethered to a wooden post. The entrance door to the house was ajar. Gereinte dismounted and left his horse to the rangers to tether and Darien joined him. They approached the door with some trepidation, as Jael already had visitors.

An unremarkable looking woman with a small child came to the door to greet them and Gereinte could just make out voices inside the house.

"I'm sorry, but my husband is tied up with another customer at present, but you are most welcome to wait inside for him." The woman spoke in Etanese with a local accent. There was something familiar about her that Gereinte could not quite place. At any other time, he would have passed her in the street without notice. He must have been mistaken, as she didn't appear to recognise him. The child pulled insistently at the woman's skirts and stared at Gereinte and Darien. Bolt, Allard and Kemal followed them into the house.

They were shown into a small waiting room with

a door that led directly into the workshop. The woman closed the connecting door as the voices beyond filtered through.

"Some drinks, perhaps, while you wait?" she said.

"That would be welcome," Darien said.

"And whom shall I say is calling for Jael?" Her voice was soft and hypnotic.

"Count Alain Merlac. And these are my companions, Darien Issoire, Kemal ed-Din, Bolt and Allard." Gereinte watched her face for signs of recognition, but her expression was just warm and inviting. If indeed he had met her before, she had forgotten the experience. Well, there were many people who had worked at Castle Helmstedt over the years, but he was usually good with faces and names.

"I'm sorry if this is inconvenient. We are staying in Kallanin for a very brief visit and would like to commission a sword from Jael," Gereinte said.

The woman smiled with a twinkle in her eye.

"Please excuse me, my Lord, while I tell Jael that you are waiting." The little boy darted out from behind her skirts to grin at the visitors, then followed her out of the room.

She returned a few minutes later with a jug of wine and some bread and cheese. Gratefully received, Gereinte and his companions sat down to await their turn to see the famous Jael. The woman poured drinks and encouraged the men to eat, while the toddler dashed about playing peek-a-boo from behind her skirts. Gereinte warmed to the child and held out his hand, at which the boy ran to him. As he held the boy's hand and turned his palm over, he noticed that he had only a stump for a little finger. The boy looked up into his eyes with all the trust of someone who has not known what hurt the world can offer. That the boy had lost a finger only made him think of his own lost brother. He lifted the child to his knee.

"When I was your age, my grandmother used to tell me a story about a giant and some little people, called Pygmies. Do you want to hear the Pygmies tale?" The child's eyes lit up and he clapped his hands together in delight. But the woman was gentle, yet firm in retrieving the boy before he monopolised their attention. It became apparent that all was not going too well with the customers in Jael's workshop. She left the room with the child and Gereinte was left to figure out whether to feel more concerned about the woman and the boy or what seemed to be transpiring next door.

Chapter Thirty-Five

Delyth breathed a sigh of relief as she closed the door behind the Prince and his party. She was sure he had not recognised her but knew that he had an uneasy feeling about the encounter. He had grown more intuitive with the years and she was more worried about him getting too close to Allan, than coming to any conclusions about her own identity.

She left Allan in his room, then turned her mind to another little problem that had stalked into her house only half an hour since. He was a Sarlatian nobleman by the name of Zartur. An arrogant man who had barged into Jael's workshop followed by two rough looking bodyguards and demanded to be seen. Delyth had dealt with his sort many times in the past and had no qualms about putting him in his place. However, the arrival of the Prince had thrown a new dilemma into the mix. Jael was aware of her past and aware of her need for discretion, but the Prince... he could not know. He must not even suspect for a moment.

"Where's my sword?" Zartur demanded.

"I have finished it, my Lord, and now I am working on a suitable scabbard." Jael looked up briefly at his uninvited guest and continued to work. "The only one I have which will fit is not appropriate for such a weapon."

Delyth slipped unnoticed into the back of the workshop. The mood between the men was tense and the air prickled with heat.

"I tell you I am not interested in your scabbard," Zartur said, "I will get my own scabbard, but I want the sword *now*." Delyth sensed that Jael was getting very tired of this Sarlatian client.

"Very well sir, the sword is yours upon the payment of the outstanding four thousand five hundred crowns as agreed."

"What four thousand five hundred crowns?" Zartur's voice rose in pitch. "You are not getting a penny more than the five hundred you have. The sword is worth no more and don't think that a crooked Carentan is going to cheat me."

"We had an agreement," Jael said in a patient tone.

"Lies, lies," Zartur said. "Where is your evidence, your documents, your witnesses?"

"As you very well know sir, we were alone and you also know I do my business on the basis of a word given in honour; not written contracts."

"You miserable peasant," Zartur said. "You have the audacity to traduce my honour?" He drew his sword and advanced on Jael. "You deserve to have your throat slit for such an insult to a Sarlatian," he said pointing his sword at Jael's throat.

***

Gereinte stood up. Darien, Kemal and the rangers were silent, waiting for some indication of what his intentions were. The voices next door were now raised to a level that concerned him. He inched open the door and could just about make out the backs of the nobleman and his henchmen. He was not at all surprised to recognise the party that had nearly ridden them off the road not an hour ago. He listened to what was being said, then beckoned for Darien to join him.

"We must do something to help him," he whispered. Darien's eyes widened at the sight of the

233

nobleman and they listened for a moment until it became evident that the situation was deteriorating at an uncomfortable rate. "Come on," he said, leading the way into the workshop.

As Gereinte and his party burst through the doors, several things happened very at once. Distracted by this sudden intrusion, the nobleman, Zartur, turned away from Jael who in turn stepped to one side. There was a flicker of motion from the back of the room, too fast for the eye to follow and a circle of steel blurred across the room. A dagger hilt sprouted in Zartur's throat and he fell instantly to the floor twitching and groaning, a fountain of blood spewing from the wound. Whilst his men watched in stunned silence, the groans stopped and it became clear that Zartur had attempted one deception too many.

Meanwhile, Kemal and Darien had spread out on either side of Gereinte. The two Rangers glided around into flanking positions and the five men formed a tight semi-circle around the Sarlatians. The henchmen looked desperate and drew their swords. A bad situation looked likely to get worse.

"Hold," Gereinte said. "There is no need for any more killing here. Your master threatened the life of the swordsmith and has paid the ultimate penalty. But, we have no quarrel with you. Take his body and leave in peace." Gereinte's words were calm, but imbued with a commanding authority.

The Sarlatians looked at the grim faces surrounding them. They sheathed their swords and with much muttering and cursing, picked up Zartur's body and staggered away.

Gereinte was aware of Jael's wife in the room

234

and wondered that he had not noticed her presence before. It also did not escape his notice that she had been concealed in exactly the direction from which the mysterious dagger had been thrown. She stepped forward and spoke in a low voice to Jael, who glanced up at the party that now confronted him.

"Count Merlac," Jael said, striding forward. "You have saved my life and probably my family's lives. I do not have the words to express my gratitude. I believe that you came to commission a sword. Well, that at least is one thing I can do to acknowledge my debt to you." He picked up the sword and presented it to Gereinte on his outstretched arm. "This is now your sword, Count. You have earned it." All thoughts about the dagger vanished from his mind as Gereinte looked at the sword that was being presented to him. It was the most beautiful and deadly weapon he had ever seen. No ordinary sword, it was an unusual blue in colour, the rippling patterns clearly showing its Damascene steel ancestry. Gereinte was speechless. He gripped the hilt and gently moved the weapon to and fro, marvelling at how comfortable and easy it felt to wield.

"This is truly the most astonishing thing I have ever seen," he said. "How much will it cost?"

Jael glanced at his wife who gave a quick almost imperceptible nod.

"My dear Count. It is a gift. For your intervention today. Besides, the sword has clearly chosen its master; see how the blue of the Damascene steel glows brighter in your hands. Look." Jael held his hand out and Gereinte passed

235

him the hilt of the sword. The minute it left his hand, the steel appeared to return to a dull grey. Jael smiled in satisfaction and the company in the room was silent with astonishment. Gereinte laughed in amazement; it was too much to have ever hoped for.

"We will see to it that you are not out of pocket for your astounding generosity." Gereinte held the sword again and watched the steel ripple like a mirage as it recognised its new owner.

"I'm afraid that this is the only scabbard I have that will fit the sword," Jael said, showing Gereinte a plain and worn item that clearly did not reflect the majesty of the blue sword. "If you are able to come by again in a few weeks, I could have something more suitable ready for you." Gereinte thought for a moment as he looked at the scabbard.

"No," he said. "This is perfect." So he sheathed the beautiful weapon, then tied the battered old scabbard to his waist, where it hung looking like a tired old king.

Chapter Thirty-Six

Gereinte and his party stood on the dock and watched the Skyelady on its approach to Kallanin. As the robust schooner docked in the port, Gereinte could just make out the stout figures of the Coustillers busy on deck.

"It must seem odd to be going back on board the very boat that took you hostage for nearly a year." Etienne said.

"Well, at least I know that there is an end to this journey. What news of our beloved barony have you gleaned whilst I have been squandering our wealth on the trivialities of warfare?" Gereinte patted the dull looking scabbard at his side and Etienne raised an eyebrow and sighed.

"Yes, quite," Etienne said, casting a disapproving eye at the scabbard. "Well, I have it on good authority that Borsa is playing to the barony through manipulating the lesser lords. The suggestion is one of no confidence in the Regency. He means to launch a civil war, but I doubt that he'll get anything significant underway whilst your mother remains in control. She has far too much influence with the barons; they dare not step out of place. My worry is that his spy network reaches further than we know. My father has weeded out a good many from the castle and some he has even turned to our advantage. However, the fear is that there may be many more working in the background that we do not know about."

"If needs be, we shall have to cut our journey short, Etienne."

"I doubt it will come to that, but I have

237

messengers in place, should the situation deteriorate."

"Good. I have an uneasy feeling about being away for so long. It is the ideal time for someone like Borsa to strike. But, then again, it is too obvious, even for him. We shall see. In the meantime, let me introduce you to some friends of mine." Gereinte lead the way towards the Skyelady where the ruddy cheeked, moustachioed Coustillers welcomed them aboard with their customary abandon.

***

As the Skyelady moved out of the Port of Killanan, a clear blue ocean beckoned before its crew like a temptress. Haro Dal had met Gereinte's party before boarding with a mixture of fond delight and restrained etiquette. The last time they had met, the Prince had been a boy on the cusp of changing into a man and as far as he or the crew were aware or indeed willing to concede, the boy had been a slave, picked up on their way and duly transformed into a valuable member of their team. It was almost as though Haro Dal did not know what to say when he was presented with a young prince and heir to the throne of Carentan. There were awed whispers amongst the crew of 'our Carentan' as Gereinte came aboard the Skyelady and it seemed as though the crew held its breath on their captain's command.

Gereinte saw conflict in Haro Dal's eyes and the way he moved his arms; should he bow or should he shake hands? In the end, he threw all caution to the wind and grabbed Gereinte roughly in a bear hug, after which the entire crew exploded onto the deck to greet their former crew member. Some shook

238

hands, some hugged him and others tried to engage him in a bit of playful fighting. Gereinte could sense the tension emanating from his companions, who didn't know whether to jump between their prince and the marauding pirate-like people or to join in with the pleasantries.

"Well," Darien said. "I wasn't expecting that." Gereinte looked over his shoulder and grinned before being dragged off by Genno and Bayant who insisted on recounting their latest adventures at sea.

The party were treated as royalty and given the guest quarters with plenty of the Chef's best dishes available and as much ale and wine as they pleased. Despite this accorded respect, Gereinte still preferred to take his meals below deck with the crew and even stepped in a few times to help out in the kitchen, feeling somehow that he still belonged to the ship and owed his passage in terms of work, despite being admonished by Kaysin and Fenner. Yet, he missed the sea and he missed the company of the Coustillers. His worries had been few and far between when he had been on the Skyelady, compared to what now faced him back in Carentan. So, he dodged Kaysin and Fenner and continued to throw himself back into crew life for as long as the journey allowed, if only to take his mind away from the prospect of the next six months of interminable official meetings.

The crew were intrigued by Kemal, who resembled a warrior-like version of the wise man, Jabir, the navigator who had accompanied the cabin boy, Griff, during his stay with the Coustillers. Kemal largely ignored the attention, amusing himself instead with the sharpening of his long

239

sword, which only served to further attract attention. In particular the cousins, Genno and Bayant, who had once given over their time to teaching Gereinte how to fight with knives.

Gereinte and Darien were on deck looking over the aft rail at the shimmering silver-blue sheen of reflected sun from the ocean, disturbed only by the odd dolphin that darted in and out of the ship's wake. Darien nudged Gereinte and nodded over to Kemal. Gereinte looked over his shoulder and saw the master swordsman sitting cross-legged on deck with a long sword and sharpening stone and a growing number of Coustiller crew sitting in parody of him with their tiny sharp knives. Before long was not surprised to see the first tentative attempts by the crew to engage Kemal in a game of tactics. Kemal, of course, took the bait and soon, a small crowd of onlookers watched as the fighters exchanged ideas and strategies.

"Well, at least they're keeping him busy enough to forget about us for a while," Gereinte said. Darien nodded and stretched his limbs in the glaring sun.

"Hmm," he said. "I could certainly do with a day's break from Kemal's gruelling sessions."

"Don't worry, my friend," Gereinte said. "The crew will keep him so busy, he'll forget the time of day." In fact, what began as a pastime for Kemal and the crew, developed into an exchange of tips and tricks of knife fighting versus the sword. Before too long, the rangers Allard and Bolt had been dragged into the melee to test their wits against their Coustiller hosts. Gereinte thought better of disturbing their sport and settled back to enjoy the smooth and calm voyage along the east coast to Sternhelm.

241

Chapter Thirty-Seven

On their arrival at the port of Sternhelm, Allard and Bolt were the first ashore to locate horses for the next leg of their journey to Dern, the capital city of Tennengaul. Gereinte and his party said their farewells to Haro Dal and his crew, then found a suitable vendor from which to stock up on supplies for their trip.

"To where are you fine gentlemen heading?" the vendor said, as he packaged their wares. He was a curious looking fellow with a round and honest face. Gereinte had the impression that he asked the same question of all his customers, though he seemed genuinely interested.

"Dern," Etienne said as he exchanged goods for coin. "Will the weather hold, do you think?" The vendor looked dubiously at the sky and shook his head.

"There's a storm brewing, to be sure. You have quite a way to Dern, you may have to take shelter on the way. I'd steer clear of the mountain ranges too."

"Oh?" Darien said. "Surely the quickest route is through the mountains."

"Aye, that be true. But there are stories of bandits and raiders taking travellers as slaves. Mostly Gaullian travellers, but I'm sure they're not fussed as long as you fetch a fair price or have anything of worth about yourself. Just be wary is all I say."

"Thank you for your concern," Gereinte said. "The raiders - where are they from?"

"Klagenstill, to be sure. They've been working

their way deep into Tennengaul for some months now."

"Is Prince Darron doing nothing to address this?" Gereinte said.

"Aye, the Prince's Royal Guard patrol the area, but the bandits operate in small groups and are usually gone within days, hours sometimes, leaving only a dead camp and destruction in their wake."

The party left with their wares and took to horseback, taking the most obvious route out of Sternhelm, despite the vendor's warning, towards the mountain range beyond which lay the capital city of Dern. The longer route would take them right to the edge of the Dernhelm Forest, which in itself was asking for trouble. Kemal had countered that their chances of survival were greater out in the open mountain ranges than in the hidden depths of the forest.

The track that they followed was well worn from traffic and cut a swathe through the deep valley that ran through the mountains. Before they reached the foothills, they stopped at a well-placed inn, called the *Road to Nowhere* to rest and water the horses, replenish their supplies and take a well-earned break from their travels. The inn was small, but friendly and quite empty of trade.

"Judging from the name, I take it that they don't expect return trade this side of the mountains," Darien said. On hearing his comment, the serving girl smiled.

"People don't stop for long here, Sire," she said. "It is a place for merely passing through on the way to somewhere else."

"Must be a lonely job for a young girl like you,

243

to be stuck out here, with no regular customers to talk to," Darien said, flashing his smile. The girl blushed at the attention and Etienne gave Darien a dig in the ribs, at which point he doubled over in mock pain. Gereinte leapt in to rescue an embarrassing situation.

"I think what my friend is trying to say, is that custom must be very quiet out here, particularly at this time of year," he said. Etienne frowned at Gereinte, as if to say, 'Is that the best you can do?' The girl laughed at the three young gentlemen who had captivated her attention.

"I am quite able to find things to amuse myself and since I have grown up in these parts and my father owns this inn, I find plenty to keep me busy." She returned to the opposite side of the serving bar and Darien watched her go with a look of appraisal in his gaze.

"Darien, please. To matters at hand." Gereinte nudged his friend who returned his attention to the map that was outstretched on the table. Gereinte took a long draft of ale, then pointed. "We are here now and this mountain path should get us to Dern by the quickest route. If we ride through the night, we may even make it there by morning. What do you think?" He raised his head to the group sitting around the table. Kemal nodded along with Etienne and Darien, but the rangers looked dubious.

"I think it unwise to travel at nighttime, especially with a storm brewing ahead," Allard said.

"I agree," Bolt said. "Even in familiar territory, travelling by night would not be recommended. Too many opportunities for brigands to attack and if we get lost or split up, how do we find each other again?"

"We could stay here the night and take to the road first thing," Allard said hopefully. Gereinte could not hide his obvious disappointment. He had hoped to arrive in Dern by morning, not wanting to drag out this trip any longer than necessary.

"All right. Say we do get split up, we shall use a calling sign. The owl signal that we used as boys." Gereinte appealed to Darien, who cupped his hands together and let out a loud hoot. The other customer at the bar looked up briefly before returning to his cask of ale. "Well, perhaps a bit more subtle than that, but yes, that's the idea."

"Here's a compromise," Etienne said. "Let's stay here for a couple of hours, sleep if needs be, then be on our way." The companions around the table nodded their agreement, though the rangers were still somewhat reluctant.

After some hours rest, they packed up their supplies by the light of the moon, paid the innkeeper and settled into the saddle for their journey through the mountains. The rangers kept up the rear, still looking dubious about both the timing of this trip and the roiling clouds overhead.

By nightfall, the party had reached the foot of the mountains and although Gereinte was happy with their progress, a heavy mist hung over the peaks and they had begun to ride into a thin veil of wind and rain. The valley was narrow and rocky underfoot which made riding in such conditions treacherous. It soon became evident that they would have to dismount and continue on foot if they were to make any more headway that evening. They had no choice but to plough ahead with the rain lashing at

245

their backs and the wind trying its best to push them off course.

Every so often, the sky lit up with forks of lightning and there followed a peal of thunder, which sounded like the mountains were being cracked in two and made the horses skitter and nearly bolt with fright. The air held a heavy, metallic scent with the underlying earthy smell of recently felled trees.

Gereinte cursed his over-zealous ambition to reach Dern by morning, which now looked unlikely and carried the additional threat of safety to his party. Over confidence, he surmised, noting the barely concealed looks of blame being cast in his direction.

There had to be a reasonable solution. Quickening his pace and slipping in the process, he caught up with Kemal who headed up the party. The sheeting rain coupled with bursts of deafening thunder made it difficult to speak. It was hard even to see through the film of water that ran down his face. Kemal looked at him dispassionately and Gereinte used his hands to signal that he was going to check out a possible form of shelter. He handed the reins of his mount to Kemal who walked on with the two beasts slipping and sliding behind him.

Gereinte had noticed a promontory jutting out between two mounds of rock which hid a path leading somewhere else. He hoped it might be to a cave or wooded area where they could possibly shelter and sit out the storm, so he duly followed it. He ducked under a small sheltered opening in the rock face, mentally measuring whether or not they might be able to coax the horses through and came out the other side into a clearing. Beyond the clearing, there were trees and some evidence of recent human activity; an old campfire, piles of dead wood, flat patches of grass and in the distance, the perfect circle of trees with enough of a canopy from their branches to afford some respite from the penetrating rain.

He turned back to the wall of mountain behind him, and the sky lit up as though the One-God himself was pointing a bony white finger. The streak of bright light split the mountain in two and the subsequent crack of thunder momentarily deafened Gereinte. He stood pinned to the spot, enveloped in an unnatural silence. Moments later, the mountain began to slide towards him with unearthly speed. He turned on his heel and ran back towards the clearing he had discovered not daring to look behind him, but registering the sound of tumbling rocks chasing him across towards the trees. The impact of a loose rock hitting him on the back of the head sent his body reeling forwards and tumbling towards the ground. His skull shrieked with pain and a black screen slid over his eyes as his body went limp.

Chapter Thirty-Eight

Caitlin had taken to her bed with what she had informed everyone was a mild bout of fever. In truth she was just so tired; bone weary tired. She needed to rest for a few days, so had left her commitments to court in the hands of Chancellor Lorquin. The medic had provided a draft of some vile tasting concoction of herbs mixed with ale and water, then had insisted on giving her a poultice for her throat which was raw from the cough.

She sighed and watched her eldest daughter, Roda, bustle about in the room, putting things straight and opening the window to let in the air.

"Mother, why are you hiding yourself away like this? A brisk walk in the gardens would relieve you of your symptoms rather than some disgusting brew and a wet cloth." Caitlin smiled. So much like herself, both in looks and temperament. Roda would make a good wife when the time was right. It was of vital importance to get the political timing right to take full advantage of moment. It had been impeccable for Nerys; a royal wedding celebration had been exactly what the nation had needed, to divert attention away from civil unrest and restore some faith in the Regency. The people love a good celebration and a public holiday had been declared for Carentan and Tordre, cementing their newfound alliance. Caitlin coughed into her handkerchief and was startled to notice a tiny smudge of blood on the cloth. She looked up and Roda was staring at her.

"What? What is it?" Roda's face had lost its pragmatic cast; she looked fearful.

"Nothing, my dear. It's nothing at all," Caitlin

said, crumpling the handkerchief into her palm. "I just need to rest, that's all. In a day or two, I'll be fighting fit. There is so much to do before Gereinte's return." Roda came around to Caitlin's bedside and took hold of her hand, gently squeezing it.

"That is some way off, mother. Don't be worrying yourself about it now. Concentrate on getting better. That is the best you can do for Gereinte right now." Caitlin smiled at her daughter's concern.

"When you have children of your own, which I am sure will not be too far away, you will understand how a mother's love affects every thought and decision in her life." Caitlin looked away and her thoughts, as so often did those days, returned to her youngest son, Josselin. She blamed herself for his assassination. If she had not been so distracted by her plan to send Gereinte away, she might have been more attuned to what was going on in her home, right under her very nose. She had tried many times to recall the face of that nurse maid, but always it eluded her memory, almost as though some spell had been cast over her to make her forget.

"I miss him too," Roda said. Caitlin gazed at her daughter whose soft grey eyes had misted over with a distant look. "You can't forever blame yourself. Maybe that is what is making you ill." Caitlin dropped her head back to the pillow and closed her eyes. Roda was perceptive enough to understand that she didn't want to talk about it, so she kissed her gently on each cheek, then left the chamber without another word.

Gods above, though she knew the chances of Josselin still being alive were virtually nought, it sometimes calmed her to believe that somewhere there was someone watching over him. Silly, she knew. But with Reiner, though she missed him terribly, there had at least been closure. She had seen the body, held his cold hand and understood that he was in a different place. With Josselin, she could not really believe he was gone. Not until she had witnessed his passing with her own eyes. She lay back, closed her eyes and allowed herself the fantasy of one day seeing him return to Helmstedt.

Chapter Thirty-Nine

Gereinte blinked his eyes open, then he shut them again as the light sent a searing pain across his forehead, culminating in a steady thump, thump, which throbbed at the back of his head. His first thoughts were, "Oh no, not again."

For a moment, he just listened. There was activity nearby. In fact, he sensed that he was not alone. The smell was rank; urine and faeces, coupled with stale sweat and horses. His hands were tied behind his back and he was lying on his side, close to what smelled like freshly cut wood. He slowly inched open one eye and saw that he was imprisoned within a stockade and there were others around him. The wooden pen was open to the air and his ears picked up all the sounds of an operational camp. People were talking, but not in a language he readily understood. He strained for a moment, then recognised the deep guttural accent of the Klagenstill. Two rough looking bandits stopped by the stockade and peered in at him. They laughed, exchanged a bit of banter, nudging and pointing at Gereinte and a few others, before moving on. The activity outside the pen carried on; tents were being raised, horses watered and tethered. Somewhere food was being prepared and the sweet smell of tender meat tainted with the sour Berris leaves favoured by the Klagenstill wafted beneath his nostrils.

Gereinte eased himself up to a sitting position, cursing his stupidity at getting caught. He wondered what had become of the rest of his party, hoping that they had remained on the other side of the landslide and were even now looking for him. The storm had passed, but his clothes were still soaked through and despite the sun starting to peek through the clouds, he shivered. He leaned his head back against the nearest wooden pole and looked around at the other captives.

There was a middle-aged man and woman who were propping each other up. The woman wore a headscarf and had a travel worn and weary expression on her face. The man was thin, dirty and looked extremely tired. A young boy was attending to them, encouraging the woman to use a cloth to wash herself. When the boy offered the same treatment to the man, he just shook his head and turned away. He assumed that it was their son, but when the boy turned to look at Gereinte it was obvious from the quality of his clothing, although dishevelled, that he came from a noble house. The boy noticed Gereinte was awake and stood up, moving to his side. He was quite slim and reminded Gereinte of himself maybe two years ago when he had been captured by the Coustillers. He was not more than about thirteen or at most fourteen years old. His tunic was tattered and grubby and he wore a cap that was more the kind of thing you would see a peasant worker wearing.

"Hello," he said, peering from beneath the cap. "I'm Jess." The Etanese accent just confirmed the boy's noble background. He had a soft feminine complexion, which on reflection, placed him probably closer to the fourteen-year mark. Jess returned his gaze. As they silently appraised one another, the two Klagenstill bandits returned to the stockade and unlocked the gate. The couple warily rose to their feet, but the bandits waved them down and instead made a motion with their hands indicating Jess to come to them. He went, casting a glance back at Gereinte before being taken away. The woman began to sob and the man stared into the sky, disengaging from the reality of being a captive.

Gereinte closed his eyes to try and dispel the pain in his head. The best he could do was to hope that his party would find him and break him loose from this ridiculous situation. Shifting his weight, he brought his hands underneath his backside and eased his feet and legs through the gap between his arms, so that his hands were now in front of him. He inspected the knot and smiled to himself as he set to work on loosening the rope. It took him only moments to break free. He turned to face the wall of wooden stakes that kept them captive and kicked out with one foot. The wood shifted easily and began to splinter with the force of his blow. One more good kick and it would surely break. The woman had stopped sobbing and was looking at Gereinte curiously. She shook her head and nodded towards the gate in warning. Gereinte heard the sound of voices and returned to his former position, looping the rope around his hands behind his back.

Jess returned to the stockade with four bowls stacked on top of one another. He was closely supervised by the Klagenstill bandits, who unlocked the gate, then re-locked it once he was inside. Jess handed bowls to the couple, then came over and sat beside Gereinte. He placed two bowls of steaming food on the ground; a Klagenstill staple of tenderised meat mixed with Berris leaves.

"They said I'm to keep you tied and feed you myself." Jess picked up a bowl and made a scoop out of his fingers, making to feed it to Gereinte.

"Thank you, but if it's all the same to you, I'd rather do it myself," Gereinte said, freeing his hands and taking the bowl from the boy. Jess was startled at first, and then settled down to feed himself, picking delicately at the pieces of meat. Gereinte watched the boy, wondering how he had managed to get caught on his own and what he was doing out there. The boy darted self-conscious glances at Gereinte.

"How did you do that?" he said, nodding towards the rope.

"Oh, I learnt a thing or two about rope knots. It's a long story." Gereinte chewed on a mouthful of meat. The boy shrugged.

"It's not like we're going anywhere," he said. Gereinte watched him silently eat the food and refrained from getting drawn into the whole history of his adventures at sea. He leaned forward and lowered his voice.

"How many of them are there?"

"You don't have to whisper," Jess said. "No one here can understand Etanese. They are all Klagenstill barbarians, apart from those two, who are just unfortunate travellers caught unawares."

"You haven't answered my question," Gereinte said. Jess smiled, evidently used to the kind of conversational banter that frequented houses of nobility.

"About ten or more. You have to careful though." He nodded over to the couple. "He tried to put up a fight to begin with and they soon beat him

254

down. Now he just stares into the sky and she just whimpers," Jess said. "They let me out sometimes to help out in the camp and fetch and carry for them because I don't complain. I just do what I'm told. Though I have managed to filch a few useful items."

Gereinte panicked when he remembered his sword and searched around the ground near where he had lain.

"If you're looking for that battered old thing you had around your waist, they took it away. More than likely, it is with the rest of their thieved items in the wagon that carries this forsaken camp from one spot to another."

"Where are they heading?" Gereinte pushed himself to his feet and went to peer out of the stockade, but there was not much to be seen apart from trees and distant mountains. His head span with dizziness and he squatted back down.

"We're on the edge of the Dernhelm Forest, heading North, I think. Where were you travelling to?" Jess said.

"Dern," Gereinte said, picking up the bowl for a second try at the muck presented to them as food. Jess leaned forward, curiosity sparkling in his eyes.

"So am I," he said. "And I intend to get out of this place one way or another. I have hidden a knife in the ground over there. And beside that post, you'll find a spare key to the padlock holding this place in chains." The boy had ingenuity; that much was clear. "But how can I hope to escape and overcome ten Klagenstill bandits with only those two Gaullians to help?"

"Don't worry," Gereinte said. "I have friends,

who are even now looking for me. Once they catch up with us, you will have some stories to tell when you return to your family."

Jess looked at Gereinte with awe but Gereinte knew that he was going to have to take a risk with the boy's life if they were to have any chance of escape. He only hoped that Jess's sleight of hand was a true talent and not just faint-hearted bravado.

"Though, there is one thing I must ask you to do for me…"

Chapter Forty

As the sun crept down behind the mountain peaks, the captives finished their Klagenstill delicacy and Jess set about collecting the bowls and dishing out water.

"They'll be back soon to tie us up and check your ropes. Here, let me." Jess threaded the rope around Gereinte's wrists and tied a secure enough knot to fool their captors. His slender fingers had a determined strength to them that reminded Gereinte of his sister, Alliane. Ally always wanted to be one of the boys and their mother had all but given up on schooling her in the delicate arts of being a lady at court. It seemed to Gereinte that Jess was the boy that Alliane longed to be; riding out on adventures and getting caught up in dangerous situations.

Before long, the barbarians returned. There were two of them, thickset and rough with long dark hair bound up in scarves, beards that hid a multitude of scrapes and scars. When they spoke, it sounded as though the words had to be physically expelled from their bodies with the guttural noise of a choking boar. Gereinte kept his gaze impassive as they reached behind him to check the knot of ropes. He caught a strong whiff of Arak; a drink favoured by the Klagenstill. He only had the misfortune to taste it once on his travels with the Coustillers and one sip nearly took his head off. It is said that the effects are tempered by the Berris leaves, which is why everything they eat is laced with it. Drunk to excess, Arak could have deadly consequences. The two bandits who were checking the captives were already starting to sway a little.

The bandits grunted towards Jess, who dutifully gathered up all the cups and bowls and followed them out of the stockade. So… tonight would be the night, if their captors were drinking Arak. He hoped that Jess would have the courage and skill to stick to their loosely laid plan as he didn't have time to wait for Darien and the rest of the party to catch up, if they were on his trail at all. He was not in particularly good favour, having dragged them halfway across Tennengaul in the middle of a storm.

Kemal and the rangers had been itching for a good fight since leaving the Coustillers and might be disappointed if he started without them. Doubt began to seep in; there were ten or more bandits and only himself, his sword and a young boy. The Gaullians were worse than useless and would most likely get in the way. He glanced at the couple. The man sat with his head propped against his wife and was snoring. She, on the other hand, was watching Gereinte with more than a little interest.

In a short time, Jess was returned to the stockade. He turned his back on his captors, who produced another length of rope and tied his hands securely behind his back. The gate was locked behind as they went back to their campfire and their drink. Shouts, laughter and tuneless attempts at music drifted across the evening breeze as Jess sat back down beside Gereinte.

"What now?" Jess said.

"Did you get it?"

Jess nodded. "But I don't see what use a battered old sword is going to be."

"Be patient, little one." Gereinte smiled. He eased his arms underneath his legs once more, so

258

that his hands were now in front and set about undoing the knot in his rope.

"How do you do that?" Jess said. "Are you some kind of jester who does tricks to entertain wealthy folk?"

"Hardly," Gereinte said, frowning at the boy. "I learnt a lot of tricks during a spell at sea with a Coustiller crew."

The boy's eyes widened. "I've heard stories about the Coustillers. It must have been exciting. I hope you can fight like one of them. I've a feeling we might need it..."

A familiar sound drifted across the camp, masked by the gruff shouting and merriment coming from the Klagenstills; the soft hoot of a night owl. Gereinte lifted a finger to his mouth and the boy fell silent. He heard it again, then nodded to himself. He cupped both hands together as though holding a large apple and blew into his hands, and mimicking the hoot of the owl. Jess was so excited he nearly clapped his hands, sitting on them instead when he remembered. They both listened for a moment and sure enough, seconds later, Gereinte's efforts were rewarded by another two hoots.

"The luck of the gods is with us tonight," Gereinte said in a low whisper.

"Where is the sword?"

"Untie me and I'll get it for you," Jess said. He was on his feet in seconds, a look of anguish in his face. "I've hidden it beneath my tunic." Gereinte held his empty hands up, wondering why the boy had become so jittery. "Over there by the large post, you'll find a knife buried. It'll be quicker to get these ropes off." Jess said. Gereinte retrieved the

259

knife, released Jess from his bindings, then started to work on the Gaullians. The man awoke suddenly and opened his mouth in protest until he realised what was going on. The woman looked as though she wanted to hug Gereinte.

"Don't thank me yet," he said, then remembered they didn't understand. "Stay here," he said in faltering Gaullian, emphasising each word. They nodded enthusiastically.

When he turned around, Jess was holding the rusty old scabbard at arm's length as though he might catch something. Gereinte retrieved it and tied it around his waist. Then Jess started to dig a small hole close to the stockade gate and pulled free a small key. He unlocked the gate, taking great care not to let the chains rattle as he laid them on the ground.

"What now?" Jess said.

"Now, we wait," Gereinte said, sitting cross-legged on the ground. Jess looked confused, but followed Gereinte's lead. The two Gaullians looked as though they might burst with impatience. The woman's eyes darted between Gereinte, Jess and the stockade gate as though she was expecting the bandits to appear at any moment. Truth was, that was precisely what Gereinte was expecting. But he was prepared.

They sat in silence for what seemed an eternity, listening to the sounds of the night, polluted only by the drunken mumbles of their captors. Then, as though splitting the very air in two, he heard two distinct whistling noises on the wind followed by.. thud.. thud.. in quick succession. Then the camp erupted into absolute chaos around them. There were footsteps back and forth, shrieks of rage and snippits of speech in guttural dialect. Gereinte thought he heard a battle cry and saw in the shadows beyond the gate, two lithe figures drop out of the trees. More arrows sang on the breeze, followed seconds later by screeches of fury. A Klagenstill warrior smashed open the gate and stood heaving a broadsword, dripping with fresh blood. Gereinte sprang to his feet and launched a surprise thrust, releasing the blue sword from the confines of its scabbard, seconds ahead of making impact with the monstrosity that blocked their only escape route. The bandit was motionless, a look of disbelief on his hairy ragged face. He looked down at the sword that protruded from his chest with a faint blue glow emanating around his wound. Gereinte put both hands on the hilt, lifted his foot to the giant's chest and heaved until he freed his blade. The Klagenstill took one look at the fountain of blood spurting from his midriff and started to bellow like a cow on heat. One well-placed boot sent him flailing to the ground where he beat his fists for a few seconds more before lying still in the dirt.

The Gaullians and Jess stood up, looking at the fearful warrior-bandit brought to rest by the young man with the glowing blue sword.

"Stay here," Gereinte said. Then he leapt over the body, pausing to check for signs of life. Satisfied, he darted out of the stockade and into the melee.

By the time he reached the centre of the camp, his friends had established control of the situation. Darien and Etienne were on horseback, running down anything that moved and swinging their swords in the direction of any servants or women of the Klagenstill, just to make sure they knew who was taking over the camp. Allard and Bolt were loosing arrows like they had not had any target practice for at least a season. And Kemal was locked in a one to one fight with a snarling, Arak drunken bandit who didn't know when it might serve him best to either lie down and die or run and hide. The Klagenstill never were the brightest race in the Western Isles.

"You took your time," Kemal said, grunting as he parried a thrust from his opponent's sword. The bandit's sword slipped from his ham-sized fist, embedding itself point down in the ground at their feet.

"Well, you know - had to make sure the other captives were safe. Besides, I could say the same about you lot," Gereinte said. The bandit looked down at his sword and reached to retrieve it, but not before Kemal landed a fist in his face that sent him reeling backwards making circles with his arms and spitting out his already rotten teeth. An arrow whisked through the air, narrowly missing Kemal's head and landed with a finishing blow to the bandit's chest. Kemal glared over his shoulder at the ranger standing on the periphery of the battleground. Allard waved a hand cheerily.

"My pleasure. You were taking far too long about it anyway," he said.

The ground was littered with bodies and there were no more takers for trouble with the uninvited party guests. Bolt had started to drag the bodies into the centre of the camp, whilst Darien and Etienne were using their skills of diplomacy to round up any connected individuals and question their loyalty to the dead Klagenstill. It seemed that most were quite happy to take their meagre belongings and disappear into the forest to take their chances with their newfound freedom.

When he was sure that there were no more Klagenstill likely to cause a problem, Gereinte returned to the stockade. The Gaullians were still huddled together staring at the body of the bandit, as though they expected it to get up and start fighting again. Jess was nowhere to be seen. He helped the couple to exit the stockade, and then told them in faltering Gaullian that they were free now. They dropped to the ground and kissed the backs of his hands, weeping and thanking him in their own language. Gereinte looked toward the rangers.

"Allard, would you help these two to find horses and supplies? They have been through a lot and may need some assistance," he said. Allard nodded and took the Gaullians around the camp to gather supplies and essentials for the next leg of their journey.

"Bolt," the ranger whipped his head around, "any sign of a young boy?"

Without warning, there was an almighty bellow and out of the undergrowth ran an enormous Klagenstill warrior, eyes blazing with fury and bloodshot from Arak. He made a straight line for Gereinte, carrying something large and immobile under his arm. He ran, sword arm outstretched before him towards Gereinte. Jess was dangling from the bandit's grip like a much-treasured rag doll. Gereinte had grown to like the boy in the short time they had known each other and besides, Jess

263

had helped him escape. A bitter anger flared up. Jess did not deserve to die like that.

The weight and commitment behind the Klagenstill's attack was his own undoing. Gereinte sidestepped the thrust and countered with a slice to the warrior's sword arm. The bellow turned into a scream of fury, not due to the pain, numbed as he was by the Arak, but more due to the fact that he had been outsmarted. But still he held tight to that poor boy, swinging the body around as though it were now an armoured shield. He turned and squared up to Gereinte with a quick shift and flick of the blade. The knife bounced off Gereinte's blue sword with ease. The bandit faltered, mesmerised by the glow emanating from the blue sword. Gereinte thrust it deep into the fleshy mound between the breastbone and the shoulder of the arm that held onto Jess. The Klagenstill roared and instinctively dropped the boy, who fell to the ground with a thump. He looked in disbelief at the glowing sword that protruded from his chest and a thin trickle of blood began to ease from the wound. So immune was he to the pain that he still had the strength left to lift his own sword and prepare to launch an attack on his now weaponless opponent. In an instant he was stopped dead in his tracks, the shaft of an arrow split his throat and a fountain of blood sprayed in an arc. Gereinte heaved his sword free and sheathed it as the bandit's eyes rolled up into his skull and he toppled to the ground.

Gereinte knelt beside Jess and gently turned him. His face was pale and bruised and his hat askew. He rearranged the hat and put a hand to Jess's chest for signs of breathing. Gereinte was startled when an eye popped open and Jess said, "Is it over yet?"

"Good grief, lad, I thought you were dead."

"It's what vulnerable animals do in the wild when a predator comes along - play dead. I was hoping he would leave me alone." Jess shrugged.

"Kind of risky, if the vulnerable animal happens to be the next meal."

"Maybe," Jess said, standing up and brushing himself off. "But I thought this one had drunk so much, he probably wouldn't have seen a dead boy as much of a challenge."

"Maybe not, but I bet you didn't think he'd try and use you as a human shield."

"Hmm. I think I must thank you for saving me."

Gereinte pointed towards the trees and Jess turned to look. A green-glad ranger waved back.

"I think you have to thank my friends in the trees," Gereinte said. Jess's eyes nearly popped out.

"A real live ranger." He turned back to Gereinte with a puzzled expression.

"Who are you?"

"I am Count Merlac and these are my friends and travelling companions." Jess looked around at the activity going on, bodies being piled up, swords being cleaned. Two noble men were riding horses and issuing orders to the remaining Klagenstill women and slaves. Kemal looked almost as fearsome as the warriors themselves, as he heaved the dead into a massive funeral pyre in the centre of the camp.

"I guess they won't be capturing any more unsuspecting travellers," Jess said.

"Quite," Gereinte said. "Now. We must get cleaned up and continue with our journey to Dern.

Prince Rupert Darron will have wondered where his guests have got to." Jess stared at him. If there had been any colour left in his cheeks, it had surely have drained away.

"Well, that is fortuitous," Jess said. "I am heading that way myself to meet up with my family."

"Excellent. We shall travel together." That solved the niggling little problem of how Gereinte was going to see to the safe delivery of this young boy back to the heart of his family.

Chapter Forty-One

The remainder of their journey to Dern was uneventful. Kemal rode ahead, keeping eyes and ears open for any stragglers from the Klagenstill bandits, while the rangers took up the rear. Gereinte was silent and Darien took the opportunity to impress Jess with his stories of growing up in House Issoire. Jess was as attentive a listener as Darien an entertainer. Gereinte smiled to himself as Darien regaled a fantastic story of a youthful hunting trip that went terribly wrong and nearly revealed Count Merlac's true identity in the process before clumsily glossing over his mistake. Etienne glanced over at Gereinte and rolled his eyes to the heavens. Jess's eyes flicked back and forth taking in the subtle nuances between them. Etienne slowed to match Gereinte's pace and lowered his voice.

"What do we know of Prince Rupert Darron?" he said.

Gereinte paused for thought. "I would say that the current political climate between Tennengaul and Carentan is one of tolerance."

"Hmm. You are probably right. They have done nothing to have us believe that they would support us if the other nations on our borders were to take up arms."

"Well," Gereinte said, "I'm not inclined to concern myself with foreign policy at present. I think our greatest concern is the civil unrest that is brewing within our own borders. Tell me, Etienne. What is the protocol for a guest that has all but disappeared and turns up late, scruffed up and complete with a vagrant boy companion?"

"Don't forget, my Prince, that you are of equal rank and standing as Prince Rupert. Besides, there is more to that boy than meets the eye, I am sure of it." Etienne nodded towards Jess, who was engrossed in Darien's tales.

As they approached the walls of Dern, Jess broke away from the party and rode ahead.

"I'll just tell the guards what happened and I'm sure we'll have no problems. My family are also guests of the Prince and will be expecting me," he said.

Gereinte watched the boy canter off ahead and gestured to Allard, who took off in pursuit at a respectable distance. He had an odd and uneasy feeling about letting the boy out of his sight. When the rest of the party eventually caught up with Jess, he was deep in conversation with one of the guardsmen at the outer gate and Allard was standing nearby.

To Gereinte's surprise, the guardsmen produced an escort for the party to the royal palace. As they rode through the grounds, common folk stopped to stare and step out of Jess's way. On reaching the inner ward, Jess was hurried out of sight by a number of attendants, while Gereinte, Darien, Kemal and Etienne were shown into lavishly equipped rooms and catered for by ample servants. They were assured that the two Rangers would be treated with great honour and would be bunking down with the elite of the Prince's Royal Guard.

After having rested, they were dressed in fine clothes, then invited to a private dinner with Prince Rupert Darron, the current ruler of Tennengaul. Shown into what looked like a family dining room,

Gereinte was impressed by the luxurious, but understated quality of the furniture and decorations. Around a magnificent round oak dining table were set twelve places. He was surprised, but relieved that the dinner was clearly going to be an exclusive gathering. A few moments later, Prince Rupert entered the room and on his arm was a teenage girl with milky skin and soft light ringlets that framed a mischievous smile. Gereinte recognised her, although without the battered old hat on her head she was unmistakeably Jess. A silver circlet on her brow revealed her royal lineage.

"This is Countess Jessamine, my only daughter," Rupert said. Gereinte bowed to both the Prince and his daughter. Prince Rupert was only a hand's width taller than his daughter, fair in skin and dressed in a flamboyant style. His face reflected a level of gravitas that concerned Gereinte. He looked over his shoulder to his companions; Etienne looked surprised, but Darien had a frown creasing his brow. Kemal was studiously ignoring the gathering and after bowing had begun to inspect the display of swords attached to the walls.

"I believe you have already met," Rupert said with a quiet smile tugging at his lips. "Jess had told me of your bravery and your blue sword. I cannot express enough how precious my daughter is to me and how concerned we all were when she disappeared." He turned to the Countess and wrapped her in his arms; quite an unusually open display of affection for a Royal Prince. But Rupert was clearly relieved to have Jess returned to him and Gereinte feared, judging by the twinkle of mischief in her eye, that this may not be the first or last time her father was left the victim of her youthful misadventures.

The evening was a relaxed and entertaining affair. The Royal jester made an appearance along with a small band of musicians and the conversation was light and free of politics. It felt to Gereinte like they had trespassed on an intimate family gathering. Jess made several attempts to catch his attention but his conversation with the Prince would not allow him to break away. Etienne was also engrossed in the banter that was flying back and forth as the serving staff brought more wine and the table was replenished with fresh meat, bread and a selection of rich cheeses. The Prince stopped mid-sentence and smiled warmly at his daughter across the table.

"Gereinte, what you and your friends have achieved here is remarkable and your actions have forged a strong bond of friendship between our two kingdoms." Gereinte exchanged a quick glance with Etienne, who raised an eyebrow at Rupert's words. Rupert continued, not taking his eyes from his daughter, who was still blissfully unaware of the true identity of Count Merlac.

"Please assure the Queen Regent that from now on, she can rely on Tennengaul's full support and help on any issue of concern to Carentan." His gaze broke away from Jessamine and he smiled broadly at the Carentans.

"Now, no more talk of politics, let us enjoy this good food, good wine and good company." Rupert broke away and sought conversation with his daughter.

Gereinte was astonished that he had come all that way to debate politics with one of the Western Isles' most influential leaders and all he had done was get lost, captured and fight with a few Klagenstill bandits and now he had Tennengaul at his feet. Etienne was looking thoughtfully at Gereinte, reading his mind.

"Do you think we might be able to just ride up to the gates of the palace at Malvas and hold a proper conversation with King Rudelle about the political situation in Carentan without having to get wet, dirty and bloody along the way?"

"Hear, hear," Darien said, breaking away from his audience of female courtiers.

It was close to the end of the evening before Jessamine finally found an opportune moment to speak to Gereinte. Aware that her attempts to reach him had been thwarted most of the evening by her father, Gereinte was wary that perhaps Prince Rupert was a little reluctant to encourage her.

"My Lord." Jess curtsied and seated herself beside Gereinte. "I just wanted to thank you for what you did and apologise for my deception." She lowered her eyes and a pink blush rose to her cheeks. Gereinte was warmed by this display of modesty but couldn't help thinking that he preferred the quick witted, cheeky character of Jess, boots and hat notwithstanding. He took her hand in his and she looked up. There was still that twinkle of mischief in her eye. He could see why she was such a worry to her father.

"You don't have to thank me or apologise for anything. I would have done the same had you been an orphan from a common family. Besides, it was you who helped me to escape and neither of us would have made it alive had it not been for my

271

companions," Gereinte said. Jess grinned.

"It was fun, though. I feel exhilarated just to know we got away. I still can't believe it."

"I still can't believe that you would put yourself in such danger, being who you are and how much your father loves you."

"Oh yes," she sighed and pulled a dreary face. "It's just so boring here, playing at being a lady. I could go out of my mind before long. I want to travel. Can I travel with you? There are so many places to see in the world." Gereinte was shaking his head before she'd even finished her sentence.

"I wish I could say yes. Your company would brighten my journey, but no. I can't take you along with me. You belong here with your father." This time, Jessamine was shaking her head. Her face dropped and her bottom lip quivered.

"But he will just marry me off the first insipid royal prince that comes visiting and that will be the end of my life," she said. Gereinte squeezed her hand and wanted to laugh despite her misery.

"Who knows what kind of prince will come to whisk you away. You remind me so much of my sister, Alliane. You and she would get on so well. One day, you must come and visit," Gereinte said. Her eyes lifted and sparkled with hope.

"That would be good. Make it a proper invitation, so my father will let me go. I would love to travel to Carentan. We could visit Castle Helmstedt, have you been before?" Jessamine was getting excited at the prospect of a journey.

"I have... had occasion to visit," Gereinte said. "I will send an invitation in the Autumn on my return to Carentan." Jess threw her arms around Gereinte

272

and planted a big kiss on his cheek. When she had disentangled herself, he looked up to see Prince Rupert looking at him with a guarded expression. At least if she were coming to Carentan, Gereinte could keep an eye on her, otherwise she might just up and go with disastrous consequences.

The Carentan party stayed a few more days to recover and re-supply whilst Gereinte chatted with Jessamine and tried to encourage her to stay out of trouble. When it was time for them to leave and continue with their journey, they said their goodbyes and mounted their horses in the courtyard. Gereinte looked over his shoulder and noticed Jessamine's father talking quietly to her. There was an earnest look on his face. She glanced from her father to Gereinte as he was leaving, then back to her father with disbelief. Her mouth opened with an inaudible gasp and her hand instinctively flew to cover it. Then she looked back at Gereinte and they exchanged a look of mutual understanding before she dropped her head and curtsied low, holding that position until the party was out of sight.

He wondered why Prince Rupert had decided to tell his daughter in the end. Perhaps he was concerned that she did not pin her hopes too much on a relationship developing between them. Or perhaps, that is what he hoped for.

Chapter Forty-Two

The journey from Dern to Molton, the capital of Malvas, although a longer distance to travel, seemed to go remarkably fast in comparison to recent events. As Gereinte had little opportunity to practice his skills of diplomacy at Dern, he was looking forward to meeting King Phillipe Rudelle of Malvas who was deemed to be a most worthy host for foreign visiting dignitaries. The pace was leisurely and relaxed, interspersed with Kemal's rigorous regime of an hour's exercise and sword drill first thing in the morning and an hour's sparring practice in the evening. Kemal had grumbled throughout their stay at Dern, that Gereinte was becoming lazy and arrogant now that he had only to kill a few Klagenstill bandits to gain recognition and respect.

It was early evening, only two days into their journey, but they had made it across the border onto the south side of Dernhelm Forest. The rangers were making camp, while Etienne consulted his notes on the Martan networks operating inside Malvas. Gereinte, still in travelling attire was eager to complete his one-hour's sparring with Darien, so that they could rest before facing another day on the road. Darien was sweating profusely, evading Gereinte's thrusts and counters with ease and poise. He was moving well, but it would only take a little more time for him to slip up. And that would be the time to take him. Gereinte wielded the blue sword like it was an extension of his arm. In fact, he didn't even feel the weight of the sword at all and moved with an alacrity that made a mockery of his exhaustion. Darien, on the other hand, was beginning to show signs of weakness. Although he was a fine swordsmen and one of the best in Carentan, Gereinte was beginning to gain the upper hand, easily flicking away his attacks and beating him to the counter. Darien's parries were weakening by comparison and the sweat was now pouring into his eyes. He missed a step, Gereinte feinted an attack, twisted his sword at the last minute taking it in the opposite direction and sliding underneath Darien's counter with a clean pure thrust to his exposed throat. The sword just nicked Darien's skin, releasing a drop of blood that trickled down his neck.

"Oh, hell." Darien dropped back, released his sword and put his hands up in surrender. He looked around at Kemal who was watching with a studious expression. "I knew you were good, but that is just beyond Carentan's best."

"Again," Kemal said, and the young men looked at each in disbelief. "One hour, not yet up." He motioned Darien away and took up a stance opposite Gereinte. Darien looked relieved to have been let off the hook, but Gereinte had to finish his hour head to head with the finest swordsman in the Western Isles, not just Carentan. By the end of the session, he was drenched in sweat and aching in places he didn't even know existed. Gereinte slumped down beneath a tree, too weary to even take himself off to the river to bathe. It couldn't be soon enough that they reach Molton, where he felt sure that the legendary hospitality of the Malvatians would more than make up for this torture.

He was certainly not disappointed. On arrival in Molton, the Carentan party was lead to the Royal

Palace and welcomed by Phillipe Rudelle, King of Malvas. He was a slender, unassuming man with soft brown hair like a dormouse. His attire was relaxed and comfortable, more practical and less flamboyant than that worn in the palace at Dern. That aside, the Malvatians were renowned for their sociability and they had organised a series of social gatherings to entertain the Carentans. Gereinte and Darien, with Etienne trailing behind were embraced by this culture, hedonistic in comparison to life in Carentan. Gereinte was keen to get the formalities out of way before the party life took over and so early during their first day, he requested an audience with the King. Gereinte and Etienne were escorted to the King's personal receiving room, which was comfortable and light, though not so elaborately adorned as the Great Hall, which was often used for large gatherings and decorated to impress noble visitors. It was, of course, only the King and his closest confidantes who knew of Count Merlac's true identity.

"We maintain a fairly cordial relationship with the Gaullians, though less could be said of their bellicose northern neighbours," Rudelle said with a wry smile. Gereinte nodded.

"An interesting way to describe the Klagenstill," he said, thinking that he could certainly tell a few tales on that front.

"In that respect, Prince Rupert and I are most certainly in agreement. We are always looking to maintain a good relationship with Carentan. Please enjoy your visit and I hope that your every need has been catered for." King Rudelle was studiously neutral when it came to discussing conflict, particularly that rumbling of discontent between Carentan and its hostile southern kingdoms. Much less, the rumoured civil unrest that knocked at the Queen Regent's castle door with growing fervour. Perhaps, thought Gereinte, he was after all going to have to slay a few bandits to establish any firm commitment of support from Malvas.

"Your hospitality is most gratefully received, your Majesty," Gereinte said with a deep bow of respect. "However, I am keen to learn as much as I can about Malvatian policy and protocol while I am here, so if I can be of service to you in any way, please do not hesitate to call upon myself and my companions."

The King had a curious look in his eye, but he smiled nonetheless and nodded in agreement. Etienne flashed a look of warning to Gereinte when he thought the King was not looking, but Rudelle appeared adept at reading social nuances and merely laughed at the pair of them as though they were squires at play. Gereinte had much yet to learn about the social etiquette of this great nation. The King appeared uninterested in any further political discussion and wanted to know all about what the Carentans did for entertainment, then proceeded to describe the succession of parties and balls that the Malvatians threw on a regular basis. It seemed to Gereinte that it was going to be more difficult than he had originally envisioned, getting the King to involve him in any kind of discussion relative to the strategic alliances in the Western Isles. So he eventually gave in to the King's whim and indulged him in small talk of the trivialities of being a Royal.

Chapter Forty-Three

So…, thought Reynald, as he watched the messenger depart. After five years of undisputed iron rule, Caitlin was dying of the wasting disease. He knew she had suffered of late from various seasonal disorders and he had it on good authority from his spies amongst the Castle medics that herbs and remedies had been the order of the day for several months. Now, he had learnt that she was indeed in serious trouble. Now was the time to strike, whilst the Queen was indisposed and her little cub was off gallivanting around the Western Isles playing his courtly games. By the time anyone realised he had amassed an army, it would be too late. Carentan was his for the taking. It belonged to him now, as it always had whilst his sister had been holding on to the regency until the time was right.

Carentan held its breath and waited for the news which might cast the Kingdom into bloody conflict. Reynald's ambition was no secret and few of the main political players expected him to accept the accession of the 17-year-old heir to the throne, without a fight.

His negotiations had been nothing if not thorough over the months leading to this moment. The moment he had received news of his sister's illness, the wheels had been set in motion. The balance of power was set to change now that others had begun to gain a foothold in Carentan. That was partly the problem with Caitlin; she had allowed too much freedom of speech. So much so, that it had enabled ambitious political manoeuvring by individuals such at Abiel Morda, the fanatical demagogue, whose power was growing fast. Increasingly, the common people flocked to his Churches to hear how their eternal souls could be saved if they truly believed, performed the sacred rites and of course made a generous contribution to the Church's coffers."

"Godlessness has come to reign in Carentan," Morda screeched in his sermons. "Carentan must return to the old ways. The Scriptures tell us that heresy must be rooted out or the One God will forsake us."

Reynald sneered. Heresy seemed to be greatly on the increase recently, judging by the number of sinners being submitted to Questioning by the Church's Inquisitors. Those who survived the Questioning seemed to have lost the desire for sin but also seemed to lose all other desires. Whilst building his power base in Carentan, Morda was playing another game. Reynald's spies had reported on the secret meetings between Morda and the other church leaders of the Western Isles; and about the plan to meld the bickering, fragmented churches into a unified Holy Church Authority capable of challenging the hereditary rulers. Morda's ambition was the driving force behind the plan and if it succeeded, there was clearly no doubt, at least in Morda's mind, about the ultimate leadership of the Holy Authority.

Then, there was Issoire. Issoire confused Reynald. One of the wealthiest barons in the country, he was past thirty and still unmarried despite desperate attempts by mothers of promising young noblewomen to alter this state of affairs. This and his solitary monastic life had given rise to a number of unkind rumours in court circles about the direction of his sexual appetites. Though mild mannered and not very warrior-like, Issoire was a quick, accomplished swordsman and had killed more than once in personal combat. Despite their rude jests at his expense, courtiers stepped carefully around Issoire and watched their words in his presence.

Conservative by nature, Issoire was said to favour the traditional ways of Carentan and might be expected to support Caitlin Andolin. But Reynald believed most of the nobility would swing to his cause when Caitlin was gone. Issoire was a realist, and might be unwilling to gamble on his ability to survive in isolation. Reynald had contrived several private conversations with Issoire about the future of Carentan. But his unsubtle advances had resulted in no more than a few murmured, uncommitted ambiguities from Issoire. He did not rebuff Reynald, but neither did he agree and as time went on, Reynald had become uncertain and frustrated.

There were also the many lesser lords, whom Reynald had been working on over a longer period of time. It had begun with the local court disputes, unfortunately put paid to, by Caitlin's introduction of the Royal Courts of Justice. This, then progressed to the current state of civil unrest that he had been instrumental in stirring up, particularly amongst the merchants and tradesmen of Carentan, who took little more than a mention of increases in taxes to get them on-side.

The demons of civil war and chaos were waiting in the wings of Carentan. Waiting for Reynald's long awaited embrace.

***

As she drifted in and out of consciousness, Caitlin re-visited the plan she had carefully laid for her son's accession to the throne. It was always Reiner's intention for him to be schooled and trained by the Easterners, Jabir and Kemal, cementing a long and distant relationship between the East and West. Reiner had been good at forecasting the future. He knew long before he died that there would be trouble ahead from the Eastern countries; long after his own reign had come to an end. At such a time, he also knew that he would not be around to guide Gereinte through the maze of international relations and so between them, Reiner and Caitlin had devised a plan to prepare their son for a future that would demand strength, intuition and ingenuity from the ruler of Carentan. However, Caitlin had not bargained on losing her husband quite so soon. And now, she herself had barely a few precious days to secure the future of Carentan, let alone plan for the prosperity of the Western Isles.

For some things she was going to be reliant on their allies in order to support Carentan and hoped that Gereinte had gained some of their confidence during his travels. She had sent out the messengers as it had become imperative to cut short Gereinte's trip; the entire Andolin dynasty lay hanging in the balance. He should by then have reached his sister in Tordre. She hoped there was time for him to make the return journey to Carentan before it was too late.

Since Gereinte had left, Reynald had been

281

stirring up trouble amongst the lesser barons and Caitlin feared that any day soon, the country could descend into civil war. Without a strong leader, the regency had no hope of stilling the unrest that was quietly brewing in the background. And, once Reynald laid claim to the throne, those barons and lords that backed him would reinforce his legitimacy and the people would side with the majority. Without Gereinte, there was no opposition. Completely bedridden now, Caitlin could no longer stand up to her brother.

She coughed and a droplet of blood-streaked spittle settled on her lip. She reached for a handkerchief and knocked over a pitcher onto the floor which landed with the sharp clatter of metal on wood. Her attendants came into the chamber, closely followed by Roda who gauged the situation and instructed the attendants to bring fresh water and handkerchiefs. Her daughter pressed a cotton square to her lips and smiled. Caitlin could see the agony in Roda's eyes, though she sought to hide it behind her smile.

"The Chancellor," Caitlin said. "Lorquin. Get me Lorquin."

"Shush, mother. The messengers have left already, we can only wait now. You must rest."

"No," said Caitlin. "There are plans that have to be put in place. Our family's future will depend upon it."

Reluctantly, Roda turned and whispered to one of the attendants. A few minutes later, Chancellor Lorquin was being escorted into the Queen's chambers, looking grave and concerned. Caitlin turned her head on the pillow to look at him and reached out feebly with her hand. He held her hand softly and his touch felt good.

"Rupert," she said. "There is something we need to do."

Chapter Forty-Four

Princess Fiamina swept her long auburn locks over her shoulder exposing the soft milky skin at the edge of her neckline. All heads turned in her direction as she breezed into the room. She spied her father over the opposite side of the hall, talking to the Carentan guests and held back for a moment to watch, studiously ignoring the interested glances that were cast in her direction. She might once have lapped up the attention, hungry as she was for approval. Perhaps at twelve or thirteen years she sought such admirers, but now at seventeen, all she felt was indifference. She was indeed beautiful and in equal measure clever; this she knew. Her father had presented her with any number of suitors over the years, but none had managed to captivate her attention.

Fiamina watched the young men from Carentan, dismissing them as another party of nobles out for a good time, touring the courts with the sometimes-dubious ambition of bagging a princess along the way. She despised those typical aristocratic attitudes and couldn't fathom why her father seemed so attentive towards them. However, she watched them with great interest, particularly the dark haired one with the cheeky gleam in his eye, what was his name? Darien. He was definitely worth a second glance. But the one named Merlac, she could not get the measure of him at all. He seemed so rude and physically turned away whenever she came anywhere near their party. She certainly would not be giving him the benefit of her attention. Her father saw her and waved her over. She did not really want to join them, but it seemed unavoidable. The tall handsome one named Darien turned out to be the younger brother of a wealthy baron in Carentan and possibly the most suitable of them all, but her father insisted on introducing her again to the despicable Count Merlac, who predictably lowered his eyes and refused to partake in even the smallest of pleasantries.

"Charmed, I'm sure," she muttered under her breath as the Count turned away to talk to one of his dignitaries. She thought she caught an angry flash in his eye when Darien stepped in and reached for her hand. Darien lowered his lips to kiss the back of her skin which sent goose bumps tingling up her arm.

"May I?" he said, indicating the dance floor. She nodded, unable to trust her voice to respond in any coherent manner. Darien was highly attentive and as he swept her across the dance floor, his charm was so effortless and practised. Whilst he was with her, he only appeared to have eyes for her, which was exactly what she needed.

Towards the end of the evening, the pace of the dancing began to wind down and the swirling became slower and more intimate as the music dropped in tempo. Darien held her close to his body, almost as though he was afraid she might fly away. Her stomach fluttered with a million invisible butterflies as he leaned in closer, his cheek almost brushing her own. She felt dizzy with the sweet scent of his breath, when suddenly... ooof! Something heavy knocked into the side of them, sending them almost spinning to the floor. Darien reached out and grabbed her arm lifting her smoothly to her feet and saving her the embarrassment of landing in an ungainly heap on the floor. She turned on the couple that had collided with them about to unleash a barrage of words hardly fit for a princess, when she found herself face to face with Count Merlac. His poor bewildered partner, a young noble woman, clearly out of her depth just stood clasping a hand to her mouth as the Count pulled aside Darien leaving the ladies standing like forgotten statues on the dance floor. The altercation between the Count and Darien was urgent and hushed and though it seemed like hours had passed since her abandonment, Fiamina was back in the arms of Darien within minutes. He picked up where he left off as though nothing at all was amiss, only to her he seemed a little pensive and perhaps more distant. She took a moment to gather her thoughts.

"May I ask what...?"

"You may ask, but an honest answer is not mine to give, Princess."

"Oh." Yes, oh. Is that the best she could do? Surely she deserved some better explanation. "I notice that your friend is rather concerned about something." Darien looked down at her, his eyes scrutinising her with a depth that sent shivers down her spine. Then he smiled as if remembering a good joke and shrugged.

"Where the Count Merlac is concerned, nothing ever surprises me," he said as a matter of fact. She looked around to try and locate the Count, but he had evidently given up on dancing as the young noble woman had now found an alternative partner who hopefully didn't have two left feet. Perhaps that was why he was so angry. He was jealous

286

because Darien was so accomplished both on the dance floor and with the ladies. He looked down at her again and pulled her tighter to his chest. Her body betrayed her feelings by shivering and flushing her skin with a crimson sheen.

"What is it with the Count?" she said, breaking away from Darien. "Does he hold some kind of power over you?" Darien hung his head, a small smile tugging at the corner of his mouth, but remained silent. "Oh..," she exclaimed in frustration. "If you won't tell me then perhaps he will." She tried to pull away, but he gently kept her within the circle of his embrace.

"I wouldn't recommend it, really. He is just angry with me, that is all." She stopped struggling and sighed as Darien fixed her with the intensity of his gaze.

"I thought as much, you know, when he ran into us like that. Perhaps I should give him a few dancing lessons, no forget that, he is too rude and I wouldn't even spare him a minute of my precious time. How dare he be angry at you for his own incompetence." Darien was looking at her with a curious expression of amusement.

"Please. Try to think more kindly of the Count. He is probably not entirely what he seems to you."

"Think kindly? Good grief. Has the age of chivalry passed him by? You can tell him from me that if and when he decides to adopt some manners, I may do him the courtesy of merely acknowledging his existence. Until then, I won't even notice he has gone." Darien stopped moving and stood very still, his mouth agape. "For goodness sake close your mouth before you start catching flies," she said, surprising herself with the force of her words.

There was not much left then for her to do, but extract herself from the very intoxicating embrace of this man and return herself to her father, who had been watching the evening unfold from the comfort of his chair in the wings of the room. Darien remained for a moment, staring after her, before regaining his composure and engaging another partner in dancing the final few numbers for the evening.

She sat down next to her father. Her mood brooding over the outcome of the evening. She shook herself, trying to think of anything other than the hateful Count who had interfered with her plans.

"Father, you seem thoughtful." Fiamina noticed that he was looking over at the Carentans. "Darien is such a fine young man, don't you think?" She hoped her voice didn't betray her desire.

"Hmnn," Alvar grunted. "I was thinking that Count Merlac might be a better suitor for you, my dear." She could not quite believe what her father was saying.

"Why, he's nothing but a mindless playboy, interested in nothing but hunting and stupid sword fighting," she said to her father in disgust.

"Well, my dear, he's not so mindless that he hasn't fooled you, amongst others, as to his true nature and what this Grand Tour is really all about," her father said.

Fiamina flushed and said indignantly, "I don't believe it. He's not that clever."

"Clever enough to have misled you once before, my love," he said, appearing to enjoy the moment. "I know you've not spent much time with the Prince

288

of Carentan, but think back carefully; particularly to that eventful trip to Holmport on the Skyelady."

Fiamina started and stared over at the Count. His face was just about visible now as he danced with another woman and now that she was looking closely at him for the first time, she could not believe that she had missed it before. Her father was watching her with an amused expression on his face as the truth dawned on her. Her emotions swept through her like a tidal wave. First disbelief, then joy, which finally settled on red-hot anger.

"Why, that... that lying, two-faced duplicitous toad," she raged. "I'll kill him."

"Now, now my love," her father said. "I've trained you better than that. You've studied your history. Did you really think that the son of Reiner and Caitlin Andolin was going to be just another asinine socialite? Look carefully at his entourage. Etienne Martan is one of the most efficient spymasters in the Isles. His network is nearly as good as mine. Then take Darien Issoire..."

"Yes please," Fiamina murmured, her eyes softening. Alvar noted this with interest.

"Darien is generally recognised as the best military commander in Carentan with a good grasp of strategy and an astute tactical brain," he said. "What do you suppose he's been spending his time doing in Sarlat?"

"Ignoring me mostly," Fiamina said with a grumble.

Overlooking this frivolous comment, Alvar continued. "I would be very surprised if Darien does not already have a very clear picture of our army and military capability. Admittedly our main strength is naval, but our land-based forces are not trivial. Finally there is our Easterner friend, Kemal ed-Din."

"He's just a swordsman surely. Admittedly a very good one, but that's all," Fiamina said.

"Well, my sources tell me that he is more than just a very fine swordsman," her father said. "In his native land, he is not only a prince, but known to be an extremely capable and experienced military commander. Now why do you suppose the eastern potentate would send one of his best warrior princes into Carentan to educate and train Gereinte?"

"To help Gereinte ascend to the Carentan throne, presumably," Fiamina said. "But why would the easterners care who is on the throne of Carentan?"

"Well now, that is the question," Alvar said. "My own theory is so unlikely and fanciful that I'm not going to divulge it even to you until I have better grounds for belief."

Chapter Forty-Five

They left Sarne in the hope of making a swift visit to Tordre, which was part of the planned journey. Gereinte was very much looking forward to Tordre, not having seen his sister Nerys for some time. After an uneventful journey, the Carentan party reached the walls of T'sar, the capital of Tordre. The gates of the city were flung open and the party were surprised by the presence of a squad of honour guards who escorted them through the streets of T'sar to the palace. To their further surprise, the streets were lined with cheering chanting city people, waving flags and shouting "Carentan" and "Queen Nerys." How quickly Nerys had won the hearts and minds of the people of Tordre.

They were shown into the Royal Hall where Morra Dreiden and Nerys sat next to each other in identical thrones. Morra looked younger than Gereinte had imagined, but he had a personal power about him that emanated calmness and wisdom, without the necessity for words.

As soon as they entered the hall, Nerys abandoned all pretence to dignity and flew across the hall to hug Gereinte, sobbing.

"Ger, oh Ger, I've missed you all so dreadfully." Morra had an austere look about him and Gereinte wondered at how cold a relationship it looked for his sister. But these misgivings were put to rest when he saw the king's eyes soften as he looked at his queen. There was a depth of emotion and understanding between them that he envied and he was comforted that Nerys was being cared for in the manner she deserved. The Carentans spent the next few days hunting, partying and meeting with the civil and military leaders of Tordre.

The morning of their departure, the Carentan party gathered in the palace courtyard in preparation for their journey to Vermondie. As they gathered their packs, King Dreiden strode briskly toward them, Nerys keeping stride alongside him.

"I know we have said our formal farewells Gereinte, but I have one personal message for you," Dreiden said. "My faith lies with you to restore Carentan to its former glory. I see much of your father's strength within you. Should you need assistance, be assured that Tordre is behind you in every way."

"My thanks Morra," Gereinte said. "For your words and your support. I hope to return one day under more positive circumstances." One final hug from Nerys and Gereinte led the party away toward the city gates.

Three hard days' riding later, the Carentans arrived at the outskirts of Verton, the capital city of Vermondie. Gereinte was relieved that at last the end to his journey was in sight. He was impatient to return home and begin laying the foundation for the future of his homeland. To Gereinte and his companions, Verton had little to commend it. The buildings were generally ugly, looked badly constructed and many looked derelict. The streets were choked with filth and there was an overall impression of squalor.

They eventually arrived at the gates of the palace where they were challenged by a pair of surly guards. On hearing who they were and the purpose of their visit, the guards opened the gates and let them enter, albeit reluctantly. The party trotted down the carriageway to the massive front doors of the palace. As they walked up the steps, the doors opened and a manservant welcomed them in, bowing and inviting them to enter the hall.

It was early evening and the party were ushered into a waiting room while orders were dispersed for the preparation of a suite of rooms. The palace had all the austerity of its infamous incumbent, King Haveritas. The King, it was announced, would be available to meet with the Carentans at dinner, once they had refreshed themselves after their journey.

"So," Darien said, admiring the luxury of the apartments and spreading himself out on the chaise longue. "How are we to progress the plan?

"Plan?" Gereinte said. "Since when did we ever stick to a plan?"

"Don't ever let your mother hear you say that," Etienne said with a grin.

"I'd like to know," Darien said, "how you plan to win over Haveritas, especially with his hound dog, Lord Dassan, nipping at your heels. Perhaps we could kidnap the princess and have you rescue her?"

Gereinte smiled wanly at his companion.

"Haveritas is not the person we should be wasting our energy pursuing. It is all about hearts and minds, my friends." Both Etienne and Darien looked quizzically at Gereinte. "You can win the minds of men through careful negotiation, but win a man's heart and he is yours to command forever."

"Well, it is not quite as simple as that in politics, your Highness," Etienne said. "You are only ever remembered for your last deed or your final word.

Goodwill can turn so easily into disgrace with one mis-placed word or ill-thought gesture. It is as well to remember that."

"And it is as much about knowing where to focus your energy as it is knowing what to say," Gereinte said, smiling at his friend.

Chapter Forty-Six

King Raess Haveritas was a cantankerous old man. Gereinte and his party were introduced to the King and his courtiers, who responded with nothing less than patronising disdain and outright rudeness. The rangers, Allard and Bolt tightened their circle with Kemal, so that the three main players in the introductions were covered from all angles. The tension in the room was palpable from the instant Gereinte entered, though the façade was of polite conduct and barely concealed envy. Gereinte shook hands with Haveritas, who sneered in his greeting, though his handshake was weak. Perhaps the rumours of his ill health were true and all he had to offer by way of offense was his attitude.

"Huh," he grunted. "You look just like your father." Unsure whether to take this as a compliment or not, Gereinte turned to be introduced to the rest of the entourage. Lord Dassan held his hand for a fraction of a second longer than was polite and his handshake was by no means weak. His smile was more of a snarl, though he did invite the men to join them in a hunting trip planned for the day after next. Gereinte couldn't help but view this invitation as more of a threat than goodwill on the part of Marcus Dassan and there were indeed a few surreptitious glances around the room at Dassan's forthright invitation.

The royal twins were by comparison the most amiable and unassuming pair that Gereinte had met so far in Vermondie. Rann was more reserved than Lirra and gave the impression that he was reserving judgment on the characters of Gereinte and his party. He was a fit young man, who evidently engaged in a lot of riding and outdoors pursuits, as was customary for many privileged families across the Isles. He had ash-blonde hair and a ruddy complexion but there was a keen intelligence behind his eyes that spoke volumes without an uttered word. Lirra, on the other hand was much more forthcoming and her quick-witted intellect, coupled with striking patrician features, soon captivated Darien's attention.

Gereinte observed his friend's approach to Lirra and also observed every eye in the room follow him. It seemed that Lirra was also aware, though her expression remained neutral and formal. Only her eyes betrayed a shadow of concern. Dassan's attention was drawn to the encounter, at which point he nodded at several courtiers who immediately joined Darien and invited his conversation, leaving little doubt in Gereinte's mind of the subtle taming of the twins that was undermining the balance of power in Vermondie. Gereinte used the opportunity while attention was diverted to initiate conversation with Rann. As it happened, Rann was most eager to hear more about Gereinte's travels and particularly his training regime.

"Perhaps," Rann said, "we can find some space in our training yard for your sessions to continue over the next few days. I would surely value the opportunity to join in with your practice." Gereinte was about to respond with positive enthusiasm when Marcus Dassan interjected.

"Perhaps that would not be a wise course of action for the young prince, given his duties of state. We can ill afford an accident, especially with his

Royal Highness being so ill at present." Dassan snorted in the direction of Haveritas who looked to be ever shrinking into a feeble human wreck. He coughed twice into a handkerchief, then his attendants ran to his side and escorted him from the room.

"I see," Gereinte said. "Well, I certainly should not want to divert the Prince from his duties of state. Rann, you are welcome to join us or merely observe." It seemed that a small grey cloud had settled over Rann, though he was trying hard not to let it show. Gereinte could sense his frustration bubbling beneath the surface, but it was not a suitable time to have that conversation he wanted while Rann was being so closely watched by his compatriots.

The following morning, Rann was eagerly present in the royal training yard to observe as Gereinte and Darien were put through their paces by Kemal. It wasn't long before a small gathering of passers-by, courtiers and knights had accumulated to watch in fascination at the alacrity and skill in sword fighting being displayed. Many of the combatants using the practice yard at the time, set down their weapons with a respectful gaze. They had possibly achieved more by inviting the prince's observation than they would have by his participation.

Kemal himself was not impervious to the attention that they drew and after drilling the pair for the best part of an hour, he took a glance at the assembled crowd and smiled. Gereinte and Darien exchanged a quizzical look, sweat dripping from their brows.

"Perhaps now is the time to really show them what we are made of," Kemal said, putting down his practice weapon and drawing his naked blade. Darien shrugged and followed suit. Gereinte hesitated for a moment, wondering how much they should really display to their potential enemies. Kemal moved alongside him and muttered under his breath, "The skill lies within the one who wields the weapon, not the weapon itself." Understanding his meaning, Gereinte put aside the practice sword and drew his sword from the old weathered scabbard. The onlookers held their breath before emitting a collective gasp. The blue sword shone in the early morning light in response to its bearer.

Gereinte took up a stance and faced his first attacker, Darien, who launched a thrust to his midriff without any faint or warning. He easily parried and the sound of steel on steel chimed loudly across the yard. There were a few excited cries from the audience, perhaps they had not expected such full commitment from two high-ranking statesmen who on the face of it appeared to be the best of friends. Darien circled back and launched a second attack with such speed that Gereinte almost missed the killing blow but managed to sidestep in time to counter, using his body position to effectively unbalance his opponent enough to send Darien sailing the ground with a thump. Gereinte was upon him immediately, the point of his sword just short of nicking the skin of his throat. There was a pause while people tried to decide whether or not to call the medics, then once they saw Gereinte help Darien to his feet, there was loud applause. The result was quick, neat and effective. He had barely given Darien an opportunity to find an opening before finishing it with such speed and deadly skill. Gereinte grinned at his friend, who grimaced in response.

"Just because you've got a blue sword," Darien muttered.

"And an adoring crowd," Gereinte said, turning and bowing with a flourish. There were cries for more and the mass seemed to have increased twofold since they had drawn their weapons.

"Pride before a fall, my friend. You still have master Kemal to deal with." Darien withdrew and Kemal took up his stance in front of the prince. This time, Gereinte was less wary of a sudden attack, knowing Kemal was better suited to a defensive style of fighting. That was his first mistake, as the eastern sword master nearly sliced his ear off with an unexpected strike, which Gereinte only just managed to avoid. There was a gasp from the crowd and Gereinte withdrew to gather his wits. No time to berate himself for making stupid assumptions, before Kemal was upon him again. This time, he sidestepped in time and attempted a counter thrust, which was blocked with a loud clash of swords sending a vibration of pain skewering the nerves in his sword arm. He ignored the pain and doubled back on himself forcing his opponent to yield to the space in between them. Kemal responded in kind by absorbing his attack and forcing back against him. The strength of his blow sent Gereinte wheeling back in an attempt to gain his footing. He dug deep within his spirit, pushing aside the pain that flared in his arms and legs, re-gaining his balance and bringing his sword back into a defensive position.

299

Within a fraction of a second of re-establishing his centre of balance, Kemal was upon him seeking to gain an advantage. But Gereinte was quick. His youth and agility worked in his favour, despite his tired limbs. He countered the next two blows and dropped back taking a defensive ploy against Kemal's unexpected and uncharacteristic offensive. That was his second mistake. Instead of taking the fight to his opponent, he allowed his teacher and swords master the respect of his years, at which point, Kemal was swift and merciless in finishing the round. Gereinte was on his back before he could determine how he had got there with the point of a long sword in the back of his neck. Kemal smiled and withdrew his sword, then shook his head. There was a low booing noise coming from the onlookers; Gereinte had evidently won some support during his first round.

"We still have some areas to work on, your Highness," Kemal said, turning his back on the Prince and returning his sword to its scabbard. Gereinte felt a keen disappointment. Not at his defeat; he could not have been defeated by a more worthy opponent. Not at letting down the crowd, although he understood well enough the benefit of having the support of the people. He was disappointed in himself. He had played into Kemal's hands and it would not have mattered if his sword were a mythical sword with magical properties, it was always the skill of the swordsman, not the sword itself. His pride would certainly recover, but could he be confident about winning a confrontation if again taken by surprise by his opponent's tactics? Sometimes he forgot he was

300

only seventeen. Perhaps he expected too much of himself, before his time. His father had many years on him before ascending to the throne of Carentan. He heard the whispers among the crowd as they made their way back to their quarters, took no comfort in the words.

"Did you ever see such a sword... magnificent."

"Ah, but it glows only for the Prince of Carentan... in another's hand it is just as grey as an Autumn day."

"So young for a crown prince and yet so accomplished..."

"He only let the old man win to make him feel better... such gentleman-like behaviour as befits a king."

It was only later that he pondered on how the eyes and ears of Vermondie took advantage of their networks to reveal to all who cared to listen of the true identity of Count Merlac.

The following morning saw Gereinte and his companions practising once again in the royal training yard. The initial excitement began to wear off, but there remained a stalwart gathering of Rann and his guardsmen each day.

Chapter Forty-Seven

The day of the hunt came and the royal party set off at first light with the Carentans in attendance. King Haveritas and his guardsmen, closely accompanied by Lord Dassan set off at breakneck speed, pushing the horses at a punishing rate. Gereinte led his party at a slower pace, preferring the relative comfort of Rann's company, though he was never permitted out of sight or earshot of the royal guard. Rann glanced at him with a withering look.

The hunt took them deep into the forestland surrounding the King's grounds and once the rangers began to nock their arrows, Gereinte was pleased to see the guardsmen glance warily at the Carentan party. Etienne rode up beside Gereinte.

"Smart move, bringing Allard and Bolt," he said.

"They are under instructions," Gereinte said. Etienne followed his gaze and watched as a diversion began. A large deer had crossed their path and now stood startled within easy shot of the party. The guardsmen, keen to show that the Carentan rangers were not the only ones who could shoot a straight arrow, turned their full attention on their prey. Gereinte watched closely as Rann fell back from the hunters and the two princes retreated from the path and cantered off at a distance before the rest of the party were aware that anything was amiss.

"We don't have long," Rann said, as they reached a clearing. "If the King even suspects that we have had this meeting, it is the guardsmen who will suffer. Much as I despise being treated like a child, no man deserves the kind of justice that Haveritas will administer."

"Agreed. I have only to tell you that should the time come when you are able to rule in Vermondie, then Carentan should not be viewed as an aggressive force. Our only wish is to establish a friendly and productive relationship with you." Rann was looking at him strangely.

"Indeed," he said. The corners of his mouth curled into a smile. "If your Queen's Guard are as highly trained as yourself and your companions, I wouldn't fancy our chances at an aggressive encounter. You astonish me for someone so young." Gereinte couldn't disguise his surprise at Rann's words.

"Believe me," he said, "youth can have its disadvantages." He was thinking of how many times he had barely managed to dodge the attempts on his life.

"I accept your proposition for a friendly and productive relationship with Carentan, but only ask that you maintain a tolerant position with the current rulers. I can do no more at present, whilst the King lives. It is a burden I will have to carry for now, though it irritates me to admit it. It is for the future of Vermondie and to protect the status of my sister and me."

"I understand," Gereinte said. "If there is anything I can do..."

"We will most certainly call upon your goodwill, should the need arise."

"Come on. I have said my piece," Gereinte said. "Let's make our way back before they notice we are gone."

The Carentans continued their stay, attending social events, accepting the occasional snarl from Haveritas and keeping their distance from the twins. Marcus Dassan was ever breathing down their necks. If it had been up to Gereinte, he would have left soon after his meeting with Rann, but Etienne insisted they stay for the extended period so as not to arouse suspicion from the King.

After a week had passed, Gereinte was woken roughly in the middle of the night. He turned over, about to express his anger when he realised that it was Rann who was shaking him. Gereinte leapt up, aware that something was wrong. The palace was in chaos, Etienne and Darien were already up and dressing. Rann gave him an apologetic look, then all but ran from the room to leave Gereinte's companions to explain.

"The King has died," Etienne said. "Rann's guards have taken control of his chambers and have clapped Marcus Dassan into a dungeon under close guard." Gereinte sat in his rumpled bed with his mouth open, trying to get his head around the situation. It was rash on the part of the prince. On the other hand, it could well be the making of him.

"He has certainly acted swiftly," Darien said, reading Gereinte's thoughts. "But he will have sent a strong message out to those who oppose him." Gereinte nodded.

"If he really does have the command of the people," Etienne said. "If not, we could have a problem."

"We have to see this through, whatever the circumstances. If the prince and princess find

304

themselves exiled, then we can offer them sanctuary in Carentan," Gereinte said. He dragged himself up and began throwing his clothes on.

The companions moved swiftly through the palace to appraise the situation and wake the rangers and Kemal. It was an unnecessary caution, as it soon became evident that Rann had been amassing support from every corner of Vermondie, whilst the King had been sinking further into ill health. He was not a well-liked man.

With Gereinte and his party's help, it took barely a day for Rann to take over the main halls of the palace, at which point he duly declared himself the ruler of Vermondie. The Carentans remained for several days to cement their newfound relationship with Vermondie, strengthened by a public declaration of their treaty. This comprised an alliance of friendship, financial and other help from Carentan, particularly in matters of trading, farming and fishing.

The next day, a messenger arrived from Tordre with a letter for Gereinte. He recognised Nerys' handwriting;

"Ger... my hand shakes even as I write this letter. Mother is dying of the wasting disease. A messenger arrived not long after you left. We must all return to Castle Helmstedt. Things are starting to go terribly wrong, as word has got out of her illness. There are people gathering even now around the outer walls of the castle and mother has called a gathering. There is talk of civil war..."

Gereinte turned his back on his friends and allowed the letter to drop onto the table, walking away to stand by the window, which looked out

305

across to the horizon from Vermondie to Carentan. His mother had sat endlessly by his bedside after he had been attacked and near killed some years ago. During that time, he had seen beyond the mask she presented every day. Something of the real woman and mother had peered beyond the restrictions of her crown. It was a lesson he could never forget.

He had asked her to see the royal medic before he had left on the Grand Tour; damn his mother's stubborn resistance. She would never admit a weakness. His thoughts flitted to the people of Carentan who he imagined were even now gathering around the town in expectation. The great and the good and the not so good would be amassing their armies and allies at Castle Helmstedt. He shivered as a frisson of inner fear crept across his skin before he banished it to the deepest corner of his thoughts. Then he turned to face his companions who stood speechless, Nerys's letter spread out on the table before them.

That afternoon the Carentan party began their journey back home.

Chapter Forty-Eight

Reynald looked down at the swirling throng of lords, knights, and assorted hangers-on crowding the great hall of Castle Helmstedt. The cream of Carentan power and wealth had gathered in response to the summons from Caitlin. Even from her deathbed, Reynald thought, my sister can command instant obedience.

In the weak evening sun, the great hall was gloomy and oppressive. The atmosphere was tense, rumours sweeping across the crowd like windblown leaves in Autumn.

"Some great lord was to be indicted for treason... Rudelle of Malvas was finally going to march into Carentan... Caitlin was going to stand down and appoint Borsa Regent."

These and other wild tales were being feverishly exchanged. Those who depended on the nobles for their status and livelihood glanced around to see which of the men of power were present and whose company they were keeping.

To the ignorant eye, the agitated mass of colour and movement in the Hall appeared to be without sense or pattern. Reynald, looking down from the royal dais at the end of the hall, knew better. He could see the focal points of power and influence around which, allies and hangers-on clustered.

The merchants in their sombre greys and browns, surrounded by their stolid guards, were muttering among themselves. Reynald could easily guess what was being said.

"What is it now? new taxes? Restrictions on trading licences?"

Reynald wondered if there were a merchant alive who thought of anything but furthering his trade.

You have cause for worry little men. But not yet, not quite yet. He had always believed that Caitlin had been much too tolerant of the merchant classes, but when his time came all that would change, oh yes, things would certainly change.

Surrounded by two hands of the Church's white clad Immaculate Knights, Abiel Morda, Leader of the Church of One God, stood silent, his thin sharp features set in its normal expression of grim disapproval.

When the time comes, which way will you jump, my ambitious cleric? Probably for anyone against Andolin. Morda had no great love for the nobility, but seemed to cherish a particularly bitter animosity toward the Andolins. He believed that they were careless in the observance of their religious duties and treated Abiel Morda with a barely veiled contempt.

Even so, Caitlin had given Morda too much scope for mischief. When Reynald came into his own, this Holy Authority nonsense would be crushed and if Morda proved difficult... well, there would be a vacancy at the top of the Church's hierarchy.

In one corner of the Hall stood Chanac Issoire with a screen of heavily armed knights. Issoire held himself aloof from his fellow lords and had few friends at Court. Carentan society had eventually become used to his inscrutable presence. *"Issoire the silent"* they called him, because of the way he doled out words like the miser he was reputed to be.

Pacing up and down, Reynald passed Fulk. As

usual when he saw Fulk, Reynald suppressed a twinge of irritation. Fulk, through no fault of his own, was an ever-present reminder of Reynald's inability to produce an heir. At first, he had appeared to be the ideal choice to succeed Reynald. Men of the Borsa clan tended to be big, but Fulk grew into a giant who towered over them all. As he achieved his full strength, Fulk matured into a powerful warrior skilled in the weapons and arts of war. By the time he was twenty, he was proven in battle, undefeated in combat or on the practice field. As well as being a peerless warrior, he was an accomplished hunter and woodsman; even the proud rangers grudgingly conceded that Fulk was as skilled in the forest as the best of them.

But, Fulk in society was a different man. Away from the battlefield or his beloved forest, the confident warrior became a shy, inarticulate, hobble-de-hoy, clumsy in speech and manner. Fulk was as uncomfortable in court as he was uneasy at formal events. Courtiers laughed and said, though not in his hearing, that Fulk was more likely to break furniture than hearts.

Reynald was disgusted to discover that Fulk was not in the least bit interested in the exercise of power and seemed unable to grasp the realities of the simplest political situation. Reynald attempted to draw Fulk into his inner circle of plotters, but gave up after he had sat silent in meetings, bored and ill at ease. So, Reynald had dismissed Fulk as a simple-minded fighting man, useful when brute force was necessary, but incapable of thinking beyond the next battle or tourney.

Chapter Forty-Nine

Gereinte's room had been transformed into a makeshift meeting room for discussions between the Andolins and their advisors. The late evening gloom and latent birdsong reflected the mood of the room's occupants.

Throughout the day, Gereinte had watched each of the Andolins being summoned to his mother for her last words of counsel. First the twins, Nerys and Alliane. Nerys had dissolved into tears after seeing her mother and had gone up to her bedroom to be comforted by the old nurse. Alliane had joined the council of war in Gereinte's room. Gereinte had stayed the longest with their mother and came out thoughtful and determined. Finally Roda went in and was still there.

Knocking gently, Ladys Autin slipped in and shut the door quickly behind her.

"Princess Roda is still with the Queen," she said in a choked voice. "The Princess asked me to tell you... that the end will be soon." Gereinte's heart quickened at her words.

Striding around the room, Warmaster Alaric paused, cursed under his breath and resumed his impatient pacing. Jabir and Kemal sat still; grave, impassive and seemingly emotionless.

"Well... we knew it would come to this sooner or later," Chancellor Lorquin said. He pursed his lips, supressing unexpressed emotions.

"Rupert, how can you be so cold blooded?" Alliane said and rushed over to Ladys to hug her. "Come and sit down Ladys, you must be exhausted after all these days of sitting with Mother. Come

310

and have a cup of wine."

"You are very kind Princess," Ladys said. "But I must get back to the Queen." As she spoke, Roda came through the door and walked slowly to the table.

"It's over," she said and then sat down as though her legs had betrayed her. "I can't say she went happily. Can you imagine mother ever being happy at being defeated, even by death? But I think she was content. We have had our instructions and I don't doubt that we will all be playing our part in her grand design." Alliane looked up at the slight note of bitterness in Roda's voice.

"It's Issoire isn't it?" she said.

"I suppose it's impossible to keep anything from you Ally." Roda sighed. "Yes. Mother had it all arranged long ago. Oh, it's a wonderful match in every way and I don't dislike Chanac, but..." her voice trailed away.

"Issoire eh?" Alaric said. "Well, he can look no higher than an Andolin princess, but by gods... with Issoire, we are evenly matched with Borsa." Gereinte raised an eyebrow, looking to Lorquin.

"Alaric, this changes nothing; we cannot risk the Kingdom on an even chance," Lorquin said. "We must take Reynald out once and for all."

"And how precisely do you plan to do that?" Alliane said. Lorquin told her and Gereinte watched her expression change from scepticism to outright horror. "You're all mad," she said. "He'll slaughter Gereinte. Reynald's twice his size and has twenty years more experience."

Undismayed by this pessimistic appreciation of his martial skills, Gereinte looked towards Kemal.

"Princess," Kemal said. "The case is not as bad as you think. The prince is fast and skilled. Traditional warriors like Lord Borsa know little of the art of true swordsmanship."

"Easy for you to say," Alliane said. "You don't have to fight that... that bully."

"Believe me Princess," Kemal said. "I would be very happy to remove Lord Borsa from your life permanently, but..." he spread his hands apologetically.

"What Kemal means," Lorquin said, "is that everyone knows he's a master swordsman and in a straight fight he'd disembowel Reynald in about thirty seconds. But we can't have it being said that Gereinte unleashed his tame killer on Reynald. It wouldn't play well in the provinces."

"So Gereinte has to risk his life because of your precious politics," Alliane said. "I can't stop you, but, if mother was still alive you wouldn't be doing this."

In the silence which ensued, eyes looked everywhere except at Alliane. She looked up, suspicious. "Oh no," she said. "Tell me it's not true."

"Princess," Lorquin said softly, "the original idea came from the Queen. But we have refined it into a plan, which we believe will succeed."

"Suppose Reynald doesn't follow your wonderful plan," Alliane said, refusing to be comforted. "And even if Gereinte wins, what about the rest of the Borsa clan? Do you think they'll just...give in?"

"We think that House Borsa will follow Fulk," Lorquin said. "And we believe that Fulk will

312

support Andolin because he is a traditionalist and for... other reasons." Normally acute to the faintest off-key nuance, Alliane, in her distress, missed the odd note in Lorquin's reply and the quick look exchanged between Lorquin and Gereinte.

"You could be right about Fulk," Alliane said. "He might seem slow, but I've never believed him to be stupid. And of course Reynald has always treated the poor boy dreadfully." A few lips twitched at the 16-year-old princess's description of the huge dour knight.

Gereinte stood up suddenly, his face grim.

"No more debate. Time to go," he said. Alliane turned into his arms hugging him and weeping silently. But she could not leave her brother with only tears to remember. "Kill him, Ger," she said, "and come back to us."

Chapter Fifty

The double doors at the dais end of the hall burst open and Gereinte strode through, accompanied by Alaric and Lorquin.

The instant he appeared, silence fell over the crowd as though a spell had been cast. Gereinte paused for a long moment before he spoke, his voice sombre but firm.

"Messires, I bring unwelcome, sad news. My mother, Caitlin the Queen Regent has died within the last hour." A collective sigh came from the crowds. The news was not unexpected, but now it had come there were mixed emotions rippling like waves through the people. "Before we pay tribute to her life and mourn her passing, I have a proclamation to make," Gereinte said. "As the rightful, acknowledged heir to the throne, and in full accordance with the laws and traditions of our Kingdom, I am claiming the crown of Carentan. If anyone here would challenge my right to rule, let them speak now."

Gereinte looked out at the sea of heads. He saw Reynald smile and imagined what might be going through the man's head. Was that a smile of exultation? He would be thinking that Gereinte was a naive young fool who had made a mistake likely to prove fatal. Throwing the gauntlet recklessly down in public like this would force a confrontation with Reynald that most people thought Gereinte could not win. Gods, but Gereinte hoped they were wrong. What if he had temporised, asked for time and then put his case before a council of lords? He had discussed all the possible outcomes with

Lorquin and Alaric and he would still have lost. But he might have saved his neck in some compromise arrangement. Had he made a mistake? Reynald was looking strong and confident; his voice cut through the confused hubbub following Gereinte's announcement.

"Messires, this is madness. How can we allow an untried stripling, more interested in books than battles, to rule in these uncertain times? Carentan is beset by enemies, both without and within. Only strong and experienced leadership can guide us through these troubled waters." Gereinte was in no doubt about the source of the necessary leadership being offered and so, apparently, were the people. In the continuing confusion, Andolin supporters were being shouted down by loud well-organised chants of "Borsa, Borsa..."

As the calls for Borsa to rule became more inflammatory, Alaric, purple with rage bellowed, "Andolin rules," in a huge voice and whipped his sword point upward in the traditional salute.

"Aye," Reynald said, "Andolin rules when there is an Andolin fit to rule. I see none here. I see a weakling; unfit, untrained and incapable of leading us forward to the greatness which is Carentan's destiny." There were rumbles of assent from the crowds as people weighed up Reynald's words. "You all know your history. The Andolin dynasty was founded on inter-marriage. When the mighty Helden Canrac died all those years ago, his daughter Caitlin succeeded to the throne. It was only her marriage to an Andolin that gave the Andolins their right to rule. Do you see history repeating itself here?" Gereinte noted some looks of confusion, as the people struggled to make the connection. "Borsa is the last line of direct descendants from Canrac. Where was the justification for my sister claiming regency, when there is still a male heir? House Andolin has no claim to the throne. That died along with King Reiner." A few claps and cheers rose above the murmuring crowd.

Throughout this exchange, Gereinte stood silent and emotionless, green eyes cold and remote. In the silence following this naked challenge, all eyes were fixed on Gereinte. He walked slowly across the dais and came to a halt within arm's length of Reynald. Reynald's eyes widened. Gereinte was looking at him eye to eye with a curiously speculative, unafraid gaze.

Then, without a word or hint of his intentions, in one swift flowing movement, Gereinte plucked a gauntlet from his belt and smashed it across Reynald's face. The power of the blow stunned Reynald and he staggered back, blood dripping from a cut lip.

"Reynald," Gereinte said. "You are a treacherous, treasonous dog; you will withdraw your words now or prove them with your sword." The Borsa knights growled and hands went to sword hilts; all except Fulk, who was watching Gereinte, his face unreadable.

Shocked, Reynald shook his head. It was not going as he had evidently planned. He was being forced into single combat, which, by the twitch of a smile in the corner of his mouth, he believed he would win. As predicted, Reynald decided to strike first. Why should he bother with all the niceties and traditions of single combat when he had Fulk and

316

three hands of his best knights behind him?

Gereinte smiled grimly at Reynald, as though he could see the thoughts unfolding in his mind. As Reynald gathered himself for the signal, Gereinte raised his left hand. The minstrel gallery above the dais suddenly blossomed with green clad forest rangers.

Hard-bitten grim-faced men, they watched from the gallery, with strung bows by their sides. No arrows were nocked, but most people present knew of the speed with which the rangers could nock and shoot. The hall was a perfect killing ground for the bowmen and if Gereinte gave the word, no one doubted that the Borsa nobles and knights would be slaughtered. Borsa's supporters moved their hands slowly away from their sword hilts.

"So this is Andolin honour?" Reynald said. "To have your bowmen impose your will against all the rules and laws of honourable combat?"

"No Reynald," Gereinte said. "The rangers are here to ensure a fair fight. They won't act unless your people seek to interfere." Reynald looked up at the gallery, and then swept his angry gaze across the assembled masses. "Well, are you going to draw Reynald?" Gereinte said. "Or is the tongue your weapon of choice? If you are going to fight, I suggest you get a better weapon than that." Reynald was wearing a slim heavily bejewelled court sword. "There would be no honour in killing a man armed with that toy."

Reynald tore his sword belt off and flung it to one side without taking his eyes off Gereinte. It landed at Fulk's feet with a clatter on the stone floor. He gestured impatiently towards Fulk holding out his hand. Fulk drew his huge two-handed broadsword and silently offered it to Reynald.

They faced each other. To most onlookers, Gereinte must have seemed badly matched to Reynald's heavy shouldered and thickset build. He was a seasoned warrior proven in battle and single combat. Gereinte's slim, loose-limbed frame appeared frail and boyish by comparison. He knew what the crowds would be thinking; few in the hall would give his foolhardy challenge any chance of surviving the duel.

"To the death," Reynald said, then swept his massive sword up to his right shoulder. In response, Gereinte raised his sword, hilt up, point down, in the hanging guard position. There was a gasp from the gathering as the sword shimmered with a sapphire hue in the prince's hands. "Who is the one holding a toy now?" Reynald said with a smirk. They circled one another. Gereinte watched and waited, anticipating his direction from every twitch of movement.

With a furious roar, Reynald launched his attack, blade swinging down and across with tremendous force. Falling away, Gereinte parried at the last moment, hesitant and uncertain. Reynald was fast for his age and bulk, but a much slower opponent than Gereinte was used to in his bouts with Kemal. Reynald launched another huge stroke, this time from left to right. Gereinte parried late again, still falling away.

Reynald pushed forward and aimed a savage cut at Gereinte's neck which he blocked by using an outside guard. For a moment, Reynald looked confused. Then he attempted something completely different. He wrenched an inside cut at Gereinte's leading leg which was easily stopped with a low inside guard. Moving swiftly, Gereinte completed the move by turning up the point of his sword, thrusting to Reynald's chest. Reynald narrowly averted the cut by leaping to one side. The fight was going exactly as Kemal had predicted. His last words to Gereinte, "Prince, you are faster and more skilled than Reynald, but he is stronger, so make it quick; in a long fight accidents can happen."

The sweat was pouring in rivulets into his eyes and his arms screamed with the pain of having to block heavy blow after heavy blow from the broadsword.

Reynald launched another fierce attack, a wide stroke aimed at Gereinte's neck. As the blade whistled down, Gereinte saw Reynald's wrists twist and knew that the cut was a feint. When the real stroke came, this time he stepped into the arc of the blade, parrying fast and early. And, following up his parry with lethal speed, Gereinte at full extension drove his blue steel sword through Reynald's heart.

Gereinte jerked his sword clear as Reynald staggered back, dying on his feet. Dumbstruck by the speed and deadliness of Gereinte's thrust, the onlookers watched in shocked fascination as Reynald fell. First onto his knees, head bowed as though in prayer, then crashing face down, blood spreading in a great pool around him.

Gereinte picked up the broadsword and turned towards Fulk.

"Lord Borsa,' he said and offered the hilt to Fulk. Fulk grasped it and as their hands touched briefly Gereinte knew in a moment of absolute certainty, that Fulk was his man. As Gereinte stepped back, Fulk swept his sword point upward with a huge bellow of "Andolin rules!" Seconds later every sword in the hall joined his salute and the great hall echoed to a tremendous roar of "Andolin rules!"

EPILOGUE

It was some time after the coronation when the new King of Carentan returned to the small village of Cannan. Jael's wife seemed to recognise him instantly, even though the rest of the villagers were fooled by his peasant's dress and seemingly innocuous companions. She looked surprised, yet kept a dignified front, as he strolled into Jael's workshop as though he had only been there three weeks ago.

"Count Merlac," Jael said, eyes flicking to his wife. "This is an unexpected surprise." His wife rolled her eyes at her husband, then turned and curtsied with her head deeply bowed.

"Your Majesty," she said. Jael flapped about apologetically, all of a sudden making the connection between Count Merlac and the many stories that had come his way about a legendary blue sword and the new King of Carentan. His face flushed as he bowed before the King. Gereinte kept his own counsel.

"I promised to return with fair payment for your gift, though I can hardly repay you in kind for the magnificence of this weapon and the part its craftsmanship has played in my journey," Gereinte said. He looked to Allard and Bolt, but they were being studiously aloof, studying the weapons on display with an objectivity that belied their pseudo identity. Gereinte nodded at Etienne, who produced a bag heavy with coin.

"Oh... no, no. I did not expect this," Jael said. "In fact..." he wandered off to the back of the room. "I have something for you." Jael came back with a

321

magnificent jewelled scabbard. "I said three weeks, but in fact it has taken me longer to produce something that would really do justice to the sword."

Gereinte accepted the scabbard with a look of wonder.

"This is much more than what I was expecting. But please accept my coin if only to assuage my own conscience and believe me... it would make me happy to recompense you at least in coin." Jael bowed his head in acquiescence and somehow Gereinte felt that the playing field had been levelled. He glanced at Jael's wife. There was still something about that woman that he just couldn't put his finger on.

Weighing up his gaze, Jael's wife excused herself, reminding them that her son was alone in the yard and quickly made her apologies.

Satisfied with the outcome of his visit, Gereinte turned his back on the little cottage that housed the smithy of Cannan and walked back to where the horses had been tethered. Allard and Bolt waited patiently beside the King's mount. Following Gereinte's coronation, they had both been offered senior positions within the King's Guard, although for the purpose of that day, they dressed in the moderate and inconspicuous dress of the forest rangers. They appeared be laughing and waving at something to the side of the cottage. When they saw Gereinte emerge, they straightened themselves to attention in preparation for the journey home. Etienne walked ahead as Gereinte glanced in the direction of their attention and was stopped in his stride.

What he saw brought a spine-tingling spark of recognition to him, which caught him momentarily off guard. It was the image of himself as a boy staring back at him; hair ruffled, mud on his shirt and a lively inquisitive sparkle in his emerald green eyes. They stood at a distance, boy to man and stared at each other for an uncanny moment, before the boy lifted his hand and waved at Gereinte, breaking the spell. Gereinte waved back, turned and walked on towards his companions. He looked over his shoulder again at the boy, then turned and shook his head, dislodging an uncomfortable thought. The royal party mounted their horses and rode away without a backward glance, though Gereinte could sense more than one set of eyes watching his departure.

The End